scowler

scowler

DANIEL KRAUS

DELACORTE PRESS

Text copyright © 2013 by Daniel Kraus
Jacket art copyright © 2013 by Vincent Chong

All rights reserved. Published in the United States by Delacorte Press,
an imprint of Random House Children's Books, a division of Random
House, Inc., New York.

Delacorte Press is a registered trademark and the colophon is a trademark
of Random House, Inc.

Visit us on the Web! randomhouse.com/teens
Educators and librarians, for a variety of teaching tools,
visit us at RHTeachersLibrarians.com

Library of Congress Cataloging-in-Publication Data
Kraus, Daniel.
Scowler / Daniel Kraus. — 1st ed.
p. cm.
Summary: In the midst of a 1981 meteor shower in Iowa, a homicidal maniac
escapes from prison and returns to the farm where his nineteen-year-old son,
Ry, must summon three childhood toys, including one called Scowler, to protect
himself, his eleven-year-old sister, Sarah, and their mother.
ISBN 978-0-385-74309-9 (hardcover trade) — ISBN 978-0-375-99094-6 (glb) —
ISBN 978-0-307-98087-8 (ebook) [1. Mentally ill—Fiction. 2. Violence—
Fiction. 3. Meteorites—Fiction. 4. Family life—Iowa—Fiction. 5. Farm life—
Iowa—Fiction. 6. Iowa—Fiction. 7. Horror stories.] I. Title
PZ7.K8672Sco 2013 [Fic]—dc23 2012005363

The text of this book is set in 11.5-point Transitional 521.
Book design by Vikki Sheatsley
Printed in the United States of America
10 9 8 7 6 5 4 3 2 1
First Edition

In memory of
Susan Laura Kraus,
1952–2005

CONTENTS

scowler

From August 23 to 24, 1981, at least three large meteorites landed in southeastern Iowa. A prison, a farm, and a bridge were damaged in the impacts. Smaller fragments are still being discovered to this day.

The Blamings of the Birds

SUNDAY, AUGUST 23, 1981

20 HRS., 10 MINS. UNTIL IMPACT

A tooth was missing and that was never a pleasant thing. It was going on thirty minutes that Ry and Sarah had been after it. When the tiny white kernel had shaken loose from her mouth, Sarah had been staring up at the sky, something she did these days with escalating frequency. The brilliance of the cloudless blue seemed not to faze her, nor did the nip of the heavy and sluggish mosquitoes. She would go blind that way, and Ry knew that was bad; also bad, though, was the unhappy notion that this flat, dull stretch of moribund farmland contained a realm of fascination that in all his years he'd been either unwilling or unable to notice.

What she was looking for were meteors. According to the radio, Sarah was a good eight or nine hours early, but none of the estimates had addressed whether or not you could see meteors during the day. Sarah was just covering her bases. Most kids her age had long forgotten their teachers' reminders of this celestial event from back in June, because those reminders had carried the unpleasant whiff of homework. Not Sarah. She had stayed up late in April to see the luminous trains of dust cast from the Lyrids; she'd had a fit when a July thunderstorm had robbed her of watching the Delta Aquariids; and two weeks ago she had noted all thirty-four Perseids she'd seen by making hatch marks in a spiral-bound notebook. But the passing of the Jaekel Belt was the big one, a cosmic event so rare she'd not witness it again until she was an unimaginable forty-four years old. To be safe she'd started craning her neck days ago—she was well aware that trusting the estimates of small-town schoolteachers and radio personalities was risky.

Interrupting this rigorous scientific observation was an event less rare but almost as exciting: the falling of a baby tooth. The cuspid had dropped while Ry had been busy uprooting the rusted Cardan shaft of a long-dead baler from the dirt, and who knows how long Sarah had gone before noticing the line of pink blood that crept down her neck. It was only when Ry barreled the soft beam of metal into the drainage ditch and whooped in victory did his sister come alive. She touched the blood and showed it to him.

Ry wasn't dumb enough to think that his sister believed in the tooth fairy; rather, she believed in money as she believed in nothing else. They all did. It was the thing that had been draining noisily from the farm for a decade now, for Sarah's entire life, and Ry knew that she hungered after it like a pirate. The whole thing was ugly and he didn't like to see it; his sister was eleven, pigeon-toed, proficient at dirtying

4

clothes within seconds of donning them, and blessed with cerulean eyes and the downy blond crown of an angel—she was the kind of kid who stared up at the sky in hopes of seeing something from storybooks. It troubled Ry that Sarah's dreamy guilelessness was boned with the sharp and cornered calculations of a handful of grimy coins.

Stiff mufflers of August heat wrapped around their necks and bleak exhales of dust bloated about their ankles as they scuffed their toes through the dirt of the McCafferty Forty. This field and the five others bordering the farm had once commanded dizzying ranks of corn, soybean, hay, wheat, oat, and sorghum. Countless times in the past, Ry had put his hands to the dirt and felt for the hidden heartbeat, but it had been as futile as searching for meteor trails in broad daylight. Only his father had ever had the ability to speak to the land.

Marvin Burke was a man whose shadow still chilled the entire county. Merchants and neighbors alike had brandished a distrust of the man of the wolverine manner, the obliterating handshake, the features that never stopped moving—pulsing veins, twitching mustache, a rubber grin that delivered the nonstop soliloquies. Marvin Burke talked too much; he was too tall, too thin; his muscles were too rangy; his head was shaved down to a gleam they found unnatural. They suspected the man was a horror and they were right.

Ry had known that what his father did in the privacy of their home was unspeakable, but how could he or anyone else dare to stop him when Marvin Burke was the one who kept the sun rising and falling, kept winters from falling too harshly, kept late-spring frosts from shriveling the delicate yellow buds peeking through the soil? Ry had visceral memories of sitting beside his father in the combine cab, their stoic cattle dog, Sniggety, further crowding the quarters. His father would push back his thick square glasses and orate so enthusiastically that the wide gap between his two front teeth appeared to melt into the black mustache and form a huge open hole in the center of his face.

From this hole would pour forth desperately important information about the functioning of the machine's cutter bar and crop elevator, as well as broader lessons about acreage, not just of their farm but of the neighboring properties too, and how the Burkes had just the right amount of land while the surrounding fools had too much or too little to produce anything but ruin; about patterns of planting and harvesting and rotation; about how to treat your cattle—they're not, after all, goddamn pets. Eventually his father's stream of chatter gave way to the humming of a song, the same one day after day and year after year, something tuneless and belligerent and exactly one bar long—*hmmmm hm hm hmmmm*—and that was Ry's cue to edge away and turn his head to watch the monsters of dust swelling in the machine's wake.

When Marvin was locked up nine years ago, when Ry was ten, the farm should have gnawed itself to the bone in mere days. Marvin had never given his wife insight into his sorcery, so she only knew of the farm what could be printed in black and white, and she shouted these banal clumps of information from porch steps and barn doors and fence posts in indignant tones, as if their repetition and volume could somehow disguise her total lack of mastery. Not one of these shouts possessed the power of a single hummed bar of *hmmmm hm hm hmmmm*. After a time, the hired hands began showing up late and taking extended smoke breaks. Not two years after

Ry's father was put away, the lead hand quit. Days after that, the others approached one by one with their hats in hands.

The dirt became just dirt. It quit clinging to roots, ceased soaking up manure, stopped drinking rain, and spat seeds. The Strickland Sixty vanished in a fell swoop, victim to a season of soy that slithered above ground like worms. Two years later, the Horvath Property was decimated when a lightning strike enveloped the lower portion in a blue fire that rushed across the dry wheat with hellacious speed. And that was how it happened, the excruciating piecemeal amputation of their land. Ry's mother tried to sell portions, but the offers were insulting. She chose instead to let the grounds overgrow and smother.

The cracks in the dirt now yawned to proportions slutty with thirst; in all likelihood, Sarah's tooth had fallen into one of them. Ry wondered if he should feel some comfort in Sarah's loss. Her tooth had been planted like a seed, and it had been years since this field had been fed as much. Now the entire farm was up for sale, and soon they would be transplanted to some desultory house in Monroeville or October or Bloughton. A house—that was if they got lucky with an offer. More likely was an apartment. Ry could barely conceive of such a thing. He glanced at his sister, maybe fifteen feet away, and tried to imagine her growing into a long-legged young lady within such cramped confines. He returned his face to the dirt. His heart hurt; he could actually feel it hurt. What was the use of resisting? He wiped sweat from his neck and transported it in a cooling wave to his shaggy brown hair. A fallen tooth in a carpeted apartment would at least be easy to find.

"Mom's calling." Sarah didn't look up when she said it. "Hey. Mom's calling."

It amazed Ry how after eleven years of being subject to her mother's hollering, Sarah still managed to muster genuine alarm.

"She's yelled three times already," she said.

"I heard."

"Then why didn't you yell back?"

"Why didn't you?"

"Because I'm the kid."

"What? That's retarded."

"Ry," she whined.

"Fuck, it's hot."

"Don't blame me. It's not my fault I have baby teeth. If you lost your teeth I'd help you find them."

"They're called deciduous teeth. Deciduous."

"And you said *fuck*. That means I can say it."

"Go fucking ahead. Have a fucking ball, fucko."

"Anyway, I know they're called deciduous." She stood up straight and gathered her hair in a motion of startling femininity. Ry didn't know where she came up with these displays of womanhood. Television seemed the most likely culprit. Kimberly from *Diff'rent Strokes* struck him as especially ladylike as she pranced around her cream-colored and pillared penthouse—now, *there* was an apartment. Of course, it was always possible that Sarah had learned such gestures from their mother, but at the moment Ry couldn't recall a single time their mom had moved in any way that made her hair or hemlines dance. If such behavior had ever existed, her husband had beaten it out of her. And after that the farm had taken up the strap.

All at once Ry was angry with Sarah, and for bad reasons, which only made him angrier.

"It's hot as hell and we're not going to find your stupid tooth. Let's just go so she'll shut up already."

"If we go now we'll lose our place," she said.

And there it came again, their mother's voice, somehow cutting through the condemnations of the crickets and the blamings of the birds. Ry squinted up at the midday sun. You could set your watch to the twelve o'clock dinner; it was a reflex left over from a decade of feeding Marvin and his ungrateful posse. Her persistence in satisfying such ghosts infuriated Ry. Would she continue these pointless drills when the farthest her kids could stray was to the other end of the apartment?

"She's so mean to us," Sarah said. "Isn't she mean?"

"Yes."

"And she's cruel. Don't you think she's cruel?"

"I do, in fact."

"And she's bitchy. She's a gigantic bitch."

A smooth dagger of pain, different from that in his heart, lanced the starburst scar between Ry's eyebrows. It was the exact location of the wound that had changed everything in all of their lives. For the most part the memory was buried, but sometimes sun exposure released a beam of recall: his father giving chase through the icy forest, the arrival of the Unnamed Three, the blood draining from Ry's forehead so that it painted a replica of his father's face-hole. Now Sarah was the one with blood running down her face, and that was even worse—it was unacceptable that she could be anything like Marvin Burke.

"No. Sarah, no." Ry pushed his shoe at a sprig of weed that could, in theory, be nesting a stray tooth. The Unnamed Three—how long had it been since he had spoken their names? "Don't say that. She's under a lot of stress. You see how much sewing came in this month? Hardly anything. She's mean sometimes but that's totally different than being a bitch."

"You're just excusing her."

"So what? You should listen to me anyway. You're the kid, remember?"

"You're excusing her because you're a cocksucker."

He shrugged. "Better than being a shit-eater. Think about it."

"Dirty cocksucker."

"Filthy shit-eater."

"Dirty poop-face cocksucker."

"Colossal maniac shit-eater."

The silence that resumed was more comfortable having been padded with these courtesies. Though it really was not silence at all; the birds were louder than Ry had ever remembered—they were screaming. Sarah looked up at them, then took the opportunity to make another quick scan of the sky.

"You know how many meteors fall every day?" Sarah asked.

"I don't want to know."

"Three or four. An average of twenty pounds each."

"Holy shit. So amazing."

"Did you know that the heaviest meteorite weighs sixty tons?"

"No. But thanks. Now I can die in peace."

"Dinosaurs were killed by a meteor, you know."

"Please don't start in with dinosaurs now."

"*Dinosaur* means 'terrible lizard,' even though they weren't lizards."

Ry stole a glance at her. She was scouring the ground, unaware. He shook his head in a mixture of irritation and amazement. Sarah might be able to move to town without so much as a backward glance, but this dirt was who he was. He could no more escape it than he could escape himself. When they departed the land would keep most if not all of his soul, after it had already taken so many of his dreams and so much of his blood. And this tooth that it had taken from his sister—

There it was. A miracle, really, finding this speck of bone in a world of dust. There was a brown spot of blood on the tooth's root, and to Ry it seemed the encapsulation of the bum deal of life: a once-perfect thing plucked and bloodied and tossed to the dirt.

Briefly he considered wrenching out a tooth of his own and offering it up—surely it would be worth double the going rate. Instead he kicked at Sarah's tooth until it slid into one of the earth's cracks. It would be the part of his sister left behind to keep company with the segments of his own body that would never be able to leave. Worse fates were everywhere. Just look around.

14 HRS., 23 MINS. UNTIL IMPACT

The birds did not quiet. Not during the mournful march across the McCafferty Forty with a grieving Sarah. Not after a lugubrious lunch of meat and bread so dry it pebbled upon the tongue. Not after five more hours of knocking wasp nests from gutters, righting wronged fence posts, and wadding and disposing of chicken wire still tufted with evidence of chickens. The birds screamed into one another's beaks and bristled their plumage, and with their own wings made cages they seemed frantic to escape. Ry sympathized.

Dusk had begun its squeeze but at this time of year would take hours. Ry was at the top of a ladder outside the window of his mother's second-floor bedroom. Her face appeared in the top-right pane. She gestured fruitlessly. Ry glared. She held up a finger—*wait*—and walked away. Ry heard her every step down the wooden staircase before losing her signal, but he knew her steps would soon resume upon the enclosed back porch.

He wolfed his last free moment. Locking a heel onto a rung, he let his body pivot like a barn door opening along a draft until he leaned with his back to the ladder. The buildings of the farm were like parts of his body; he had to concentrate to really see them. To the left of the house was the multipurpose dairy barn, once the center of the farm's sounds and smells. At its peak it had housed sixty-five Holsteins, shuffling and edgy behemoths that had been the only creatures on the planet bold enough to eye Marvin Burke with outright distrust. The dislike was mutual. Each cow was artificially inseminated in a process Marvin seemed to enjoy making as uncomfortable as possible. Births were no more pleasant. Ry himself had reached into at least a dozen hot wombs to grab purple and quivering babies, and he'd seen more than one get stuck in the birth canal, which often meant killing the mother or child—a task Marvin took up without hesitation. His trusty twelve-gauge Winchester 1200 was always at the ready.

To the right of the house was the vacant northeast pasture. It was in that field that the males had been castrated and dehorned. The former was somehow bearable: The calves had an underbelly doughiness that ceded testicles effortlessly. The removal of horns, though, was a feat of carnage that haunted Ry each day. Sometimes when the first blast of water hit him in the morning shower he mistook it for the jets of black blood that would strike his face during the dehornings. The steers knew what was coming; they lowered their heads as if trying to elude the holocaust stench. It did not help. A hired worker would pull the animal into position and Marvin would regrip his implements and take aim. It was Ry's job to apply caustic to the deep and spurting wounds, and he'd do it pretending that he was merely reaching his hands into another womb, that this was the torture of birth, not the first stage of an ignominious death.

Beyond the pasture stretched three hundred acres of dead farmland. Each field was ruthlessly named after the farmer from whom it had been purchased, a litany of conquest: the Costner Eighty, the Strickland Sixty, the Bowman Plot, the McCafferty Forty. And beyond that was Black Glade—the largest forest in the state, a place without light, the origin of a hundred schoolyard legends. Ry had only gone past its edges once and it wasn't something he liked to think about, not ever.

The only thing not pelted with dust or rust on the entire farm was the For Sale sign, which whistled sweetly in the breeze. Ry heard it, blinked himself awake, and hid his eyes so that he would not have to see it. This was the Burke farm, over four hundred acres of nothing, and he was terrified to leave it.

13

14 HRS., 11 MINS. UNTIL IMPACT

The screen door sounded like another angry bird. Jo Beth Burke's shoulders dipped side to side as she walked into view, as if she were carrying an extra fifty pounds of weight, and her muscles, even those in her face, slouched toward the earth. But she had a good face—nothing could change that. Her eyes were heavily lidded and that was their burden, but in the rare moments that those lids fully withdrew, you became sure she was going to reach out and tickle you. And all throughout his youth she had done just that. It was yet another thing that Sarah was missing.

"Why do you make me walk all the way down here?" Jo Beth's arms hung slack at her sides; this was her most exasperated posture, as if even posturing were a wasted effort. "Just open the window so I can ask you. I can't open it from my side—that's the problem."

"I know what the problem is." He looked away from her and across the yard. The doghouse next to the garage was empty; the coiled-up, never-used chain where the dog usually rested his muzzle sat undisturbed, as did the chain's padlock, which had lain open since the key vanished a decade ago. Sniggety had never recovered from his master's abandonment and was just riding out his time, sleeping for twenty hours a day, deaf and twitching in the shade. His absence was unusual.

"And you're going to fall," Jo Beth said. "Look at you."

"You want to do this?" He bucked his back so that, for a moment, only his heels touched the ladder. It was a deliberate incitement and he saw Jo Beth draw back in fear. Instantly

14

he regretted it and took a firm grip of the top step. "I'm not going to fall."

"If you could just raise it an inch," she said. "Then I could grab it from the other side and we could try together."

"And then what? Have you thought this through? Then you'll have a window that won't close. The wood's all warped. If I get it up, it's not going to come back down. When it rains it'll get all over your floor. You really want that?"

She sighed and wiped hair back from her sweaty temples. She spoke quietly, perhaps to herself. "Yes."

He wondered if it was true. Because the more things went wrong around the farm, the more his presence was required. This was the terrible unarticulated truth. Jo Beth Burke was thirty-eight, which meant she had been Ry's age when she gave birth to him. At nineteen she was married, living with her husband, feeding farmhands, keeping house, and nursing a child. He, on the other hand, was a year past graduating near the bottom of a class of forty kids, and he'd yet to make a single feint toward a life of his own. There were community colleges within a few hours' drive. There were jobs holding road signs in Bloughton. There were other farms that, despite the hard times, would pay him hourly wages. They might keep a close eye on him for a while—the son of Marvin Burke, poor messed-up kid—but eventually his pedigree would be overlooked. His hand strayed from the ladder and touched the swelling of a new pimple alongside his nose. It seemed symbolic of the issue: Was he an oily-faced kid, or was he a man?

Sarah's head poked out from under her mother's arm. A faint pinkness of eye was all that betrayed her earlier crying.

One thing was clear: She had gotten paid. It glittered all over her.

"Mom's got stuff for the Crowleys," she taunted. "Don't you want to go to the Crowleys'?"

Four miles was a long way to go for your nearest neighbor, but that was the distance to the Crowley farm. Sarah had somehow gotten it into her head that Ry was in love with Esther Crowley, the eighteen-year-old daughter with a mane of black hair that sometimes caught under her ass when she sat down. He was not, in fact, in love with her, but he had, in fact, nearly had sex with her two years ago, a traumatic incident that marked the only attempt at physical relations he'd ever had with a girl. He refused to think of it, ever—he'd think of algebra, baseball statistics, anything to keep the memory away. How Sarah suspected the truth was beyond him, but he was pretty sure Jo Beth had never picked up on it. He'd like to keep it that way.

"We do have some mending for them. A nightgown. A beautiful nightgown." Jo Beth paused. "But I can drive it over if you want."

That pause—did she suspect after all? His mother imagining him putting his clumsy hands to a girl's bare skin made his ears boil. He took the hammer from his belt loop. "I'll do it. It's fine. It'll take me like twenty minutes."

"You should take longer," Sarah suggested. "You and Esther could watch the Jaekel Belt together. It's very romantic."

Ry sighed. "But I can't do it tonight."

"Then I'll have to do it myself," Jo Beth said.

"Well, enjoy the walk."

Her face fell. "The car? Oh, Ry."

He gripped the hammer more tightly. "Don't give me that. The car what? The car is not my fault."

"But you said you'd have it done."

"What am I supposed to do? Grow spark plugs next to the strawberry patch? I put the order in with Phinny and he'll be here."

"When? I just feel so bad about that nightgown; she must be wearing something of Kevin's—"

"Tonight? Tomorrow? He'll be here when he gets the part."

"Ry, how many times is this going to happen?"

"That depends on how many times you plan on incinerating the spark plugs."

"Can we order more than one box?"

"Can we get a new car?"

"Ry." She shielded her eyes even though the falling sun was behind her. "Can we order more than one? Is it too late?"

"Will you calm down? Phinny's bringing a bunch. The Crowleys can wait for their damn pajamas. I'll install the plug and drive over there tomorrow morning, end of story."

Ry chanced a look at his mother and saw both resignation and gratitude. He should have felt good about that, about solving yet another of the farm's myriad problems, but instead felt only the sensation of further sinking. He was six foot three and shaved every day; his continued presence here was becoming a mockery. He mashed his lips and told himself that he deserved an extra year of childhood—a year at the very *least*—for all those months stolen by doctors, psychiatrists, and the Unnamed Three.

"Fine," Jo Beth said with hushed complacency. Beside her Sarah had twisted so that she could stare at the sky again, and

her mother's arm supported her weight with offhand exper-
tise. "Sarah lost another tooth. Didn't you, Sarah?"

"I know," Ry said.

"I'm worried it's infected somehow. She's all snotty."

"You don't want me to stay up!" Sarah accused. "You want
me to miss the Jaekel Belt!"

But Ry heard it too, the nasal buzz that presaged a sore
throat and cough. It seemed that for every two weeks Sarah
spent bursting with energy she spent another throwing up
into a bowl.

"She's going to have perfect teeth," Jo Beth said. This
slide into dreamy prognostication announced a tempo-
rary cease-fire. She pressed Sarah's head into her side and
began waddling back around the corner of the house. Ry felt
snubbed. He swung himself back toward the window and regarded his misshapen reflection in the aged glass.

Swiftly he withdrew several nails from his pocket and
transferred them to his lips. He made sure the sash was
lodged solid against the frame and centered the first nail over
the weatherboard. He raised the hammer, aimed, and with
one mean blow sunk the nail. No matter how many times the
bedroom window jammed, his mother insisted on trying to
open it. Well, no more. He drove another nail and sad flakes
of paint scattered. She would have to be more creative in her
assignments of busywork. A third nail, a fourth, each like the
sealing of a coffin.

The detestable job done, he lifted the inside of his elbow
to wipe at eyes so sweaty they felt full of tears. That was as
far as he got. There between the brooder house and calf shed
was Sniggety, winding his way around abandoned machine
parts and the tractor wheel that had once housed a miniature

rose garden. The dog moved with his trademark limp, but with hackles raised. It was the birds. Ry had forgotten them again, but there they were, still screaming.

It was only because he was facing the doghouse that his gaze swept the front yard. He paused, blinked, and looked again. The long shadows thrown by the trees made it difficult to see, and the driveway itself was a quarter of a mile long. After a time, though, Ry became convinced. Standing on the road, next to their mailbox, was a man.

13 HRS., 46 MINS. UNTIL IMPACT

At first Ry was sure that it was Phinny Rochester. The man ran a shop out of his garage about twelve miles west. Phinny got a good price for his salvage and a fair commission from his special orders—at least, that was Ry's impression. He had visited Phinny's plenty of times with Marvin. The men loathed each other, and when Marvin loathed a man he visited him as often as possible, displaying his shaved scalp, flashing the gap in his teeth, talking uninterrupted for staggering amounts of time—thirty, sixty, ninety minutes. Phinny, to his credit, never backed down, and would nod as many times as was necessary. Most of these encounters would be scored a draw.

The first time Ry visited the shop after Marvin's incarceration, Phinny Rochester looked as if he had exhaled a long-held breath. He beckoned Ry with oil-stained fingers, grinning behind kaleidoscopic whiskers. He cut Ry no better deals than he had cut Marvin, which made Ry trust him; in fact, he had quickly become Ry's only real confidant. Ry had plenty of secrets—the severity of the farm's debt, his

19

regretful sexual encounter with Esther Crowley, the untold lengths of his father's depravity, the Unnamed Three—and if he were ever to tell anyone about them, he figured it would be Phinny.

Ry had put in the order for two packs of spark plugs six days ago. Over the past two years Ry had grown increasingly embarrassed of the family car, a school-bus-yellow 1973 Volkswagen Beetle. Jo Beth was defensive of it; once the fate of the farm had calcified, she had wasted no time selling off the F-150 that exhaled Marvin's odor each time you sat down in it. Ry's long legs barely fit in the Beetle. He had to admit, though, that the vehicle would be right at home battling for parking spots in town.

Ry jumped off the ladder, still four rungs from the bottom. He took a few steps toward the driveway, felt strangely vulnerable, and slapped his thigh to engage Sniggety. The dog scratched his muzzle but otherwise made no move. At least there was the weight of the hammer at his side. Ry wiped his palms on his shirt and began the walk around the eastern side of the house. The man waiting at the road did not move. Ry risked a wave. Still nothing. You did not live this far out in the country and not wave at others. Even Marvin Burke had done it.

Twenty feet away features began to distinguish themselves. Ry slowed. The man was old, maybe in his seventies, and had gray hair crisscrossing his skull, thistles and bits of leaves caught within the wisps. His thin legs wore what looked like pajama pants, the shins fuzzy with burrs and striped with dried mud. His shoes were flimsy and had been all but cut to ribbons. The only pristine item on him was a black overcoat far too big for his skinny frame, zipped to the neck despite the heat. The man stood with his hands behind his back.

Ry stopped ten feet away. He put on a smile. The man met his eyes only for a moment. His chest beat up and down and he breathed through an open mouth only half-stocked with teeth.

"Howdy," Ry said.

The man nodded. He paused and nodded again.

"Nice time for a walk." Ry weighed this pleasantry and judged it sufficient. "What can I help you with?"

The man parted his lips. They were trembling. Ry leaned away. There were red scratches on the man's neck and face.

Ry heard his sister's cry far behind. "Mom! Ry's talking to a man!"

Ry's chest tingled. They had been spotted. Sarah would be on her way. He heard a screen door slam.

"Everything all right, sir?" Ry asked.

"Obliged," the man said. "Your family."

Ry heard feet crunching through the gravel behind him. He took a half step forward to urge the conversation along. "Say again? Something about my family?"

The man raised his face. His stubble was pure white and sprinkled his haggard cheeks like snow.

"I been watching you," he said.

Sarah arrived panting at Ry's side and on instinct he threw an arm around her. She slingshotted forward, then back.

"Sarah, go inside—"

"Hello," she said. The man's watery eyes lowered to Sarah's level and his mouth hung agape. He leaned toward her, too close, within grabbing range, biting distance. His hands, though, remained clasped behind his back.

21

"I'm Sarah." She sounded stuffy.

Back at the house the screen door slammed again. Jo Beth was coming.

"Mister," Ry said. "Maybe you better keep on."

"Are you here to see the meteors?" Sarah asked. "They're easier to see in the country."

"I . . ."

"Where were you hiding?" Sarah searched the road, the nearby trees, the ditch.

"In plain sight," the man said.

"Mister," Ry repeated.

"You're missing teeth," Sarah continued. "I lost a tooth today. A front one. Well, sort of near the front. It got lost in the field but I got money anyway."

The man cocked his head as if mystified by this creature. He turned his attention back to Ry. "I saw you had a pretty little miss, a young sir like yourself, a lady, and a dog. It reminded me of kindness. I mean that it reminded me of my home. The home of myself. Where I'm from." He winced and looked at the ground.

There was the sudden disruption of gravel. The man's eyes shifted upward.

Jo Beth had arrived. She inserted a shoulder in front of Ry and wiped her hands on the apron she still wore. There were pockets in the apron; Ry wondered if they were big enough to conceal a knife.

"How do you do? I'm Jo."

"Obliged," the man said. "I am Jeremiah. I'm troubling you for water and food. I know I'm troubling you. But I've come some way and desire water and food. This is my request."

Jo Beth took in the entirety of Jeremiah's appearance with a slowness that did not disguise itself. The man tipped his knees together like a child who needed to urinate. Ry, meanwhile, felt the shame of youth. He had danced around this man to no avail, while it had taken his mother six words to establish control.

"I can give you water," Jo Beth said at last. "Sarah, why don't you go fill that red thermos on top of the fridge."

Sarah coughed but did not move.

"And a bit of food?" Jeremiah's eyes twinkled hopefully. "If it's not too much trouble? To sit down to some food would be . . . It would be something I could not ever repay."

"Where are you from?" Jo Beth asked.

Jeremiah looked pained and turned his head to gaze down the dusty road. "I come from Wisconsin way."

"That's very far."

"Yes, ma'am."

"You came directly from there?"

"No." His eyes became dejected. "No, ma'am."

"Where did you come from, then? Today."

Jeremiah's shoulders were shaking. "If I've bothered you, ma'am, I am sorry. I will be on my way—"

"You haven't bothered me." There was a command to his mother's voice that Ry hadn't heard in a long time, as well as an undertone of sympathy. "But you're on my property. I have a little girl."

"Eleven," Sarah said. "That is my age."

"So." Jo Beth stopped kneading the apron and let it drop. "Where did you come from today?"

"The woods," Jeremiah said.

"Black Glade?" Her voice betrayed her surprise.

The man looked confused.

"That's the forest over yonder," Jo Beth said. "At the end of the property there. Goes for miles and miles. Was that the woods you were in?"

"No, ma'am."

She considered this. "Where else were you?"

"Fields."

"Fields," she repeated. "And where did you sleep?"

"I did not." Jeremiah was shaking his head in a miserable figure-eight pattern. "You are kind, ma'am, very kind."

Jo Beth laughed lightly. "Because I'm asking you questions?"

"Yes." Jeremiah's voice was phlegmy. "No one's asked me anything for the longest time."

"Well." Jo Beth nodded as if this was what she had been waiting to hear. "How are you with cars?"

"Mom," Ry said. "It's not me; it's the part."

"Right," she said. "I keep forgetting."

"I'm no help with engines," Jeremiah said. "I never was a farmer."

"You're in the wrong part of the country then," Jo Beth said.

Jeremiah nodded at the ground. "I expect I am."

"Bluefeather?" Jo Beth ducked her face to try to find the truth in his eyes. "That's where you lived before now, isn't it?"

Jeremiah nodded. His shoulders shook so violently that Ry wondered if the old bones might jar loose from their whittled sockets. *Bluefeather*—the word was familiar, though Ry couldn't remember why.

"And they didn't give you a set of civilian clothes when they released you? That doesn't seem very kind."

24

The man looked bewildered. He angled his head but held his tongue.

"My husband's in Pennington," Jo Beth said. "There's a man who doesn't deserve to be released. But that is simply not the case with everyone. That's probably hard for you to believe after so many years, but you have to try." She gave him a small smile. "Why didn't you wait until we were asleep and just take what you wanted?"

"I thought it," Jeremiah said. "Lord forgive me, I thought it." He raised his woeful face to blink at each of them in turn. "You look like such fine folk. I couldn't do it. I swear to you I couldn't do it. I'll sit—" With his spittle-covered chin he indicated the drainage ditch. "I'll sit beneath the telephone pole. Anyone drives by, I'll hide. You can bring out whatever you want and I'll be grateful."

A breeze sent the hair on his head flying. The hand Jeremiah brought out to pat it down was not a hand at all. It was a pincer. Sarah gasped and Ry dug his nails into her shoulders. A few seconds later Ry realized it was not a deformity; rather, the man's index, middle, and ring fingers were gone, and in their absence the surviving pinkie and thumb seemed abnormally long. Loosed from its clasp, Jeremiah's other hand now hung free at his side and it was just as troubled, though in different formation: Only the index and thumb remained, giving the hand the look of fleshy tweezers.

Silence fell across the group and it took the man a moment to realize the cause. He looked down at his insectile appendages and turned them over in the fading light. "Cell doors, that's what done it," he said. "Would I have clung so hard if I were guilty?"

Bluefeather—Ry finally remembered. It was the prison in

25

nearby Lomax County. When Marvin Burke had been sent far across the state to a facility known as Pennington nine years ago, Ry had become aware, for a brief period, of the state's penal system. Bluefeather, if Ry's memory was accurate, was high security. This man's striped pajama bottoms and slippers were state-issued prison garb; that nice new overcoat was stolen; and those missing fingers had been sacrificed by a man desperate not to hear the cold finality of a door locking into place. It was the worst thing Ry could imagine—a wandering ex-convict happening upon their defenseless farm—yet he saw the tension escape from his mother's bearings.

"I was just about to get started on supper," she said. Ry knew it was the man's hands that had clinched it. Jeremiah was old and weak and those were points in his favor. But hands like that could not wield a weapon. This man was at their mercy, not the other way around.

"There's chicken," Jo Beth said. "Dumplings, green beans, milk. Come along and we'll fix you a plate. Then you can be on your way."

12 HRS., 56 MINS. UNTIL IMPACT

It was a strange hour filled with the rattle and thuds of Jo Beth's food preparation, the wheeze of the old fan on top of the fridge, and the incessant stream of chatter and coughing coming from Sarah. While Jeremiah sat hunched at the table with his hands in his lap, the girl crawled like a monkey over the rest of the furniture. Jeremiah tried to answer her first couple questions—*What is your middle and last name?* and *Do you like our dog?*—but before he could arrange the correct order of syllables, Sarah hurried on to topics of even greater import. Within minutes a pattern was set that both of them could live with: She would ask questions and he would sit there too shell-shocked to respond.

There must have been at least a few boys of Ry's age in Bluefeather, because Jeremiah found him the easiest to behold. Dozens of odd moments passed between them; it was as if the man could sense the convict blood that beat just beneath Ry's skin. While Sarah badgered their guest with more rhetoricals—*If you could be shorter, how much shorter would you be?*—Ry wondered what this man had looked like before prison had stolen his fingers, bent his back, sucked the color from his flesh and the life from his eyes.

"You could stay in the TV room," Sarah said. "We have a couch in there that's pretty good for sleeping."

"Sarah," Jo Beth said.

"What? It would just be for one night."

Jeremiah shook his head miserably.

"Did they have beds in jail?" Sarah asked.

He nodded his head.

"Were they hard? I bet they were hard." The tip of her tongue explored the new vacancy in the corner of her smile. Ry found it hard to look at. "If the sofa's too soft there's lots of floors. We have so many floors!"

"Sarah, this man has places he has to be."

"We have wood floors, we have cement floors, we have carpet floors."

Jo Beth turned from the counter, her red hair shades darker because of sweat, and approached the table with a serving bowl of green beans. Sarah recoiled as if the beans had made threats against her life.

27

"Do you have somewhere?" Jo Beth asked. "If not, maybe it's best you do stay one night."

"I've no fear of grass."

"Well, we have a barn for that matter. At least you'd be out of the elements."

"No. No."

"I understand. I do." Jo Beth turned back to the counter and produced the sound of knife against board. "It just doesn't seem Christian to let you out there tonight, that's all."

"No. . . . No. . . ."

It took them too long to realize that Jeremiah was crying. Unwilling to display his hideous hands, he did not wipe away the tears that carved four distinct paths through his face paint of dust. His warped back jagged in silent hiccups and his bottom lip fretted around as if attempting to gather the tears and stow them.

Jo Beth set the knife down and turned. "I'm sorry. It's not my business."

"I knew it from the road. I could tell you were kind. I passed so many homes, went so many miles."

"Don't cry." Sarah's voice was hushed and fragile. It had been so long since anything but irritable outbursts had disrupted the farm's atmosphere that Ry had forgotten how his sister became awed by shows of emotion.

"My shoes split," Jeremiah continued. "My ankles bloodied up."

"We'll get you a new pair. Ry's got some old clothes that I bet would fit you. Don't you worry. And you're staying here tonight and that's final."

"Yes, ma'am."

"We've got an old army cot somewhere."

"Yes, ma'am."

"It's in the attic," Sarah offered. "Hey, that's another place you could stay."

Ry hoped that his mother would recommence her work at the cutting board; she did not. He hoped the sizzle from the stove-top chicken would continue to distract everyone, but it had been removed from the burner. Even Jeremiah's sobs had softened, so all that remained was the echo of Sarah's words. If her legs hadn't been curled up beneath her, Ry would have given them a hell of a kick.

One did not make cavalier offers about going into the attic. You didn't even talk about it without first measuring the temperature of souls. Not because it was a room associated with Marvin's cruelty but because it was the exact opposite: a closed-off space that housed the most sacred object owned by any of them.

It was a dress. Sarah, who named everything, had been four when she dubbed it the White Special Dress, and the name more than stuck—its infantile moniker was the only thing that made it bearable to speak of at all, because you could laugh at such a name, make fun of it. These were bluffs. It was not a folly, this dress. It was as radiant and as real as the sun and just as easy to feel—all you had to do was go into the attic and remove the dustcover.

People all over the region knew that Jo Beth Burke could sew. Her domination of county fairs throughout her school years marked her as someone with the kind of blind artistic instinct that in the country was treated with the same wariness as mental retardation. In one way or another Jo Beth had sewn her way into most of the families in her school district, and she hand made the long skirts she wore to school dances, the dresses she donned while being courted by Marvin Burke, the gown she wore while getting married. It was a shock to her that once the honeymoon was over, Marvin wanted her sewing kept limited to the darning of his socks, the replacing of his buttons, the pressing of his shirts. It took only one transgression—the letting out of the waist of a neighbor's pair of slacks—for Marvin's threat to become physical. As quickly as she had become ingrained into the lives of those around her, she vanished. *I don't have time anymore,* she told them. *Farm life,* she said, *it is what it is.*

Marvin Burke had insisted on tidiness, but Jo Beth Burke preferred the inspiration of chaos. Nine years had gone by now with nearly every inch of tabletop in the dining room blanketed with her commissions. She repaired jacket elbows right through lunch if the fancy struck her, and hemmed skirts with hands still soapy from the baths she gave Sarah. Neither Ry nor his sister would ever think to ask her to give it a rest. The looping motions of her fingers were the circulation of her blood, and the tightening of fabric was the pursing of her heart's ventricles. As long as she sewed she was alive.

The idea of some kind of special project was laughable at first. Not when the farm was falling apart, not when money was so scarce. But it was born of frugality, of leftovers. A scrap of chiffon from a confirmation dress taken in a few sizes. Eight feet of diamond lace left over from the repair of a set of heirloom place mats. A beehive of yarn flecked with the brightest silver. An entire skirt's length of silk duchess satin. A scattering of ivory pearls—she had no memory of their origin.

From these hoarded remainders grew the first gestures of art. Nightly she placed pieces together to evaluate their collage potential, pinning by hand and passing sections beneath her machine, only to rip free the stitches with her teeth the next day and start over. The project was eventually moved to a dressmaker's dummy in the attic, supposedly because it was delicate but really because it had the force to command a room of its own.

After three years of intense but sporadic work, it looked more or less like a wedding dress, though whose wedding remained unclear. After five years, anyone else would have sworn it was finished—if anyone else were allowed to see it, which they were not. After seven years, the dress hit you with a beauty that was almost rageful. Hundreds if not thousands of hours of toil had passed since its inception and still, almost weekly, Jo Beth adjusted and tweaked. Now it had an empire waist. Now it had leg-o'-mutton sleeves. Unlike every other aspect of life, over this one their mother exercised total control. White Special Dress, the labor of her life, of all of their lives, would never be finished, and Ry was only beginning to appreciate its constant change as fundamental to its power.

This was the real risk of an apartment in town. Where would White Special Dress live? Surely not in the open, thought Ry, not on a coatrack, not draped over some ratty chair, not in a closet or trunk—its fire would be snuffed. The only solution was sale or abandonment, and Ry wasn't willing to entertain either option. If it meant the dress could have enough space, he would finally strike out from his mother and sister and face the noxious world. He felt made of scraps too, but none so breathtaking.

Supper was a spectacle. Jeremiah's left hand, the one with pinkie and thumb, was useless except for providing balance. It clamped the plate edge in order to anchor it. The right hand, the one with index and thumb, was his primary weapon. The mushiest of the green beans he was able to spear, and he was able to scrape off bits of potato. The chicken breast, however, was a conundrum. Orbs of sweat dotted the man's scalp as he fought for decorum. In Bluefeather he would have gobbled it down in any way possible, but he was a free man now, and if he couldn't play by society's rules then he did not belong. He sighed and palmed his roll, his only true friend.

Sarah broke the silence. "Where's Bluefeather?"

Jeremiah looked thankful for the excuse to drop his fork. He wiped his brow with a forearm. "Couple hours' drive. Roundabout. Don't recall exactly."

"Yeah, but what town is it in?"

His eyebrows drew so close that opposing strands, long and white, interlocked. "It weren't in any town."

Sarah turned to her mother. "It's got to be in a town. You can't be nowhere."

Jeremiah took advantage of the split second of inattention. Ry saw him swipe his potatoes with his thumb and transfer a dollop into his mouth. The thumb was instantly sucked clean and returned to the side of the plate, looking innocent.

"That's true," Jo Beth admitted. "I suppose it's closest to Bloughton."

"Well, why isn't it *in* Bloughton?" Sarah twirled her knife against the table as if it were a top she was trying to keep spinning.

"Stop that; that's bad for the table," Jo Beth said. "And you eat those potatoes or you'll have to eat them cold."

Sarah carved a pea-sized bit of potato with her knife and inspected it like a jeweler. "But why, Mom?"

"Because they're vegetables and vegetables are part of life."

"No," Sarah groaned. "Why's the prison not in Bloughton like it should be?"

"Warden's from there," Jeremiah offered. "Staff, too. Just a ways outside of town is all."

Sarah transported the bit of potato into the spot where her tooth had been. It was a convincing replacement.

"Some people," Jo Beth ventured, throwing a tentative glance at their guest, "might not feel comfortable with a prison near their home or close to their school. So even though technically the prison is in Bloughton, it's easier on everyone if it's out of eyesight. You understand?"

"Yeh, ah uhuhstah." Now that she had a potato tooth, she didn't want to mess it up.

"It was the kind of thing that drove my husband crazy—people trying to hide how they made a living," Jo Beth said. "I don't like to agree with anything Marvin said, but in this one case, I do. Bluefeather provides a lot of people with good wages and there is nothing wrong with that. There's nothing wrong with prisons, either—people serving their time, becoming better people." She turned to Jeremiah with a smile. "Nothing wrong at all."

Jeremiah's mouth hung open. The slime of green bean coated his tongue. They all watched as his thumb and forefinger slackened and the stem of the fork slid away, crashing to the ceramic.

"Marvin?"

Jo Beth flinched. Hearing her husband's name from a stranger's mouth was like taking buckshot.

"Marvin Burke." He said the full name as if it were a psalm.

Jo Beth swallowed whatever was left inside her mouth and it went down hard.

"He's in Pennington."

"No." Jeremiah was saying it before she finished. "He's much closer."

Ry tensed for the violinistic terror that should accompany this threat, but instead his body felt heavily blanketed. Sounds dwindled; physical awareness of his family faded to nothing.

"Bluefeather?" Jo Beth's head made vague circles. "He's in Bluefeather?"

The alien appendages twitched. "Yes, ma'am."

"That's impossible."

"Had I known your name was Burke—"

"How dare you." She tried to close her mouth but her upper set of teeth rattled off the lower.

"If it were on the mailbox, I didn't see—"

"How dare you frighten my children."

"No, ma'am, oh, no—"

"In my house. My *house*."

Tears sprung to his eyes. "Please . . . oh, please, I meant nothing by it. You . . . you are upset. I spoke too . . . I don't know why; I'm not accustomed to . . . my mouth is not accustomed to talking. You should not forgive me. You don't even know what I've done. What I've done is terrible. If I told you, you would not find it in your heart to forgive me and you would be right. You're all so lovely and kind."

Jo Beth found she was still holding her knife. She placed it alongside her plate of useless food.

Jeremiah swatted down the bad air that had risen; his four digits worked the air like large albino insects. "You've been so kind and I wanted to be kind too, not to make you or your children scared—not of me, not of Marvin Burke, not of anything."

Jo Beth was pressed into the back of her seat. The soft placement of her voice was for Sarah's benefit. "Tell me why we might be afraid of you."

"Because I did not serve my time, not all of it." It came out fast, as if it were the only way he could bear it. "I got out. There was an explosion. I got out."

The metal fan rang with each fatigued revolution. Ry was grateful. It gave a measurable length to a silence that was otherwise endless. He remembered a snippet of high school Shakespeare. My kingdom for a transistor radio.

"An explosion?" Half-chewed food sat cooling in Sarah's mouth. "Like a bomb?"

Ry's lips moved over the same syllables—*An explosion? A bomb?*—but the dryness of his mouth prevented sound.

Jo Beth whispered as if to herself. "What are you talking about?"

"A hole in the wall. An explosion. I didn't see it. You don't see anything in there. Just your four walls. Or a different four walls if it's supper. Or a different four walls if it's shower time."

"There was a bomb." Jo Beth heard her own voice and was awakened by the preposterous ring of it. "There was a *bomb*?"

"Please, please, that's what I want to explain." Jeremiah took a deep breath and tried to slow down. "Laundry—I was on laundry detail. I was pushing my cart down the hall. There were a noise. A great noise. It sounded like an explosion. And there were shouting. And smoke. So much smoke. I went right into it. I don't even know why. That's the way I'm supposed to go with my laundry cart, that's the laundry hall, and if they caught me heading the other way . . . I have a good record, ma'am, I'm not violent, I believe in rules."

"This was a . . . what?" Jo Beth looked around the table for help. Ry just blinked at her, empty of words. She licked her lips and forged ahead. "Some kind of prison break?"

"No, ma'am, please, no. Don't for a moment think that. Fellows talk about that sort of thing all the time—about dynamite. That doesn't mean that's what happened. I don't believe that were it at all. A boiler, maybe. Bluefeather is old. Or else there's gas pumps outside the fence. I don't know; there was nothing to see. I went into the smoke and couldn't hardly see because of all the light. It was like morning. Only it were too early for morning. Just a hole. And fire. Fire everywhere. The exercise yard—it was on fire as well. You could've driven a truck through the hole. Two trucks. The wall was gone also."

Sarah was agog. "The entire wall?"

"If it were dynamite, it were a great amount."

"And you ran away," Jo Beth said. "You escaped."

The harder Jeremiah nodded, the more energy that squeezed from his old joints, the veins in his face, the corners of his eyes. "No one else were there with me. That's not true—I'm sorry, that's not true. There were one man. A guard, I could tell by his boots. Rest of him was all burnt, though. I'm afraid I kept going. The fence . . . Mrs. Burke, the fence was—I'd never imagined—it was curled like paper when you burn it. I'd never . . . I'm sorry. But ma'am. I'd never seen such light. I walked through it. I did."

"Others got out. Is that what you're saying?"

"The shotgun." Ry's voice was a croak. "Where is it?"

Jo Beth didn't even look at him. "That thing's a hundred years old."

Ry was numb. "But where is it? I don't remember."

"No." Jeremiah shook his head firmly. "There were guards everywhere. The hole was in Laundry and Loading, not the cell blocks. No one got through."

"Just you."

Jeremiah shrugged and in it was a faint note of pride. "I was first at the hole."

"It's too far," Ry blurted. Everyone looked at him and he became aware of his curled lip and vulture posture. He straightened, exhaled, and tried to temper his thundering pulse. "I mean, that's like three days on foot. You must have had a car."

Jo Beth looked at Jeremiah. "You stole a car, too?"

Jeremiah covered his face with both hands; the four digits offered beggarly cover. "It were a service truck. The door was open. The engine was running. I suppose the driver ran out when he saw the explosion. I just—ma'am—it was right in front of me. . . . I just walked into it. Hardly remembered what the wheel was for. Been so many years. But it all came back. Just luck, ma'am, just a little touch of luck after a whole life that had no luck at all, not none."

No one said anything.

"And I was innocent!" Jeremiah proclaimed.

Jo Beth looked at Ry. Her lips looked very red against her face.

"You don't put a man in there for that long for something he did not do," Jeremiah pleaded.

Ry looked at his sister. She seemed confused but energized.

"You don't do a man like that and then ask him not to walk into a hole that just opened up," Jeremiah continued.

"Where's the truck?" Ry said. "Where'd you leave it?"

Jeremiah shook his head. "Ran out of gas. I couldn't say where. Walked all through the day. Kept to the trees, found this coat on a hook. Might've asked them for help instead but didn't much care for the bark of their dog."

"On top of everything else," Jo Beth said, "you stole a coat."

Jeremiah hung his head.

Together the four of them panted in unison.

"You shouldn't steal so much," Sarah observed.

"But it's divinity." Jeremiah lifted his chin, his eyes sparkling with some new notion. "Don't you see? Divinity brought me here to tell you of Marvin."

Jo Beth took up a napkin, wiped her hands with deliberation, and then stood and crossed over to the phone mounted on the wall. Each footstep sounded final. She put her hand to the receiver.

"No, don't call," Jeremiah said. "Not yet, please; they'll come and take me."

"I'm just going to call the prison. Find out what happened. I'm sure you heard wrong; Marvin isn't there." She lifted the handset to an ear and lodged a finger in the rotary dial.

"Shaved head, sometimes." Jeremiah strained for control. "Glasses. Mustache, when they used to let him grow it."

Jo Beth's frame folded like the closing of an umbrella.

The old wound between Ry's eyebrows began to sting.

Jeremiah's tears began to dry as he picked up steam. "He used to talk of you. All of you. That's how I know. That's how everyone inside knew. If he got within earshot he'd talk and talk—you couldn't stop him—and he'd always talk about the same thing. Me and Marvin Burke had kitchen duty once. Year or two back. Maybe we shared five, ten words before he starts in. I got this wife, he tells me. This son. And how they wronged him something terrible."

"Maybe it was jail talk." Jo Beth held the wall for support. "Things change in your mind once you're out. Isn't that true? Isn't that how *you* feel?"

Jeremiah shook his head slowly. "I can't say, ma'am. When Marvin Burke talks you feel obliged to believe him. Couple fellas who called him out got beat down—least that's what they say. And it were not the first time. Marvin Burke transferred from Gingham. Not Pennington. Gingham. You ought to know this. I don't know why you don't."

"There were letters," Jo Beth said. It sounded impulsive.

Ry looked at her in surprise and felt a dagger of betrayal. His mother had known things, important things, and kept them. He saw in her glance a panicked apology, and she leaned in toward Jeremiah—now it was her turn to plead.

"They come every now and then. I don't open them. I read one once and it was about something awful he'd done and why on earth would I want to know that?" She appealed to her son. "Why would that be something I wanted to know? So I stopped reading them. You'd do the same thing. The last thing I've ever wanted to hear was his name, you know that. I never knew anything about any transfers, I swear."

"They done it because he maimed a man in Pennington," Jeremiah said. "Cut both Achilles. Did one one week, waited for him to return from infirmary, did the other. That takes patience. Of course I've also heard that's hogwash. Men say a lot of things—that don't mean they're true. Pennington was no good for him, so off he went to Gingham. Ma'am, I don't know truth from fairy tale when it comes to Gingham. But they say there's a Negro in Gingham with half a tongue after Marvin went after it with a fork. By the time—ma'am, I'm sorry, I know he's your kin—but by the time he got to Blue-feather the boys in charge must've lost track where he came from. Or maybe just ran out of options. Or maybe Marvin Burke planned it—there's men I know who would swear this was all his druthers."

"Can I be excused?"

Ry heard the voice as if it had come from someone else. But he was standing; his chair was backed away from the table; his lips were still parted from the request. Looking up at him were three sets of eyes, all glassy and smooth. He had seen such voids of comprehension in the eyes of sentenced cattle.

"I'm going to be excused," he said.

"Okay," Jo Beth said. "Okay."

He dove from the yellow glare of the kitchen into the comparative murk of the dining room. Four long steps and he was across it. Six steps more and he was down the hallway, tussling with the regular and screen-door locks of the front entrance, and then his feet were clapping across the porch and down the stairs. After that he was lost in the twilight, falling to his knees somewhere beneath the tree he had so often used to escape the abusive sounds of his father. He knelt and let the vomit pour. He was bent so far that gravity ran it through the cleft of scar tissue between his eyebrows. He wiped and blinked. Finally he crawled several feet away and settled onto his back. The first stars of the evening were out, and he wondered if he might see an early meteor—a good omen, maybe.

He lay there for a while, just him and the screaming birds.

Palms were used to wipe clean his face and neck. Grass was chewed and spat to conceal the bilious odor. Sniggety came around to investigate the puke.

Ry's legs were shaky up the stairs; they were stronger in the hallway; in the dining room, the purple dining room, they mimicked how they were supposed to move and sound. He seated himself wordlessly at the kitchen table. The others noticed nothing—he had been gone no longer than an ordinary bathroom visit.

"Ma'am, there is no need for panic," Jeremiah was saying. "He's there, yes. But he is not getting out. His behavior, ma'am—it's not the kind to earn parole. You have yourself such a wonderful house of kindness. You can't even think of leaving it."

"We already have so much packed," Jo Beth mused.

"Such a shame," Jeremiah said. "So much beauty around these parts. But you know the best path—don't listen to a word I say."

Ry felt a kick under the table.

"You barf?" It was Sarah, whispering in a frequency that sheared beneath that of adults.

He glanced at her and felt a surge of comfort from her squirrelly presence.

"No, I'm Ry."

41

She grinned. Her potato tooth was gone.

Jeremiah stood up.

"Of course," Jo Beth said. "I'll fix up the cot."

"No," he said. "Oh, no, ma'am. I ruined supper. I'll be on my way."

"I won't tell them about you," she said. "When I call Bluefeather. Which I have to do. You understand that. I have children."

Jeremiah's chin bobbed curtly, but he did not look convinced. "Obliged. But I'll be on my way."

Jo Beth held her head in one hand and sighed. "At least let me find you a change of clothes. At least let me do that."

Jeremiah looked longingly through the window at the night that had fallen, newer and darker than even his filched overcoat. Ry saw the calculations of risk and reward tug at either ends of the man's temples, and then the hopelessness that rounded his back.

"I'll wait out on the road." He spoke it as if it meant defeat. "That's what I'll do if it's all right with you."

11 HRS., 39 MINS. UNTIL IMPACT

Ry walked with Jeremiah down the gravel driveway, past the machinery shed on their left and the defunct orchard on their right. Both of these areas had automatic floods, which raged with moths just as they always did, only this night the illumination seemed weaker, as if a power grid somewhere had strangled the voltage. Each step they took sounded like the snap of dry bones.

There was a certain silence that went agreed upon among

men. Ry counted on this to get him through the next few minutes beside the mailbox as they waited for Jo Beth. Not a single word had been spoken since they'd left the kitchen, so it was a surprise when he felt Jeremiah's hand upon his shoulder. The pinkie and thumb pressed into him like jaws of a vise.

"It's you most of all," Jeremiah said.

"I know." Again Ry was surprised by the words that came out of him.

"He's not getting out. Not now. But someday—he changes his ways, plays by the rules, who knows? He never killed anybody. They can't keep him forever. He gets parole, it won't matter where you live."

"Understood."

"You make your mother read those letters when they come. You read them *to* her."

"I will."

Jeremiah shook his head as if Ry's assurance was insufficient. "He told me you played him a fool. Attacked him like a coward."

"That's . . . I don't think that's—"

"He told me it was you who would get the worst of it."

"I wasn't a coward. I was a kid."

"Awful things he told me he would do to you. I did not want to say it in front of the females."

Ry turned with enough briskness to buck the man's hand. He was becoming scared, and that angered him.

"Why'd they lock you up?" he asked.

Jeremiah looked stricken. "I told you. I did nothing."

"What did they *say* you did?"

43

The old man furrowed his bushy brow with a resoluteness that surprised Ry. When Jeremiah took an indignant breath, his bottom lip nearly touched his nose.

"They said I killed a boy."

"A boy?" Ry felt superior and it was like choking on fire. "You're as bad as him—as Marvin. You're worse."

"No." Jeremiah shook his head sadly. "I've got no vengeance in my soul. I'm clean. He's got so much that his soul's nearly gone. You can see that plain, just by looking. No, son, the question is you. Do *you* have vengeance?"

Jeremiah leaned in and began to sniff the boy—a long, dry inhale that lasted as long as it took the old man to inch his nose across Ry's face, neck, and shoulders. Revolted, Ry stood motionless. Finally Jeremiah exhaled with a disappointed smack of his bloodless lips. The wafted breath smelled of pickles and yeast.

"You haven't got *any*," he said.

It was a judgment and a challenge. Ry was up to neither because the drawn conclusion was true. He had frustration and petulance and jealousy and shame and impatience and resentment; he had these in gory torrents. Even added together, though, they were not equal to a single rich lode of vengeance. There was one time, as a boy, that he had held such power in his hands, and though it had saved his skin it had been but a brief interlude in a life of gutlessness. Standing in the open air, with the lush cologne of Black Glade loosening his will, Ry could no longer hold back the memory: the bat, the woods, the Unnamed Three. He shut his eyes.

Interlude

JULY 1971–JANUARY 1972

Marvin treated his son as a man even when he was far too young to accept the burden. His father took him everywhere, and not just the fields and the pastures and the barns. He took him into the bathroom: This is how you hold your dick to pee. He took him to the store: This is how you squash men a dollar at a time. He took him into the church: This is how you hum through a hymn so later you can pump the hands of your enemies in the foyer. Ry was expected to learn things on the first try and when he didn't, it's true, sometimes he was struck. The hits stung, but that's it.

It was Jo Beth who got the real beatings, crisp and dutiful and applied with the same brisk relish as aftershave. From the time of Ry's first memory to the age of nine, the sound of these smacks against his mother's cheek or arm or back were no different from the occasional spanks farmers gave to their misbehaving pets and livestock. They were the sounds of progress.

Everything changed with the introduction of the bat in the summer of 1971. The white ash of the Louisville Slugger was stained a rich burgundy. Maybe lots of bats were red, though Ry didn't think so. Holding the Slugger before him like a sword, Marvin stood before a twenty-five-foot castle of baled hay that exhaled dust into blinding beams of sunlight. It was a spectral sight and the nine-year-old Ry approached with awe. The passing off of the bat was done with as much tenderness as when Jo Beth would hand Ry his baby sister. For a moment Ry was sure that he and his father were going to hug. Then Marvin's eyes flickered, became cooler. It had been a silly thought—they had never hugged, not to Ry's knowledge, and at this point it was better not to open that door. Ry convinced himself that this was true.

He spent a week of early evenings swinging away at a stringed ball he had hung from the branch of his favorite tree, with the assumption that it would be an irresistible lure for Marvin, who would come out, smoothing his mustache in appreciation, and expound upon the physics of a good curveball. Instead, the shouts and slapping noises from inside came more frequently than usual.

For the first time in Ry's young life, the yields were off. The recent wheat harvest was thin and the hay crop seeded beneath already showed signs of frailty. If the hay was weak, the cows would eat poorly. If the cows ate poorly, their milk production would suffer. If Grade A production suffered, more time would be spent outside the milk barn to compensate, and they might be caught off guard when the state health inspector made his surprise visit. In fact, a jealous neighbor might see to it. Each night Ry heard these theories coming from the eastern windows. He could not think of anything to help the cause, aside from becoming a better batter.

That was not to happen. One night after supper Marvin stormed outside in bare feet and ripped the bat from Ry's hands. "Security!" he hollered as he made his way back toward the house. Rounding the corner, he shook the bat at the stars: "Security!" Not only was the taking of the bat sudden but to Ry even the logic seemed strained. The baseball bat would somehow deter vindictive neighbors better than the Winchester? Ry didn't believe it, but he was only ten. What did he know?

Whether or not Marvin's original intent was pure, the bat soon took on a more sinister purpose. What set him off the first time was the discovery of a small mending job that Jo Beth had taken on for Mrs. Horvath down the road. The idea that their imbecile neighbors might think Marvin Burke's family needed a single goddamn cent more than what he brought in was abhorrent. Ry immediately noticed the change in the quality of nighttime noises. Impacts had a lower pitch; what formerly snapped now had the sound of a sad and gigantic heartbeat: *Thump.* An epic length of time later, the second beat: *Thump.* Ry fell asleep counting the seconds between the beats and wondering what kind of animal could live with such sluggish blood.

After the first night of this new abuse, his mother was never the same. Ry heard her make a call to Mrs. Horvath, saying she was so sorry but didn't have time to fix up that blouse after all, could she suggest the stitchery in Bloughton? Soon he began to notice shiners expanding from her elbows and anklebones. Her body would seize up in the midst of odd movements—lifting a jug of milk from the fridge or turning the faucet to the left. She still smiled at her son in a way that insisted it was nothing, only now her own eyes didn't believe it.

It was a surprise when he found her sitting on her bed one day working the handle of the bat with a square of sandpaper. He asked her why. He didn't know any better. When she looked up her eyes were pouched in soft purple tissue, and she winced while making the smallest of turns in his direction, as if there were things inside her that had been hurt. She smiled and told him she wanted the bat to stay pretty—or maybe handsome was a better word for a baseball bat; pretty was a girl's word. He stood there in the doorway as she kept on about how it had been Ry's bat first, and that it was still his bat secretly, and that one day he would get it back, just wait and see—but shhh, wait quietly. Ry didn't know what to say. She kept talking and sanding and crying.

The end came on a January weekend. They were inside, the entire family, because it was a night cruel with snow and armed with wind like slapping hands. Things were nevertheless going well: Calves bedraggled by some mysterious ailment were making a spirited recovery. Marvin leaned back in the living room rocking chair and hummed his satisfaction: *Hmmmm hm hm hmmmm.* Mom prepared food in the kitchen, Ry and Sarah played on the living room floor, and there was peace on Earth, at least until the humming stopped.

Ry glanced over from where he sat scrunched on an ottoman, pretending the floor around him was a river of lava. Marvin's rocking chair lurched, empty. He was up and moving. The blue TV glow slid off his shaved skull as he swept into the dining room. Ry leaned over the lava to watch. His father reached beneath a correspondence desk and removed a small, folded pile of fabric that Ry had never seen before. Because of the dimness and distance Ry couldn't be sure, but he thought Marvin put the material to his face and inhaled deeply before adjusting his glasses and thumbing through his mustache bristles. Ry leaned farther and his knees sunk into molten rock. Marvin carefully folded the fabric—it was pink, Ry could see that much—before stuffing it into his pants pocket. Not a word was said. Minutes later, the family sat down to dinner.

Ry slept well that night. He would never forgive himself for that.

Eight hours later he got dressed and went outside while shaking off bad dreams about the new kinds of noises coming from the bedroom above. January, after all, was a month that always made the house squeal and moan. He went through the motions of early-morning chores trying to move as little as possible. His knees, brutalized by glaciated dirt, slowed his trip back to the house, or at least, he told himself it was his knees. He dallied for so long that eventually Marvin emerged from the house and passed him on the way to the garage, face obscured inside a white hood of exhalation, his gloved fingers pawing through a key ring.

"Your mom's sick." It was a grunt from behind a coat collar. "Don't pester her."

Ry turned on his heel. "I heard her—" he began, but Marvin was already stamping the snow from his boots at the garage entryway, then slamming the door behind him. Ry paused to hear the truck engine shudder off its armor of frost before lowering his face against the cold and heading indoors.

It wasn't until he was shivering in the kitchen that he

came up against the reality of no breakfast. Marvin was gone; his mother was sick. He heard movement above but knew by its aimlessness that it was Sarah. He shucked his coat and boots and went upstairs. Sarah had only recently been given her own bed, and already this morning she had abandoned it. She sat near the window groping at toys. Watching her fumble with brightly colored plastic always rankled him. He had his own toys, army figures and superheroes and race cars, but Marvin had made it clear that such trinkets were not for the heirs to mighty farms.

Plenty of toys remained, though, and lived in a wilted cardboard box printed with the words "Corn Flakes" and crammed into the space beneath his bed. Sometimes, if he knew Marvin was far out of range, Ry would take out the box and pour the contents onto his bedspread. He would sift through the characters, pair them off for unfought duels, and bask in their million tiny facets. Soon they would seem to be as big and as real as he was. Ry had been jealous of his sister's happy banging, but that was the wrong approach. Forget chores. Forget meals. Forget his mother. They could bang toys together until the snowy world outside faded to absolute white.

It was a fantasy interrupted by the blank gaze of his parents' bedroom door. Ry held his breath, leaned in, and listened. Sarah's clatter made it hard to hear. He closed his eyes and let his warm ear seal against the cool walnut. There—he heard a tentative bedspring. Somehow relieved, he retreated, picked up Sarah, and carried her downstairs.

They ate cereal. Ry had to wring the milk out of her shirt. Next, there was a special stool for washing hands and on the sink there was animal-shaped soap. Traumatized by an

50

improper ratio of hot to cold, she barely noticed as he dressed her in coat, hat, snow pants, and boots. She held on to him with a mittened hand and together they took a thousand toddler-sized steps to the dairy barn. When those chores were completed, they cut across the center of the property toward the chicken house, but made a pit stop in the garage to feed Sniggety. The dog, still curious back then, left a wet nose-trail across the girl's face. This dismayed her and she tried to air her grievance. Ry pretended to listen but was distracted by the space in the garage where the truck used to be. Marvin Burke had mentioned nothing the day before about going into town. For that matter, Jo Beth Burke had shown no signs of illness. Everything felt wrong.

Soon it was one in the afternoon. Ry felt a flash of annoyance at his mother. Never, not even during the worst bouts of illness, had she failed to fix them food. Her desertion was profane and left him with no choice. Ry's gut was hot and the stairway banister, when he took it, was cold. Once at the unhelpful bedroom door, though, his indignation dissolved.

"Mom?" It was too soft. He cleared his throat and raised the volume. "Mom, you okay?"

He pressed his ear to the wood. Icy air howled through some breach in the defenses. Downstairs, Sarah was yielding to the dull drone of a resolute cry. There was a consistency to these noises that had the texture of sleep; his mother would never know if he snuck in, stole a quick peek. He put his hand to the brass knob and was surprised by his varnish of sweat.

"Honey." It was his mother's voice. He stopped turning the knob and it clattered back to a neutral position. "Honey, is that you?"

Ry's heart was pounding. This conversation went right in

the face of Marvin's warning. If they were caught, he knew full well that his mother would get the brunt of the punishment, and that itself was punishing. He spoke quickly. "I wanted to know if you felt better."

"No." The response was instant. "No, dear, leave me alone. Is that Sarah I hear? Is she all right?"

"She's fine. I was thinking of making lunch."

"That's a good idea. You do that. Don't worry about me. You just let me rest and feel better."

Ry did not move. She sounded like she was holding her breath.

"You want me to bring you soup?" he asked.

"No," she said. "Did you feed the chickens? You better do that."

"I already did. You need some water?"

"And what about the cows?"

"I did them before Dad left."

There was a pause.

"I have water," she said. "Plenty of water. Now go take care of your sister. You left your comic books in front of the TV. Go read your comic books."

The bedsprings creaked. He thought he heard a gasp.

"You don't sound sick." This was bold. He clamped his teeth.

"Well, I am." Her voice carried equal parts disorientation and anger. "I *am* sick. I am *very* sick. What else do you want me to say?"

That he hit you again. That he used the bat. That it's not a virus that's keeping you hidden but a bruise or welt or something so bad you won't let your children see it. Say that, any of it, and the door will open and we can deal with it, you and me; we'll figure out a way, even if he comes home and finds us—somehow we will deal with it.

"Now you go look after your sister and let me rest."

He was ten years old and always did what he was told.

It was just this once that he disobeyed.

He seized the knob and cranked it. It would not open. He wrenched it harder.

"Ry, no! No, honey! I'm fine! I'm fine!"

Not once in his life had he found a door in the house locked. The old house had keyholes everywhere, but Ry had never suspected the existence of actual keys. He stood and kicked at the door, at the knob, the jamb, the hinges. He slammed his palms against the wood. Nothing gave way.

"Stop! Ry, please! Just stop!"

But he was already running, downstairs in moments, through the house in seconds, her protests fading. He hopped into his boots but did not lace them; he hurled on his coat but did not zip it. As he threw open the back door he heard the softening of his sister's cries as she grew sleepy. With any luck she would doze through the whole thing.

His parents' bedroom window was above the back porch. Ry tried to think of it, with its siding and sills and rain gutters, as just another tree to be climbed. Once he found himself standing upon the roof's sparkling shingles, he took a quick inventory of the nests of snow, the runners of ice. He moved swiftly, stretching his torso over the edge of the roof, reaching out for the storm window that was now at shoulder level, and putting his hands to the pane. It was unexpectedly hot. He dug his nails under the sash and lifted. It opened cleanly for the very last time.

Ry pushed himself up and over the windowsill. This angle

of approach did not allow him to prepare for the various waiting impediments: the rapier of a radio antenna; the rocking chair and its long teeth; and the red bat, which clattered to the floor and sketched a territorial arc. Ry shook off the traps like Sniggety emerging from a rain-beaded crop and rolled away, gaining balance against the dresser.

She was too ashamed to look at him—that was his first thought. She lay on her left side facing the far wall, a thin sheet draped over her body. His second thought was that it was too cold for such a measly covering; he couldn't imagine why she hadn't burrowed beneath a few blankets. He began compassing the foot of the bed.

Wadded near the headboard was the pink fabric, the one his father had stolen from the dining room the night before. Another step closer brought a new detail into focus: It was bloody. Not soaked, just spotted, as if it had been used to stem the welling of minor nicks. Ry realized that the fabric was another sewing commission. How could she have been so stupid? He did not feel the rest of the steps it took to bring him to the far side of the bed. The sheet, when he lifted it from his mother's torso, had no texture or weight—it was as if he were shooing away smoke. His mother's naked body was a surprise, though not fundamentally disturbing; she was, after all, in the privacy of her own bed. Nothing appeared to be wrong, and Ry leaned over to whisper apologies.

Her ear was sewn to the bed. It was an amateur job, though Ry could imagine Marvin insisting, as he laced the brown thread in and out of the cartilage, that that was the whole point—it didn't take a genius to sew. Jo Beth made an attempt to look at her son, but even the slightest move tautened the ear. One of the four loops of thread had already snapped; the others proved that Marvin Burke at least knew his knots. Ry lifted an arm to offer some kind of assistance and his mother winced. He winced back. With fingers as clumsy as his, she was sure to emerge from the ordeal slotted. Frustration splintered into impatience. She was the one with dexterous fingers. *Use your hands*, he thought. *Can't you just use your hands?*

She could not; he felt bad for even thinking it. More brown thread snaked through the webbing between the thumb and index finger of each of her hands, drawing them tight to the mattress. Ry took a step back and was mesmerized by the brown shimmers of thread he suddenly saw in dozens of bodily locations. Marvin had lashed his wife into a posture so natural that, had it not been for the discarded pink cloth, Ry might have taken it for sleep and tiptoed out without thinking twice.

More than pain, it was numbness that Ry sensed from his mother. Sensation had left his body, too. He didn't feel the bolt shift when he unlocked the bedroom door from the inside. When he withdrew the twelve-inch sewing shears from the bureau inside the walk-in closet, the metal was without temperature. Before returning to his mother's side he lowered the window to stem the icy breeze, and it jammed a half inch from closing. He put all of his weight on it but no farther would it budge; nine years later, only nailing it shut would finish the grudge. Blood worked its way back into Ry's fingers, though, and that was important considering what he had to do next.

With exquisite care he removed the sheet from the rest of her body. Though her skin was blue, he felt the heat of her shame. Her body's meat hung heavy and shone with perspiration. Her thighs were tacky with urine. Ry felt the prim fealty of a nurse as he took up the pink fabric, shook out its crusty folds, and quartered it. Blood had ruined it, though Ry was of the opinion that it was being repurposed for nobler service. He found a clean edge and swept beads of sweat from his mother's lip and brow. Then he refolded it again and wiped the urine from her thighs and blotted what he could from the mattress. He discarded the fabric in the trash can and took up the shears.

It was the most intimate thing he had ever shared with anyone. He began with the left ear, raising the pink flesh and extending the point of the shears to make three minute snips. Freed, she immediately wrenched her neck to stretch the cramped muscles. Ry continued his scrutiny; not an inch was left to chance. A single thread made four passes through her left armpit, and the act of pinching that skin away from the bed was not unlike the morning milking. A tidy knot cinched her left nipple to the mattress, and Ry took care to rest the blade against the areola before committing to the cut. The thread passing through the upper curve of her navel had previously broken free but she had no idea; Ry faked a slice with the shears and watched her stomach pound in relief. Most serious were the four trips the thread made through her hip fat. After he freed it, the flesh spasmed as if just that part of her were sobbing. Everything else was easy to liberate: the thread that passed through both folds of her private parts, the loose knots that strung the underside of her knees to the mattress, the eight meticulous circuits Marvin had sewn through the skin between each and every toe. When Ry finally rose with an aching back and shears shining with blood, he knew that he had freed more than skin.

Jo Beth sat up, grabbed the glass of water that had sat out of reach for who knew how many hours, and chugged it. She shook stubborn drops from the bottom of the glass, took several deep breaths, and then stood. It was the last thing Ry expected. Two dozen threads dangled like extracted veins. She reached to her ear, pinched her fingers, and began to withdraw each string. It was an unchaining: Each wisp swam away on invisible currents, and she grew stronger with every body part that was emancipated. For the first time Ry felt shy. He lowered his eyes, then felt the encircling of two arms and the nestling of breasts. His feet nearly left the ground with the force of her back-and-forth rocking. Behind her, he glimpsed the white mattress and saw the dotted red outline of her perforated body. It was the residue of a person left behind; this new woman holding him was whole.

"Gather your sister," she said.

Difficult to do, with a baseball bat in one hand and shears in the other, but gather her he did as his mother dressed and hurried downstairs. Barest essentials—bottles, medicine, diapers—were stuffed into a bag. Ry's main job was to carry the weapons, but the bat was eerily smooth and kept slithering from his grip like an eel. It would require both hands. He slid the shears into his back pocket.

His mother's coat was unzipped when she ran outside. Ry heard the sputter of the car engine cranking, heard it die. Bile surged up his esophagus—it wouldn't start; they would never make it. When he heard it catch he almost sobbed. Jo Beth knew the vehicle's quirks as well as anyone; in weather like this it needed five minutes minimum to warm up or it would die before making it past the driveway. Ry set Sarah on the floor and began lacing his boots. They were leaving. It was happening. The knot got sloppy and Ry had to start over.

Jo Beth burst in, grabbed Sarah's shoes, coat, snow pants, and hat, then dropped them in a pile in front of the two-year-old and went to work. Ry knew from experience that it took several minutes to dress Sarah. That meant there was time to save something that mattered to him alone. He hurried through the dining room and entered his bedroom. Every object cried out for mercy but he felt a masculine disregard for their pleas. Ry took to his knees and reached under the bed.

But when he picked up the box it wilted, and the "Corn Flakes" stamped on its side accordioned into a nonsense of consonants. Ry dropped it on the bed before the bottom gave way. There was no way this box was going to make it. He felt the snotty choke of a child's stubborn determination. This was his birthday, Christmas, and the last day of school put together. He would not be denied.

"Let's go." His mother clapped from the kitchen. "Now, Ry."

"Wait!" He took the box and dumped the toys onto the quilt. Hypnotized by chrome and rubber and painted faces and sculpted muscle, Ry found choice an impossibility.

"Meet us outside," Jo Beth warned. The front door creaked. "We're leaving."

Ry sunk his hands into the pile and felt the loving bite of fake weaponry and robot circuitry, the prickly scruff of stuffed animal. He shoved a handful into his coat pocket. Another handful into the opposite pocket. One, two, three more crammed down his left pants pocket and four jammed down the right. The ridges of plastic faces, of posable arms, of hands with notches for accessories—they excited his fingers, were the very textures of joy. He could not stop now. Several more characters went into his underwear.

He heard what sounded like a car door. No, not yet! A sob tore through his shoulders and he swiped up the baseball bat and turned away. Action figures ground against his groin as he dashed through the dining room. He banked through the kitchen, kicked through the back door, and rushed across the porch, feeling like a toy himself—stiff and operating with the simplest of jointed limbs.

Leaping down the stairs, he expected to find the car idling in the driveway, Sarah waving at him from the backseat. It was not there and Ry wondered if he had been left behind. Then he saw the creep of exhaust from the garage and realized they had yet to make it out. Ry ducked under the clothesline and came upon the car. It chugged dutifully. There was no one in it.

He turned at the sound of voices and saw, thirty feet to his left and near the junk shed, his mother scuttling backward across the snow with Sarah clutched in her arms. A purring truck blocked the narrowest stretch of driveway and Marvin Burke stood in front of it, boots planted, overalls poking from his wool coat, green stocking cap sitting comically low upon his head, gloved fists placed on hips like a schoolmaster. Jo Beth was screaming something. Ry couldn't make it out and stepped closer.

"Don't touch her!" That was her refrain. "Don't touch her! Don't touch her!"

Whatever conversation Ry had missed had been enough for Marvin. For once he was not in the mood to talk.

"Get out of my way!" A strand of saliva hung from Jo Beth's lip. "We'll run you over!"

Ry realized he was still moving. Toys poked at his legs as if nudging him along.

Marvin held out a palm to his wife, as if expecting to be given her hand, or even the baby.

"Burn in hell!" Jo Beth roared.

Ry was fifteen feet away now. He passed his mother and sister. Marvin did not look at his son; instead he made clenching motions with his outstretched hand.

"No!" Jo Beth screamed. "No! No!"

Ten feet, nine, eight—Ry choked up on the bat, his fingers and wrists recalling the lessons of all those swings taken over all those nights. He raised the bat to his shoulder. Seven feet, six, five—he drew it back. Here it was at last, the violence he had always expected and secretly wanted, a violence that if pulled off correctly might just free his sister and mother. His heart lost its tempo, improvised.

Marvin looked at him.

"Son," he said.

Ry smiled—an apology—and swung.

Until the final instant, Marvin did not believe it. That was the sweetest part, the mustache twitch indicating how the master calculator had miscalculated. The moment, however, was brief. The sickly strike passed a few inches in front of Marvin's nose. Ry was left drastically twisted. He blinked and coughed and wondered if, apart from everything else, his father was disappointed that he had raised this magnitude of pussy. A shadow fell over Ry; Marvin took the bat. There was nothing else to it. Ry appraised his empty hands. Red welts glistened upon each palm.

He looked up. The gaping black hole of the man's face was warped by the unfamiliar contours of betrayal. The bat, however, looked natural in Marvin's grip, particularly when he lifted it to his shoulder.

"The rubber tubing." Marvin sounded choked. "You flushed it?"

Ry acknowledged that it was a perfectly sound question. After the curtain was drawn on this scene, Marvin Burke had a farm to administer. Unfortunately, the morning's chores were impossible for Ry to recall. Marvin's defeated sigh was aimed at all parties, including himself.

"This is not how to run a farm," he insisted.

The bat left a red mark upon the air. Ry was struck between the eyebrows. He was aware of a black flare like that of the camera flash during school photo day; then, at a great distance, his mother's howl. He saw trees, clouds, the roof, the ajar second-floor window, clouds again, trees again, snow. The puny plumes of his own breath. Sniggety, upside down, skulking from the upsetting scene. He felt for his body and found nothing. After a time, blood began to run into his eyes. It made sense to close them and he did.

Sixty seconds at most passed in darkness, though it felt like sixty years.

Ry resurfaced. Through lashes glued together with blood he made out his mother crouched against the side of the garage. She held Sarah's face to her chest as if to shield her from the outlandish Wild West vision of Marvin Burke hopping from one foot to the other. He was hollering all the while, though to Ry's busted head it was but wet and fuzzy nonsense. Ry shook himself, watched his vision go wild, and felt hot blood sluice down his collar. For some reason this made him aware of the shears lodged in his back pocket. He took a handful of dirt and dragged himself closer for a better look.

Now Marvin was making jabs with the bat close to his wife's face. Jo Beth was not crying, though, and not shrinking. Ry was proud. His mouth opened in a smile and he felt blood coat his bottom lip.

Snow fell. A truck rumbled past on the road and gave a neighborly toot; Marvin waved his bat like an overexcited kid. He did not look around, though, and Ry was glad. He pulled his junked body another foot, then another. Marvin started clobbering the ground at Jo Beth's feet as he tried to explain a complicated point. Ry felt mud spatter from the backswing—his crawling had drawn him even nearer than he had realized.

He brought himself to a seated position and reached for the shears in his back pocket. The metal burned his hand and tears exploded from his eyes instantly. He could no more drive the shears into his father's back than he could his mother's neck or sister's heart. The sink, the squish, the jut—his muscles refused to be a part of it. He was not a killer; he was a little boy—he was ten and he was useless. The shears, in fact, had already slipped from his fingers and were lost in the snow.

If he ran away at least he would not have to watch what happened next. Ry's first steps were foul; his knees bobbed as if they were toys floating in water. Marvin noticed him standing and was so surprised that he dropped the bat. Ry felt the pinch of a grin. Running: It was not cowardice; it was inspiration! His father would be forced to chase him! Ry gulped a sob of pride. His foot kicked through the flimsy wire fence bordering an erstwhile flowerbed, and his legs, midsection, and torso worked together in acceptable fashion. He shuffled across the lawn dizzily. The exact location of his mother was unclear—he could no longer see her due to a black spot in his vision—but he pointed at what he hoped was the garage and whispered a prayer: *Drive away, Mom, drive away.*

Ry heard the *shunk* of a Louisville Slugger being snatched from sidewalk cement and he gasped in delight—his father was taking the bait. Ry picked up his speed and careened between the thirty-five-foot silo and the corn crib, everyday landmarks along a path he could traverse half-blind, which he was. His father gave chase—Ry could hear the footfalls. Far away, he thought he heard the opening of a car door.

"Yes!" Pink froth sputtered from his lips. "Yes!"

Both seventy-foot silos, the old grain shed, and the dueling manure pits blurred by in neon scribbles, and then the architecture of the farm gave way to the endless brown of one hundred and sixty acres, the white corkscrews of snow. Ry elongated his stride and laughed at his speed. What spirit and endurance! With each pump of his leg, toys worked free from his pockets and scattered. Bravery! These kamikaze soldiers! He would earn their sacrifice.

It was a distance that never took more than seven minutes to cross, but that was walking. At a dash, Ry covered the winter ruins in what felt like seconds. Beyond the low-hanging limbs of Marvin's beloved Osage-orange trees, so thick they made fences unnecessary, awaited the caliginous magnificence of Black Glade. Green ash walnuts stood like old gods, flexing their bone wings against shag bark and bitternut hickories. Ry dove beneath these skeletons and daylight was obfuscated. The pelt of snow became haphazard scatterings.

For half an hour he dodged among the trunks and branches. No sooner did Ry find himself slowed by a deeper thicket than he heard the distant firecracker blasts of Marvin taking out intrusive limbs with the bat, and the ice crackle of similarly obliterated thornbushes. They were the sounds of furious defeat: Because of the son's unexpected burst of speed, the wife and daughter had escaped and soon police would be sent in pursuit. Marvin had lost control and there was nothing else of equivalent value to lose.

"Hmmmm hm hm hmmmm."

This song was the only way to keep focus in the face of such failure.

Marvin was twenty or thirty yards away, in some perilously indeterminate direction, and Ry bucked himself away from the flaky bark of a red pine and kicked through the beetle-ravaged hull of a fallen hickory. Two action figures fell from his pockets; he felt the decrease in weight. Moments later a leap over a small creek released the last of the toys he had shoved into his underwear and they splashed down like turds. His toys, the future merriment he was owed, all of it would dissolve like shit in water. He gasped for breath with his hands on his thighs, and wondered if this was what it had felt like for his mother to be hounded day after day and year after year.

Living was a burdensome impulse. He kept moving for one incredible hour, then a fantastic second. Then three, then four, or more, he lost track—his body was a miserable machine and time passed like a slowly breaking bone. To throw off his father, he made every unpredictable turn that he could, but Marvin always came roaring back. Sunlight dove away and still neither father nor son slowed his pace. Beneath the braided and purpled canopy, sharp things ripped at Ry's ears, obstructions cracked his kneecaps, and barriers sent him clawing for alternate avenues. After stuffing a gritty handful of snow into his mouth in place of water, he used his cold fingers to probe, just for a moment, the site of his wound. His forehead was spongy and swollen. A concussion, was that what he had? Or was it something worse? His thoughts were unclear; they were just clear enough to know this.

More than anything he was freezing. Both shoulders, his back, and his legs ached from shivering and his exposed skin was inelastic and numb. He wasn't stupid. He knew he couldn't keep up this evasive effort. Full darkness had fallen, and there was no way he'd survive an entire night so inadequately clothed against subzero temperatures. He knelt alongside a hill and watched each joint of his body quiver with the promise of surrender and the welcome onset of hypothermia. He lowered his butt to the bank and enjoyed the comforting hitch of relieved sobs—it felt so good to give up. The birds of nightfall wailed a lullaby. He couldn't remember them ever sounding like that before.

Patting at his empty coat pockets led to a crushing realization. It was his toys that had given him away—dozens of them, their chilly little corpses creating a trail far better than breadcrumbs. Ry laid his head down in the cold twilight, set his arms at his sides, and gazed up at the branches that made cracks in the smoked glass of the sky. If he removed all suggestion of rebellion, perhaps his father would kill him quickly.

There was something in his left pants pocket. Forcing in his knuckles and fingers was like stuffing in rocks and twigs, but after some fumbling he withdrew not one object but two. No—even farther down, a tiny third object as well. This was curious. He debated tossing the traitorous toys into the snow. On the other hand, he felt an idle interest in the identity of these survivors. After all, it still might be a couple of minutes before he was overtaken.

He laughed at the motley sight. A gathering of odder bedfellows would have been difficult to produce. The first one was Mr. Furrington, a portly turquoise teddy bear with a sewed-on bow tie and bowler hat. He had been a baby gift, and Ry had warm memories of taking him along to the bath and potty and dropping him into both when Furrington asked to approve the contents. This cheap wad of cloth and stuffing had guided him through scary bedtimes, ominous mealtimes, and episodes of sickness and worry. Marvin had implemented a zero-tolerance policy on stuffed animals a few years back, and Ry had placed each offender in a garbage sack with eyes clear and dry, though his mother, for some reason, had cried. That night, Furrington reappeared in Ry's sock drawer, and though Ry knew it was his mother who had salvaged the toy, he preferred to imagine Furrington himself scaling the trash can and brushing off the filth in regal distaste before readjusting his hat and strolling back into the house. To keep him hidden, Ry put him in the cardboard toy box, where men with guns and mutant villains soon overwhelmed him.

Jesus Christ was the second toy. Ry recalled that the figure had come as an unexpected bonus from the stupefying chants and papercraft drills of Sunday school. Jesus Christ was an eight-inch bendy figure in the Gumby mold, entirely pink save a white swaddle of cloth around his midsection, a brown beard of nodular texture, and the painted dashes and dots of his face and stigmata. When Ry had seen the Jesuses being handed out, he felt a rush of fantasy: He would break out the blue and black markers from the arts-and-crafts bin and turn Jesus Christ into Marvel Comics' Reed Richards, a.k.a. Mr. Fantastic. It was a disappointment when he got his hands on Jesus Christ and found that he did not stretch at all. He only bent. Ry had stuck Jesus Christ's legs behind his head and knotted the arms, and when he released the plastic messiah from his tortures the limbs snapped back into place. There was a disarming intensity to Jesus Christ's pupil-less white eyes, and yet there was also something peaceful in the blankness. Ry felt a quiet. In truth the contemplation of Jesus Christ's features was the closest thing to a religious experience Ry had ever had at church. This did not mean that Jesus Christ was fun to play with; Ry gave up after just a few attempts. Throwing him out, though, seemed like sacrilege, and over time, when he saw the pink skin peeking through layers of more popular toys, Ry could not shake the hunch that there remained in Jesus Christ a Mr. Fantastic potential.

The third and last toy was Scowler. Ry stared at it, fearful of making any sudden move. Mr. Furrington and Jesus Christ he may have remembered if asked to mentally catalog the contents of the cardboard box. Scowler, though, he had will-fully forgotten. It was a toy only in the broad technical sense. There was nothing fun about it. Ry had found it in a dusty apple box that his mother had brought home from an estate sale. He had been lifting aside yellowed issues of *Life* and swirling a hand through a metal soup of pulleys and hinges and buckles, when suddenly he saw a mouth gaping up at him. Ry withdrew the figure carefully. Its insides crunched like cornmeal. It was naked and humanoid, a collection of rancid lumps, and no more than four inches long, with half of that length owing to its cone-shaped head. The waxy texture of its skin suggested oilcloth, and though its intended color was yellow, it had bleached to a hue almost fleshlike. There was a crisp outer film that had once adhered to the skin with waterproof tightness, but now blistered away like sausage casing. Dominating the head was a huge downturned mouth, a dry open hole defended by dozens of daggered teeth made of seashells. Shallow depressions, imprinted by the artisan's thumb, served as its empty eye sockets. Its abbreviated limbs were gnarled like roots, and tiny nails erupted from repair zones like patches of iron acne. Sharp sawed-off pipe edges poked from the ankles and wrists, evidence of the thing's metal skeleton. It felt to Ry like a dreadful talisman—for what purpose, he did not care to know.

He had begun to lower it for instant reburial when his mother craned her neck over his shoulder.

"Look at that," she said. "That's folk art."

"It's dirty," Ry said. Attacking the object's cleanliness was a savvy tactic.

"Someone worked hard on that," Jo Beth said. "Look at the workmanship. Look at that slipstitching. There's not a single gap between those teeth. Somebody loved this little guy."

"I don't like it."

"Well, you're spoiled. The person who made this probably didn't have money for real toys. They had to make do with their imagination and whatever they had handy. You keep it. I'll bet it outlives every other toy you have."

Ry rolled it over in his palm. Its weight seemed deceptive.

"What does it do?"

"What does it do? Does it have to *do* something?" She leaned over and squinted. "He scowls."

"He scowls?"

"In fact, he kind of looks like you."

He turned to her in alarm. "What do you mean?"

Smiling, she pointed at her son's expression. "Right there, see? You and Scowler are like two peas in a pod."

Ry looked back down at the thing. The eyeholes offered nothing.

"Okay," he said. He set Scowler on the floor and later placed him facedown at the bottom of his cardboard toy box. He assumed it would go missing along with the turquoise teddy bear and bendy religious icon. Through brisk shuffling of the box's contents, it would even dismember and disintegrate. Death—that's what boxes were for. Only it didn't die. Scowler showed up repeatedly throughout the years, its hollow eyes and voracious mouth poking their ways into the topmost space of the toy box, the knives of its exposed skeleton spearing gun belts and jet packs. Ry would extricate these entanglements and assure himself that they were accidental.

The fat one, the tall one, and the small one: Ry fanned out the trio beneath the moonlight. How odd that he would spend his final moments with these companions. He gathered them to his chest and struggled for the icy breath that would be one of his last.

You can do it.

Ry smiled. This encouragement was pleasant, even if it came too late.

I believe in you, old boy.

It was a jolly falsetto with a punctilious British accent. Ry was warmed by it, even tickled.

There's no telling what you could do if you just moved your bloody bum!

Ry laughed. He raised an arm and regarded Furrington. The brown marble eyes winked in the dawn. That couldn't be right; Ry pressed the heel of his other hand to his forehead in consternation. This agitated the mushroom swelling of his wound, and his vision splintered into rays of color. He fought to hang on to his last thought. What was going on? Oh, yes, this stuffed animal was speaking to him—of course it was; it was his old friend Mr. Furrington.

I'll never give up on you, Furrington said.

"Thank you," Ry whispered.

Give it a go, old chum.

"Should I?"

Why not? You might be surprised.

For Furrington, he'd try. He ignored the advancing *hmmmm hm hm hmmmm* and tightened the muscles in the small of his back. He found himself sitting straight up, his extremities tingling with—could it be?—a kind of warmth. He smiled down at the turquoise bear. Furrington tipped his bowler, or maybe Ry did it for him. Either way, he was moved by the chubby little guy's modesty and decided to repay him with effort. Ry took to his feet—a miracle, a miracle. There was no feeling in his toes but there remained some compliance in his ankles, and he chanced a couple shaky steps down the bank. Another miracle. His teeth ached in the evening air and that's what told him he was—miracle of miracles!—smiling.

I love you, said Furrington, *dear friend.*

"I love you, too," Ry gasped. Tears crystallized at the corners of his eyes. His foot landed wrong and he went scrambling sideways.

Balance, chap, balance!

"Sorry," Ry said. A black oak bounced off his face, but then he was righted.

Crackers! Watch the old bean.

"The old bean," Ry said. "You got it."

Ry gazed down at the three figures in his hands and was overwhelmed with the thrill of camaraderie. Yes, he would cavort through the timber with friends of his own choosing, and no, he didn't care what his parents thought of his playmates or the places they chose to play. He wedged the three beneath his belt. Ry and Furrington and Jesus Christ and Scowler: best friends. He skipped and the bad landing vibrated all the way up into his jaw. In these conditions careless tomfoolery could lead to death—he recognized this—but why not die by splitting himself in half with the force of his play rather than suffer a tedious and predictable murder?

The euphoria fueled him for five more astonishing hours. Then his feet became rocks. Then, worse, they became trees, planted so that each step was an uprooting. A cold ripped at his ears like pulled duct tape, and a fluid, maybe cranial, drained from his forehead. Furrington kept up the droll chatter but it was hard to hear over the shriek of the cold. The police, where were they? Bad question. He knew where they were. Black Glade had them, too. He strained for an audible sign, but all he heard was the humming. His father was closer than ever, a short sprint away if only the brambles would let up.

Thou art lost, observed Jesus Christ.

Ry stopped moving, dislodged the plastic figure from his belt, and looked at the pink face, the all-seeing dots of its eyes. It was time to admit the truth.

"I'm going in circles," he said.

Do not despair, Jesus Christ responded. *Remember thy teachings.*

Oh, yes, Furrington added. *Capital idea. Capital!*

Though he could hear, so incredibly close, his father's fingers ripping through frozen briar, Ry did not resume his flight. Instead he took up Furrington in the other hand and faced him toward the elastic savior.

"Furrington, this is Jesus Christ," he said. "Jesus Christ, this is Furrington."

Blessings unto thou, said Jesus Christ.

Right, right, said Furrington. *Aces.*

"Now." Ry tried to control the trembling in his voice. "You said teachings. I don't remember any teachings."

Thou dost.

"No, I don't." The humming was as loud and jagged as a lawn mower. "He's coming. Help me."

Thy teachers have toldest thou how. His voice was deep and soothing, each syllable placed with unhurried assurance.

Ry opened his mouth to protest, but there was a glimmer of light in the swirling blackness of his mind. Hadn't there, in fact, been a school unit on wilderness survival? The point of light grew and Ry could see it, his second-grade classroom. He could even see his desk, how his too-long legs struggled against the unfair perimeters. On the desktop he saw his Pink Pearl eraser, absent of any pencil stabbings; he saw his canister of paste, as yet uncrusted by sloppy handling. All of this meant that it was the first week of school—that's how important this lesson was—and though the words "Black Glade" were never uttered, the students implicitly understood. Perhaps if Ry concentrated hard enough now he could hear just a few of the teacher's instructions.

"Yell three times in a row," Ry remembered out loud. "But I can't do that. He'll hear."

What else, my child?

Ry squeezed his eyes shut and listened some more. "Leave markings on trees so search parties can find you. But I can't do that, either."

Thou art wise.

There was something else; Jesus Christ was just waiting for him to find it. Ry pressed his two friends against his temples as he tried to block out his father's humming.

"Keep moving in a straight path. There's a way. You can use the North Star."

Willst thou show us? Jesus Christ asked with polite deference.

Ry nodded. Ignoring Marvin, so near now Ry could hear the ragged whistles of breath drawn between the song's every verse, he stumbled around with his face turned upward until he found an exposed patch of sky. It had to be close to eleven o'clock, an ideal time for stargazing. The North Star was the last celestial body in the handle of the Little Dipper, but as his second-grade teacher had warned, the Little Dipper could be difficult to find. Better to try to find the Big Dipper, which pointed to the North Star with its outermost cup. Look, there it was. That was easy. Now imagine a line drawn from the North Star to the forest floor. That was north.

Blimey, Furrington said. *You've done it!*

Go on, my child, Jesus Christ said. *Deliver us from evil.*

The humming was right there at his heels, so close that he expected the browns and grays of his peripheral vision to be slashed by red at any second. But if he could just hold to a northern trajectory instead of making mad circles, escape would be imminent, and these eight or nine straight hours of motion would feel more like one or two, he just knew it.

With the cheering of his two friends, he nearly accomplished just such a miracle. Midnight passed, followed by four hours of the harshest conditions. He did not notice when ice began to razor his fingers. He did not notice when noncirculation turned his face to wood. He had long since stopped shivering and only dimly remembered being told in school that this was the body's last-ditch attempt to save energy. Death, for so long counted on to be delivered by a fast, hard blow from his father, might instead come from winter's soft, slow smothering. Either one was fine; he would not survive the next hour and knew it, but he would at least die among friends.

When the North Star led him to a rubbish bin with a fire still burning itself out, he felt not jubilation but rather further resignation. The corroded metal barrel sat fifty yards away in a clearing, and that clearing was no doubt attached to a farm. Yet he could not approach the tantalizing folds of low flame. Shortly after Ry had stopped moving to gawk at the fire, the humming and sounds of pursuit had stopped too. Somewhere nearby, Marvin was watching the same bin and waiting for Ry to betray his location. It was possible that Ry might enjoy thirty seconds of warmth before his father descended. He dug his numb fingers into the clammy caves of his armpits and shuddered with the dry facsimiles of sobs to which he had grown accustomed.

Warm thyself. Take of us.

Oh, yes, agreed Furrington. *Indeed!*

Ry's eyes had contracted into ball bearings. They rolled downward to look upon his friends. They were lovely.

"I can't. I couldn't."

Thou art welcome to my body.

74

Guv'nor, you'd be bollocks for burning. I'm the one, hey?

Ry reluctantly removed the stuffed animal from his belt and looked him over. Each of the limbs was attached with old thread that had long ago loosened. He could imagine biting down on the bear, tasting the sour plush, tearing loose the appendage like he was some kind of wild animal. But wasn't that what he had become?

The popping of the threads was musical against his teeth. *Tee-hee,* Furrington giggled. *Oh, how it tickles!*

Ry was sobbing by the time he had removed the bear's left leg, real liquid tears dredged up from some mystery reserve. The lump of turquoise cloth, topped with a pouf of stuffing, sat in Ry's nerveless palm. He waited until all five of his fingers were able to close over it. This noble sacrifice could not go to waste.

"I'm scared," he confessed.

Fear not. Jesus Christ's painted eyes were a study in serenity. *His kingdom come, His will be done.*

You could not call it a run. The feet were too draggy, the knees collided too frequently, the fists jounced at his sides like heavy bags. It was still faster than either father or son could have expected. In just seconds, Ry was crashing into the bin and coughing within the swirling galaxies of expelled sparks. He shook his head to scatter the smoke and plunged Furrington's dismembered leg into the center of the fire. It did not immediately catch and Ry began shouting because, what the hell, Marvin could *see* him. He shouted "Help!" over and over until he saw the edges of the stuffing begin to brown. He shot away with the leg, cradling the new fire against his chest and knowing that it would not burn out because Jesus Christ was saying so. Marvin's panting rose up from behind, then softened as the man paused at the garbage bin, gasping and unsteady. Ry did not squander his lead. The black of the forest blotted out the sapphire of the sky.

He carried fire. His hand became hot and he rubbed that warmth over his face, then any other patch of exposed skin, barely able to suppress the laughter. He had not even considered what the fire would do for his sight, but the effect was glorious. The dim glow of the makeshift lantern made every step a sure one and every route foolproof, and though Ry's father could also follow the torchlight, he could not enjoy the full benefits of its illumination. Marvin, his overtaking of Ry inevitable just moments ago, slipped far, far, away, until his tantrum thrashing was indistinguishable from the soft crackle of Furrington's fur.

The stuffing incinerated quickly but the fabric itself smoldered for so long it was downright magical. When it was close to gone, Ry gathered a bouquet of dry weeds, and soon these were lit too. With a tingle of inspiration he touched the flame to other dead weeds and watched them alight. Soon the woods behind him twinkled with loci of light, any one of which, to Marvin's eyes, could be Ry. He lifted his nose to the air and smelled the grease of a country breakfast, heard the lowing of wakened cows. Like any good farm boy, he recognized dawn when he saw it. There was no stopping him now.

A hole grabbed his foot and twisted. His body wrenched with such violence that all breath was expelled prior to impact with the ground. Ry sputtered, his face burning with snow and his feet—where were his feet? He flopped over and found one foot pointing upward; the other throbbed from its hiding place inside a snow drift. Ry sat up and cords of pain fastened themselves around his leg. He scooped at the snow until he saw his ankle snaking into a narrow tunnel left by some burrowing creature. When he tried to withdraw it he heard a gritty crackle. He leaned forward, lifted his pant leg, pushed down his sock, and saw a hood of flesh that had popped open where leg met foot. Ry writhed. He could feel the chill of wind directly onto bone.

Gurgling frantic pleas, Ry clawed the dirt around the hole until he could slide free the foot. The appendage sounded like a bag of marbles when placed upon the snow. Ry lay back down, held it in for a minute, and then screamed. It seemed to alleviate the pain so he did it some more, screeching with such force that he tasted blood. He heard the sputter of a distant tractor motor. They would hear him if he just kept screaming. He blared like a siren and pounded the hard earth with his fists.

Pray calm thyself—

Shhh, friend. Oh, friend, shhh—

"No! No! No!" His crazed repetitions drowned out the smaller voices and their sensible suggestions, as well as the rustle of his father's advance. Ry knew he should not be upset. Sarah was safe; his mother was safe too. That was the whole point of everything. Yet the wicked unfairness of sixteen hours spent fighting for life in arctic temperatures consumed him with childish outrage. He was angry with God, angry with himself, angry at the failures of Furrington and Jesus Christ to deliver him safely home.

He was just about to faint, he could feel it, when he heard a noise coming from the center of his skull. It sounded like a rat trying to escape: high-pitched snuffles, agitated squeaks, the acute ticking of claws across a paneled floor. It was a breathless, hysterical sound. Ry's heart raced to keep up with it.

St—d—p-p-p—sk't, sk't, sk't.

The torture would never end! Ry stopped screaming and into that void of sound leapt Furrington and Jesus Christ.

Good golly, don't listen to him—

Thou beware thy third companion—

It's no bloody good to do what he—

Thee shall fall at the hands of—

Sk—pk, pk, pk—pk, shuf, pk, shuf, pk-pk-pk, up, up, up.

Ry pressed his hands over his ears and sobbed. Then he removed Scowler from his belt. Polyps inside of its mealy body shifted around the steel skeleton like rearranging organs. The wounds of its eyes gave up nothing, but the shell teeth of its shark's mouth gleamed—the only things sharp and clean within the tiny, yellow, curdled body.

"What do you want?" Ry whispered.

Tk, tk, tk.

"Say it."

Tk, tk, shg. Tk-up.

"No. No, I don't want to."

Pk, pk, pk, pk, shg, shg, tk'up.

"Why?" Ry sobbed. "Do I have to?"

Tk!

A nearby tree helped. Ry lifted his wasted body with exquisite slowness until he was balanced. His snapped left foot hung limp as a rabbit carcass. His vision rocked. First he saw only the shimmies of victimized plants, but then he saw the Louisville Slugger darting like a cardinal setting off from tree limb to tree limb. Not once during his flight had Ry dared to look back but he was doing it now, and there was Marvin

Burke, right on schedule, bashing a path through Black Glade as if it were no more than one of his cornfields.

Lk, lk'shup. Lk, lk'shup. Tk, tk, shup. Gg!

Marvin emerged from a line of bitternuts and stopped when he saw his son standing not fifty feet away. Never had the great farmer looked worse. His pants were torn and his stocking hat had unraveled into fuzzy strands that swayed like antennae. His face was blue and his eyes were red and sunken. Most shocking of all was his mustache, no longer so powerful when a day's growth of beard eased it into the rest of his face. The worst of it, though, was that he had become somehow *inhuman*; his flesh was scored into grotesque dinosauric segments and quaked with the pulse of ancient blood. Ry realized that this was how Scowler saw Marvin Burke—as a piteous and revolting monster—and though Ry knew it was a false vision, he found himself unable to resist it. A monster is something to be stopped, no question about it.

Marvin pushed back glasses that were gray with grime and straightened his exhausted posture.

"Dad," Ry said.

"You," the monster replied.

Frostbitten fingers choked up on the bat—Ry remembered that being his father's sole piece of swinging advice. A second hand joined the first and throttled the handle, a proper two-handed grip. Marvin took a deep breath and exhaled so that his untrimmed mustache billowed. Damp leaves smacked as he began advancing.

Wk-it-tk-it, sk-sk-sk-sk—

Warm droplets oozed from Scowler's skin.

Marvin charged, faster now, his feet booting rocks and sundering white brambles. He did not look triumphant; this was merely how you made a success of yourself. You set a goal and you stuck to it. It was an example for Ry to learn from, the final example.

Pk—d, pk—d, pk-pk-pk-pk, st-st-st-st, b-b-b-b-b—

Thirty feet away, twenty feet, fifteen, ten—and Ry struck dumb by the wild specificity of the Marvin-monster, so flecked and flawed, so freakishly tall compared to the tiny friends who had repeatedly saved Ry's life. Snot fluttered from Marvin's nose as he heaved a great breath and drew back the bat so that it angled away like a devil's wing.

Tk, tk, tk, tk, tk, tk, tk, tk, tk, tk, tk, tk, tk, tk, tk, tk—

Ry opened his arms to embrace his father.

Three feet away, Marvin was thrown off by his son's invitation. The red bat wavered. Ry smiled, his face gooey with liquid, and moved in for the hug that Marvin had always denied. Ry's busted left foot forced him to hop, and the abrupt closing of distance made Marvin—the detestable monster—flinch. Scowler rode in Ry's right hand, pleased and eyeless.

"Now?" Ry recognized his own whisper as despicably defeated.

TK!

Something about Marvin's glassy-eyed horror suggested that he saw in that final instant the truth of Scowler, discovering not a harmless homemade trifle but a troll starving for blood. The whetted edge of the doll's exposed metal pipe sunk into Marvin's neck. It was what Ry had failed to do with the sewing shears and, once done, it sickened him more than he could have imagined. Everything supernatural about Marvin instantly vanished. He tucked in his quivering, stubbled chin to get a look at the protruding figure. A few seconds passed. Marvin twitched and reddened. Then Scowler's piping took over and blood began to dribble from its other leg and both arms. Marvin's chest hitched and the movement increased the flow. Now the piping ran like faucets and, worst of all, Scowler's mouth began to brim.

Marvin lifted a hand but seemed unable to bring himself to touch the rotten thing.

Ry moved his lips in silent apology.

Every spurt of dark syrup seemed to infuse Scowler's husk with vivid color. Blood streaked through the fine white teeth. Marvin's knee buckled, and the bat barely made a sound as it slipped away. He began to sway and Ry reached out and took hold of Scowler. The steel leg dislodged with a spray of crimson, and Ry fought for balance upon his single good leg. Marvin pressed a hand over his bubbling neck.

The doll squirmed inside of Ry's palm. Horrid images of further violence forced themselves into his brain: Marvin's tongue ripped out, Marvin's chest sliced through his coat so that blood and cotton and flannel formed a thick brown stew. Ry felt his arm jerk about wildly as Scowler fought for these damages. He couldn't allow it. Ry flung himself to the ground, hiding the doll in his stomach.

Scowler yowled—a glottal choke mixed with the squeal of infuriated swine. Ry grit his teeth and shoved Scowler back into his belt. He, Ry Burke, was the monster. The blame rang up his arm as if he had struck brick. Scowler's exposed leg of metal, Ry's exposed ankle bone—what was the difference? He lifted a knee and invented a three-legged method of crawling. Physical pain, though, was a weak distraction from Scowler's tirades. Ry—*failure*—had left Marvin alive. He had failed—*failed*—to finish the job. Scowler saves Ry Burke's life and this is how Ry Burke repays Scowler? Ry kept the apologies coming as Scowler wept and spat of unforgivable acts.

These scoldings did not let up when Ry pulled himself past the forest edge and left a trail of blood through the pristine snow of a back lawn. A woman moving toward her woodpile ejected an inadvertent string of cuss words when she noticed the ten-year-old threshing through the snow and mud; her words, sadly, were not loud enough to cut through Scowler's high-pitched rebukes. When Ry was being carried by unknown parties and deposited upon a family-room davenport, he could not fully appreciate their concern because of the doll's continued gobbling. Water was poured down his throat. He sensed bandages twining around his forehead and ankle. Covered lamps gave way to sunlight, sunlight to the dim bulbs of an ambulance carriage. Glass cylinders tinkled as the vehicle rollicked over gravel, while medics slapped at his arms, pressed his jugular, and held open his lids to ask him important questions. Ry smiled sheepishly. He promised to answer them right after this doll screamed itself to sleep.

The Night Surgeon

11 HRS., 29 MINS. UNTIL IMPACT

There was more to the memory, an epilogue even more painful in some respects, but Ry couldn't drag himself through that, not right now. He inhaled the night through his nostrils, blinked away the ghost of pain between his eyebrows, and tried to imagine the superhuman Marvin Burke wearing the same color pajamas as this old man—Jeremiah, if the name was to be believed—while scrubbing dishes, stabbing hot piles of laundry, lowering the press that imprinted numbers upon license plates. Ry just could not see it. Regardless, this strange senior shared some sort of history with Marvin Burke, and that made Ry closer to him than their silence and six-foot distance would suggest. Jeremiah locked his malformed hands behind his back.

"Thinking I would head south," he said.

Ry touched his scar. "Not much south but grass."

"That right? No woods? No corn?"

"Some. Grass, though, mostly. You may be better off north or west."

Jeremiah's chin made a defiant jerk. "The wide open— that's what I want. This—all these trees—and the insects and, lord, the *birds*—it's not . . . I'd hoped . . ." His head moved in aimless loops. "For some reason I got it in my head I can hide best right out in the open."

"There's a place called Canen Clearing." Ry tried to sound encouraging. "It's south, just the way you're headed. It's not a day's walk from here."

The man's eyes were distrustful. "Canen?"

Directions were things empty of emotion, ideal for men, and Ry jumped at it. "It's a big stretch of wild grass right out in the middle of a bunch of farmland. Big as a football field. You want the wide open, that's it."

"That sounds . . . fine."

"Okay. Just—you know what you should do? Head down the road here and after about ten minutes cut through the Crowleys' corn. When you come out the other end you'll be on a road that doesn't have a name, but if you take a right on that road and cross the bridge, then you'll be heading right for it. Just keep walking. Tomorrow in the sun you'll see it."

Jeremiah blinked his milky eyes. "I don't see how I thought it were appropriate. Bringing up Marvin. Just caught me by surprise is all."

"It's okay."

"It's not." His lips swayed where there were no teeth. "Being with people like you, *good* people—it's not for me.

Quiet—that's it. Quiet, loneliness." His words fell cold to his feet. "Maybe I should not have run."

The crunch of a woman's shoes upon gravel rose from the quiet. Ry and Jeremiah looked at each other and then turned to watch the approach. Ry knew it was a quirk of the moth-bothered light, but there was prettiness to the shadows of his mother's cheeks, the lines of her jaw, the blade of shadow that plunged down the front of her dress. She had a hand on Sarah, who balanced in her arms a stack of folded clothes. She lifted it high, steeled for the sight of those feelers that Jeremiah had no choice but to extend.

The old man inspected what he took. The bottommost garments were a pair of Marvin's brown slacks and the pit-stained top half of a set of long underwear; on top of that were a red flannel shirt Ry recognized from his own collection, some socks, and a pair of his old boots in fine shape all directions but earthward. Jeremiah picked up one of the boots and put his eye to the hole worn through the rubber.

"I can't guarantee the boots will fit, but everything else should," Jo Beth said.

"Oh, they will, I just know it." Jeremiah smiled.

Jo Beth nodded. "I'm pretty good at eyeballing sizes."

"I missed clothes." His cataracts seemed to retract at the surprise of this truth.

Jo Beth's lips unsealed but found nothing more to say. Sarah coughed and it did not sound promising. Ry prodded the pimple about to break the surface at the side of his nose. All of them became aware of the birds—the sound clattered down like enough loose change to fund hundreds of complete sets of teeth.

"They're mad." Jeremiah looked at the trees. "They know something we don't."

He hitched his bundle into his armpit and began to walk away.

"You don't want to put those on?" Jo Beth asked.

"In the dark, up the road a piece." Jeremiah pointed his index finger. It looked supernaturally long without its siblings. "Where it's decent."

He took another step and stopped.

"You don't have a cigarette," he said.

Ry did, actually, back at the house.

"No," Jo Beth said.

"There were this guard. A good friend. Always had the kind I liked: Luckies. Miss that, too." He considered this for a moment, tipped an imaginary hat, and was on his way. It was scary how quickly he was painted over with nighttime colors. The Burkes stood for a minute, listening to the gravel scuffs.

"I think I just saw one," Sarah said.

"One what?" Jo Beth asked.

"One meteor. The Jaekel Belt. I need my notebook."

Jo Beth drew her daughter to her side. "No good for you to be outside sick."

"I'm not sick," Sarah protested.

"Of course you are," Ry said. "You're always sick."

Jo Beth laughed and looked at her son. "We'll find out soon enough."

Sarah glared at her brother and mouthed: *Cocksucker!*

The seven digits took an eternity to dial.

"Hello, Peg? This is Jo Beth. Good, thanks. I'm calling—hmm? Oh, yes, of course. Everything is fine. Why, sure. Bless you for asking." Pause. "Well, everything is *very* well. How are things for your group? Oh, really? All of them?"

From the kitchen table Ry monitored his mother's face. She sat perched atop a stool with her feet locked behind the crossbar like a schoolgirl. The inadvertent twirling of the cord completed the illusion. Ry pictured the other end of the call: the unsmiling Peg Crowley, a rail-thin woman with a black pod of hair, the exact opposite of the flowing contours and grace notes that gave her daughter Esther such allure.

"That's right, I'd forgotten. This is Esther's big week. What's the lucky school?"

Hills and valleys of womanhood Esther Crowley had in embarrassing abundance. When it came to book smarts, though, she held only a slight edge on Ry. He tried to take some savage satisfaction in it but it was hard to maintain—she was, after all, a year younger than Ry and already heading to college, while he stood in place doing whatever it was he was doing. Peg's nasal buzz filed at his brain until he was ready to admit to anything. Fine: Esther was better looking than he was, and smarter, and funnier, all that.

"Oh, I know what it's like to get your heart set on something. I was a girl once too. I'm sure she'll make it worth your investment. Listen, Peg—"

More buzzing. Jo Beth's response made it sound like she had lifted her eyebrows, though she had not.

"Kevin's back, too? Well, there you go, then. I for sure

thought I remembered something about him heading to the fair. . . ." Jo Beth listened; she nodded. "Time flies, I guess. Well, I don't envy the one on dishwashing duty tonight. Dishwashing duty. Dishwashing—that's okay, I probably mumbled. So listen, Peg, I've got kind of a strange question for you." A twitch—in her forehead, like she had been beaned with a pebble. "Thanks, Peg. I appreciate that, but no, it's not the mending. I'll get that to you tomorrow. It's . . . have you heard anything about what happened over at Bluefeather?"

Ry and Jo Beth held their breaths.

"No, everything is good. We just . . . we heard from someone passing by that there had been a . . . I guess an explosion? And I tried calling the prison and just got a busy signal and—"

Peg took over. Jo Beth's mouth hung open within a half-formed word.

"I called the police first but couldn't get through. And then I tried Marjorie and Betsy. But they didn't—Betsy Strickland, down the road. You're my fourth or fifth, Peg. I just seemed to remember that you had a, you know, one of those satellite dishes and may get the Bloughton news out there." Jo Beth settled her lips to see how this would play. She listened, nodded briskly, made the shapes of a grin. "Okay. Well, if any of you happen to see something about it, you might give me a ring. I—"

For a moment it seemed as if Jo Beth had convinced herself into cheeriness. Peg, though, did not like the sound of things; you could hear it in the sound of Peg.

"No, there's no reason. There's nothing wrong." A pause on both ends. "There is nothing wrong, Peg." Buzz from the

Crowley household; Jo Beth squinted. "My husband *what?* Peg, that was . . . a lot of time has passed since then." She rubbed at her eyes; Ry's knee bounced. "No one makes that kind of generalization about this area, and if they did it wouldn't be because of him. It would—well, I'll tell you. If you'll listen, I'll tell you. It would be because of, and I don't mean offense, but it would be because of people like you who won't let it go. Everyone out here is hurting. To blame it on one family, or one person, Peg, is just—"

Jo Beth's eyes, upon reopening, were pink. Ry's legs writhed beneath the table. He felt like a kid again, trapped in a pew by the boulder-like force of an interminable sermon.

"There's no *safety* issue. Peg, listen . . ." Pause. "I've got my children here too. You think if there was anything unsafe about any of this I would be sitting here talking to you? No. I'd be taking care of my kids." Pause. "Well, thank you. I guess. I suppose I *do* have a tiny bit of sense, thank you very much for noticing. I . . . look, I just called to see if you'd heard anything. If you haven't—" Pause, this one radiating heat. "Well. If you do. It is of interest to me. But I can wait until the paper comes on Tuesday. No skin off my back."

Pause, this one as slow and rough as frost.

"All right. Give Kevin and the kids my best. Tell Esther good luck at school. And you'll have that nightgown tomorrow. No, I'm not hurrying it on your account; I don't hurry things that I sew. That's fine. Okay. Good night."

The cradle took the phone, and Jo Beth watched the cord swing. Ry was nodding as if blind affirmation alone could hurry this ritual past the pain.

"Well," Jo Beth said. "That went poorly."

"Try the Horvaths," Ry said.

"No." Jo Beth stood up and smoothed her pants. "Let's not do that again."

"We can walk there if you want." Ry was still nodding; anything was possible, anything. "If it makes you feel safer."

The way she shook her head made him feel like a child.

"Right now? In the dark? With Sarah? With a chill like there is, and with her already coughing? That sounds like a good idea to you?"

"And where's the shotgun? You never said."

"Oh, Ry, let's not talk about guns."

"It'd just be good to have it."

"I'll get it," she said. "In a while. But that's not going to solve any problems."

"There's no problem." Ry tapped his chest. "*I'm* fine. But if you want to figure out what happened, one of us is going to have to walk down the road, and I'm happy to do it—gun or no gun. I could've just walked down to the Crowleys' with Jeremiah."

"With the convict. With the escaped convict. Just traipsing down the road alone at night. You really think I'd let you do that?"

"Let me?"

"You heard me."

"I'm not a kid, Mom."

"You're not as old as you think."

"Why don't you relax? We'll figure it out tomorrow. I'll wait until morning and then just walk over to—"

"No." Jo Beth's eyes were steadfast. "We are done asking for help from these people."

"Mom."

"We've done nothing to them. Nothing. And they treat us like this? Year after year? Like we're criminals?"

"That's ridiculous."

"You weren't on that phone!"

"I was sitting right here, Mom."

"I'm done with it. We're gone. We're leaving. Pack what you need because tomorrow we're out of here."

Jo Beth Burke was not an impulsive woman and pronouncements of this weight did not come from nowhere. She was already turned on her heel and heading for the dining room. Ry knew he was faster. His chair screeched outward, and swooping around her he jammed an arm in the doorframe—a frame he had fixed two years ago, dammit, and repainted last month. The imposition was startling enough that Jo Beth's nose bumped into his bicep, and in that moment of contact they both felt the vulgarity of this feckless display of strength. She took a half step back and stared up at him. It was a moment straight out of the repertoire of Marvin Burke.

The dimpled scars along her ear and between each finger no longer seemed so faint. Ry let his arm slide down the doorframe. He felt the veins of paint, the clots of coagulation. It was not a good paint job, not really.

"Phinny will be here tomorrow?" Jo Beth controlled her voice and Ry felt his face burn.

"He'll be here, but—"

"Then we'll pack the car, install the part, and then we'll leave."

Ry gaped at her. She meant it. Moving out was supposed to be a lackadaisical process; he had imagined a month or more of packing that, in Ry's fantasies, would bond mother, daughter, and son as they lifted forgotten artifacts from the backs of drawers and held them up, laughing.

"You have a place for us to go?" he asked.

"A couple options, yes." There was no fear in her gaze, none.

"So this is something you've been planning all along or what?"

"Keep your voice down," she said. "I made Sarah look out the front window for her meteors. There's no point in scaring her all over again."

He listened and heard the flutter of his sister's notebook. Jo Beth rolled her neck.

"Maybe you don't feel it," she said. "I'm not blaming you for that. Maybe it comes with being older. But we're clinging. Ry? We are clinging to this place. We have been for nine years. And I'm through. Just now. Just like that. It's no wonder we can't sell it. We're afraid to. It doesn't even make logical sense to the brain, selling your house out from under your own feet. But there is a place. More than one place, actually. They're in Monroeville. Don't bother me for details; this isn't something open for discussion. I know you're upset. But this isn't really about you. I cannot live here. It has nothing to do with your father and if he's at Bluefeather or if he isn't—I couldn't care less. I cannot live with these *people*. These so-called neighbors who throw me a few dollars and pretend to be my friends. Have you seen their crops? They're nearly as bad off as we are and that's not our fault; it's the land. I can make real money in Monroeville, Ry, and it can start tomorrow. It can all start tomorrow. You see? All we have to do is do it."

Ry opened his mouth and felt a lake of tears lapping at the back of his throat. He took a moment to swallow the salty water.

"And then what?" he asked.

Jo Beth reached out and tugged the hair at the side of his head as if checking its fixedness, something she hadn't done in years. It was comforting, her knuckles so tight against his scalp. He let his head be yanked this way, then that.

"And then it's done," she said.

9 HRS., 47 MINS. UNTIL IMPACT

Christmas in August was unintentional; it just turned out that way. By the time Ry had entered the living room, his mother was already speaking to Sarah in tones of such skillful persuasion that she could have been suggesting a suicide pact and Sarah would be nodding along just the same. A surprise trip to Monroeville was how Jo Beth put it, except that they were going to stay awhile and see how that went and wasn't that exciting? Ry knew that his mother was underestimating Sarah. Insight twinkled in the girl's eyes, but she knew when it was advantageous to fake gullibility, whether it was in the tooth fairy or a supposedly innocuous visit to what was in fact a new home.

It was more exciting than one hundred little lights from space. Sarah wanted to pack right away, but Jo Beth assured her that there would be plenty of time for that in the morning and, besides, anything they wanted to come back for later would still be here. Jo Beth headed upstairs; they heard the telltale rattle of the attic door being pulled from the ceiling and then the thud of the ladder unfolding. Five minutes later their mother was back, not with White Special Dress but with a cargo so exciting Sarah dropped her precious notebook: two full shopping bags, one old and sprouting the telltale chutes of wrapping paper, and one brand-new and bulging with promise.

"Can't haul these all the way to Monroeville without you seeing them," Jo Beth sighed. "Who's up for presents?"

Ry's heartbeat accelerated with the realization that he was in the presence of genius. With a single audacious move a night of anxiety had been transformed into festivity. The living room door was closed to gloriously exacerbate the rustle of wrapping paper and the squeal of drawn tape. There was a string of colored lights and Sarah knew where it was stashed. Ry headed out to the machinery shed, where weeks ago he had uprooted a small evergreen after its roots had begun to interfere with the septic tank. Back inside, he kicked aside the kitchen stool and propped the tree in front of the phone. Sarah strung the colored lights across dead limbs that refused the weight, and it was with some deal of smugness that Ry made it work.

"That tree's going to burn us down," Jo Beth moaned.

"What do we care?" Ry said, laughing. "We're out of here, right?"

The gifts, purchased on one of Jo Beth's rare trips to Monroeville, maybe the same one during which she procured their mysterious new housing, were piled in the center of the table. Sarah's Walt Disney record player journeyed from her room to the kitchen counter; Mickey's arm was placed to the groove and out came Bing Crosby attesting that it was a silent night. It was anything but. The previous dinner was sent into the trash with a clatter of cutlery, and a dozen cooking tasks were in progress before Jo Beth bothered to take a vote on what the hell they should eat. This mild dip into profanity, on Fake Christmas no less, had Ry and Sarah howling, waving their arms through their frantic gasps to make sure the word *pancakes* was heard. *Chocolate chip pancakes,* even. "Liver and onions? Okay, if that's what you really want," Jo Beth said. Their screams of terror were unparalleled.

By the time Bing was wishing rest upon merry gentlemen, batter was bubbling and bacon was sizzling and Sarah, showing inspiration, removed three Coca-Colas from the fridge. Pancakes and bacon and pop—he was surrounded by masterminds. He danced along to Bing until the crooner began to skip—*I'll be home for, I'll be home for, I'll be home for*—and when Ry redropped the needle Bing was already on about jingle bells. Better, much better.

While Jo Beth and Sarah sang and opened presents and licked maple drippings from their forearms, Ry rotated his head to take mental photographs of the house so that he could remember it in case he never saw it again: the incognito cans of generic or partially damaged food, the spotless heartbreak of the ice cream maker and fondue set stacked hopefully in the corner, the crusted runners on the stove front that were somehow the very fingerprints of his mother. He wanted to remember it, all of it, the life contained until the moment that the night surgeon came and snipped it away.

He felt delirious; he heard laughing and joined in out of hope that his contribution could sustain it. Their faces—yes, it was *faces* he wanted to memorize, openmouthed and crinkled with happiness, and here of all places. Sarah opened the back door and called for Sniggety. Pancakes were the dog's favorite and it should not have surprised anyone that he hauled his old bones up the steps to gobble the leftovers. It was his nirvana. It was theirs, too—feeling each other's warmth, looking over Sarah's shoulders to watch the food disappear into the soft brown muzzle.

0 HRS., 40 MINS. UNTIL IMPACT

Velvet dreams scraped away to reveal a soft scuffling coming from the other side of Ry's door. Probably Sarah, her routine out of whack from spending half the night buzzed on caffeine and staring at an uneventful sky. When Ry had gone to bed, her pen had still been hovering over a fresh page unmarked by a single hatch mark. But he was thankful that the noises had awakened him. Just because it was his last day on the farm didn't mean there wasn't work to be done. He had a whole laundry list, starting with Phinny Rochester. The repairman was a notorious early riser, and Ry figured he might as well call him right away to make sure those spark plugs were coming today. Not just today, but this morning. The faster they did this, the less it would hurt. He winced while dressing; the floor was cold. He opened the door.

Sniggety lifted his nose from the tile and let his tongue flop from an idiot grin. Ry just stared. Never in Sniggety's seventeen years had he set paw inside the house. Even when temperatures had plunged into the negatives, the best offer had been the doghouse, a pile of musty blankets, and a heat lamp. Yet here he was, a begrimed and slobbering alien plopped down within a clean and orderly world, and by all appearances elated at the opportunity.

Music rumbled from the next room, no doubt another

album placed upon the Walt Disney record player. This indicated that it was Jo Beth who was up, not Sarah, though Ry couldn't imagine why his mother had allowed Sniggety indoors. Not that it mattered—Ry was surprisingly happy to see the old boy. He took a knee, gripped the pennant of fur that sprang from the dog's cheek, and examined the tumor swaddling the left rear hip. Maybe this was the gift of their newly revised life: Old was new to the eye, the sick could be saved. Today Sniggety would be among the car's passengers. Ry chastised himself for overlooking the dog before.

His hand brushed over the dog's collar. Years of rabies tags tambourined, and then Ry felt something unexpected. He brushed crud out of his eyes and leaned closer. It was twine, knotted around the collar and trailing off across the floor like a leash. A leash? Sniggety had outgrown those fifteen years ago. This thought, disturbing enough on its own, was followed by a realization even colder. That music—he recognized it and it wasn't an album. It was a voice, and now it was directly in front of him.

"Hmmmm hm hm hmmmm."

The strap of twine lifted from the floor. Ry craned his neck to follow its arc but got no farther than the toothless maw of their shotgun. A sob broke from Ry's chest, but he yanked the sob back because it was a release he did not deserve. Instead he gave himself a single moment to enumerate his failures, and rapidly, for he had only seconds. One, not insisting that they follow Jeremiah into the safety of the night. Two, not remembering to search for the gun, not for even five lousy minutes. That was as far as he got; the heavy barrel pressed into his temple. Ry swallowed a lump of hard air, pulse racing, the delay of oblivion a torture, while the memory of old Bing made nonsensical laps in his head: *I'll be home for, I'll be home for, I'll be home for*—

Marvin Burke never changed his tune, either.

"Hmmmm—"

"Fast." The word escaped Ry's lips, dry and quick. "Do it fast."

Ry felt the warm gust of voided anger at the interruption. An apology gagged up Ry's throat, son to father, weak to strong; how swiftly it all came back.

A deep inhale, another try: "*Hmmmm hm hm hmmmm.*"

"Can't you just do it?" Possibly Ry referred to his own fate, possibly to the fate of his family. "Do it. Do it!"

"Hmmmm hm hm *hmmmm*. Hmmmm hm hm *hmmmm*."

Sniggety wagged his tail and made sprightly figure eights, the most energy he'd displayed in a decade. Ry lost himself in the appalling demonstration until a click, soft as a mother's whisper, signaled the disarming of the shotgun's safety. Yes, good—*now*. Ry thought of all the farm animals, old or infirm, that the twelve-gauge had executed.

"Hmmmm." The barrel moved, so unexpectedly Ry gasped, and the cool metal tapped his ear, once, twice. "Hm hm." Now it nudged his neck. "Hmmmm." Finally it poked at the starburst of his forehead, making things explicit, urging him up. Ry didn't know why, but he put his hands to the cold floor and pushed himself to skittish knees. The warm walnut of the shotgun stock touched against his cheek, effortlessly angling him toward the staircase, which fed upward to the confident, lazing bodies of his mother and sister. The muzzle lodged comfortably around a vertebra and prodded.

Ry didn't get a single look at his father as they climbed the stairs. Nor did he get a peek during the calamity of his mother's awakening. After a minute, the humming infected her dreams, and then her eyes shot open, and then she was throwing the sheets around like they were someone she was strangling, and doing plenty of screaming, and all Ry could think about was the last time these spouses had shared this room and what had happened. To Ry's knowledge, the mattress had never been changed, only flipped.

Sarah appeared at some unnoticed moment, drawn by the furor, and stood by the door sleepy-eyed, trying to make sense of the mom who had gone crazy and the brother who was in the wrong bedroom, not to mention the stranger. Ry got no sense that she knew for sure who the man was, though her dawning expression of rapacious curiosity meant she had a pretty good idea. The humming continued as if oblivious to all of this, and the muzzle pushed Ry, and Ry's body pushed Jo Beth, and Jo Beth clutched Sarah, and in this centipede fashion they moved down the hall and staircase.

They spilled down the back steps into a pretty country morning, and a canny shove from the Winchester sent the three of them sprawling. Jo Beth sprang back up like a wrestler, her chest heaving and hands open. Sarah followed suit, noticed a grass smudge on her mother's nightgown, and fingered it to gauge whether or not it would stain. Ry found this gesture touching and yearned to bring his sister into his arms. He brought himself to a knee, and Sniggety blasted him with a putrid snort before shouldering about the legs of his resurrected master, happily distracted at last from the aural agony of the birds. Ry stood.

It was Marvin Burke, all right. A pale tongue emerged to slake blanched and riven lips, and this alone provided proof that he was not a corpse, or a ghost. He looked awful, though—chewed up and regurgitated. His prison garb, baggy, striped, wrinkled, and filthy, was identical to Jeremiah's, except crudely flayed, and Ry could imagine him wriggling beneath several sets of barbed-wire fences. The patterns of color were mosaicked but not hard to identify: Brown was blood, gray was mud, black was soot. Though no critical wounds were visible, evidence of injury was everywhere, especially in a dark red crust covering his heart. Marvin Burke had torn, or fought, his way out of something terrible.

The familiar facial features were disguised with wrinkles, which struck dozens of anguished new intersections. Most shocking, though, was the hair. No longer trapped beneath a dome of tight skin, the hair ran dangerously wild. No areas of thinning, no lines of retreat; in fact, the hairline was lower on Marvin's forehead than on Ry's, giving the father the swept-back pelt of a silverback. There was something insidious about how long Marvin had hidden this lushness; it recalled the unchecked growth of Black Glade. The trademark mustache was gone too, replaced by a wiry month-old beard that began high on the cheekbones, circled the mouth like a ski mask, and dove into his shirt collar. The glasses had also changed over the years but remained too big for his face, as if attempting to conceal what little skin his hair had not already eaten. Nothing, of course, had changed with the teeth—teeth revealed you. Big square blocks fed into that same ravenous gap.

"Did I ever tell you about the time I bagged a bear?"

The words grinded out like crushed ice. The gun was pointed at a place near their feet, while Marvin's red eyes roved to see who would answer first. Would the winner, Ry wondered, get shot? He glanced at his mother to see if she was taking the bait; she, though, seemed to have been paralyzed by the question's absurdity.

"Well, let me tell you." Marvin's tongue came out again and made its languid rounds. "I bagged and bagged that bear to let me go."

Ry blinked as if subjected to a pulled punch. Jo Beth choked like she'd seen something revolting, and Sarah extended her epic silence. Not even the joke's teller chuckled; he frowned and raised the weapon until it was pointed at Ry's chest.

"I worked on that for three years." Marvin's voice was tightly controlled. "The Professor heard it so many times he swore he'd slice my throat. But he was the one who convinced me I ought to say it to you if I ever got the chance. The Professor was brilliant, brilliant, but on this? On this I thought he was nuts. Until I got here and I looked around at what you did—what you've *done*. Only right then did I see the poetry. A little humor before the pain—it might focus you. It might focus *me*. It might make it all the more meaningful. Don't you think?"

Jo Beth moaned. "Let's be calm. Let's talk. Please? Can we?"

"You're a sight for sore eyes, Jo." Marvin did not allow himself to look at her. "But right this second's not the time for us. I've got serious business with our son. I'm sorry but that comes first."

"Ry, is it okay?" Sarah whispered. Of course she whispered. It was how the two of them communicated anything of real importance.

"Yes." This response was his duty.

"No." Marvin shook his head. "No, see, it is not. This is my farm—surely you haven't forgotten that. So there wasn't any debating about where I should go. My reasons were simple. The first was to get some money. The warden, the guards—they're good at their jobs and when the dust settles they'll come after me, and I'll be on the run. I'm not worried about that, but a little money would ease the journey. And then I saw. Even in the dark, I could see—the colors and how they were all wrong. Everything supposed to be green was yellow. Everything supposed to be white was brown. The fields are—I still can't believe it. And I'm going to *take* something? What on earth would I take? There's not a single thing left. Then I go inside, and the kitchen? There's garbage, scraps of paper everywhere. There's syrup all over the counters and there's ants in the syrup. There's a—and I can't believe this. But there's a tree. A tree in the kitchen. This is how savages live, you understand? You took the farm that I built with my own hands, my own back, my own brain, methods I invented myself, and you did not nurse it. Now it's too late. Now it's overrun. You let that crazy forest out there get a foothold, son, and that, I can tell you, is all it ever wanted."

Ry had forgotten the craft behind these walls of words, laid one brick at a time with the patience of a master mason. It was how Marvin Burke had filibustered merchants, discouraged uppity field hands, silenced his family with checklists of everything he had done right that day, the things he would do righter the next. It was somewhat courageous, a speech of this kind given under such duress, and Ry realized that he'd been foolish to reduce the man to a voiceless monster. He wasn't even sure how it had happened. Scowler's doing, perhaps.

"Evidently this place means nothing to you, but I'll tell you something," Marvin continued. "Thinking about these fields, these crops, kept me alive for thousands of days. *You* are the murderer. That's why the second thing I came to do—to take care of you?" Marvin grimaced. "Can't even feel bad about that anymore. Just one minute, that's all I want. Not even one minute—thirty seconds. To see if you have any- thing to say for yourself, any explanation whatsoever."

"Marvin." Jo Beth took a deep breath and swallowed. "All you've done is run away. They'll be lenient. I know they will, and I can speak on your behalf. But they won't be lenient if you harm a child."

Marvin removed an unsteady hand from the stock and scrubbed it over his weary face. Soot and blood coalesced to a muddy orange.

"You know everything there is to know, son." His eyes conveyed genuine sorrow. "I saw to it. So I'm sent away and you don't care. That I understand. But to throw away an edu- cation like that? To just let this place rot? I see no logic in that, and I've looked. I've spent the whole morning looking. Tell me now what I've missed. I want to hear it."

Ry knew that his muteness was suicide, each beat of si- lence making space for the forthcoming bullets, yet he could find no words. This would be acceptable if not for the ques- tion he didn't want to ask himself: What would happen to Jo Beth and Sarah after he was dead?

"I'm sorry," Ry managed. "I'm sorry."

"You're sorry. My God. You have no idea what you've done."

"He's scared," Jo Beth said. "You're being extremely aggressive."

"Aggressive?" Marvin's face was not easy to read beneath the beard and glasses and blood and grime, but the muscles appeared to rigidify into a pattern of disbelief. "Jo—there's going to be shooting. It's going to be very aggressive."

"Marvin, no." She was through reasoning. "Marvin, stop."

Something about her pleading pushed him beyond patience. The butt of the gun squared with his shoulder. The weapon's shadow, thrown across the lawn, was already at Ry's head.

"There's nothing for me here." The raspy remnant of his voice crackled in a struggle for control. "I've never seen people with more nothing. Not even in prison. All you got is Old Snig, and you know what? Old Snig is coming with me."

Hearing his forgotten nickname, the dog whined with pleasure, the twine leash snaking after him through the grass.

"Marvin, no, please," Jo Beth said. "Marvin, please, no."

"No way my dog would die without me, that's what I told the Professor." He reaimed the gun. His right eyelid twitched behind the sight, and he knuckled away a clot of soot. It left a mark, black and horizontal, as if he were a man who shot fire instead of dripped tears. "No one—*no one*—buries this dog but me. You understand that? No—"

Marvin broke off. His eyes had wandered to Ry's right, but the person who had arrested his attention was not Jo Beth. It was Sarah. The girl stood perfectly straight with her chin tilted and neck craned, brazenly ignoring the threats, the gun, her father's very presence, instead devoting herself to gawping at the morning sky. Marvin looked baffled, even offended, and Ry opened his mouth to tell his sister to snap to attention, and quick, but then he noticed what his sister had noticed first.

The birds, at long last, were silent.

Into the void came a sustained and piercing shriek. Without even thinking, all four of them clamped their ears and twisted their necks. Fire was splitting the sky. They braced against it. A sword of yellow eviscerated the clouds and struck the telephone pole that ran alongside the road. The pole detonated. Ry heard the sizzle of sparking cables and saw curls of black circuitry head for the trees. Somewhere in the house, two windows shattered simultaneously as the projectile came in like a landing plane. It slanted over the house and the two trees directly above, the limbs blooming with red smoke, and then the people below were whipped by a storm of heat and ash. Sinuses were baked and throats seared; they lurched and felt one another's confused hands. Toes stubbed steel— the shotgun was loose. Jo Beth tumbled, swatting at a tongue of flame in her hair. Ry whirled, breathless, and found himself staring at the McCafferty Forty, the location of Sarah's lost tooth, at the very instant the fiery object buried itself into the field, spraying a half-mile curtain of earth into the blue canvass of a perfect morning. A slam of air hit their torsos and the four of them dropped like rocks. For a while, dirt continued to rain. After that, nothing moved.

Interlude

JANUARY 1972–MAY 1972

The doctors spoke to Jo Beth as if Ry were not there. Ry noticed this. He also noticed how his mother, when greeting visitors, repeated the doctors' stories with the giddy volume of one who has narrowly avoided tragedy. She used the doctors' words and relished them: Her son's story was a *miracle* of *survival*; his was an *astonishing* display of *courage*. The guests—mostly neighbors, folks from church, community well-wishers—would at this point invariably look to the hospital bed, seeking evidence of this paragon of human resilience. Instead they found a sullen, incommunicative, regular old boy. Ry didn't care. He tucked himself farther beneath tight white sheets and brought Mr. Furrington and Jesus Christ closer. He wasn't deaf and he wasn't stupid. He just wasn't much interested in adult conversation. Tentatively he took hold of Scowler's clammy belly and brought him closer, too.

"See his lips move? See?"

Tiny specks of scab marked the incision points between Jo Beth's fingers, and similar scabs ran along the ridge of her left ear. But she smiled with wanton happiness. She thought her son's hushed powwows with his three companions were cute. They were not cute. Ry would die for these friends, each of whom had saved his life.

A nurse tasked with changing the dressing on Ry's forehead was the first to find out how not cute they were. She scoffed at Furrington's missing leg, tsked at Jesus Christ's grimy skin, and went silent upon uncovering Scowler and his blind contemplation. She tried to remove them, ostensibly to make room for the unrolling of bandages, but Ry snapped into action. He clacked his teeth and pounded his feet against the railings; his left foot, encased in plaster, was louder. Later, when the nurse detailed the episode to Jo Beth, Ry was disappointed to hear his behavior described as a "crying fit." He had intended it as something more forceful.

No matter. He inhaled the familiar funk of his companions and felt pleasantly dizzy. Never in his life had he felt so secure, and everyone noticed. The very things that frightened children about hospitals Ry Burke took like warm milk: the unnerving cleanliness of the white walls and beige tile, the malodor of the elderly, the clockwork shock of nurses and their invasions. His friends made it all okay. They told him how to breathe when he awoke from nightmares; they gave him advice on which medicines to take and which to feed to the pillowcase. Trays of food went ignored until his friends deemed certain items edible (milk, potatoes) and others trickery (fruit, greens). They told him how to be tough, and when he cried anyway they sang along until his sobs turned to laughter.

The toys were present for the first police interrogation. It did not go well. The uniformed men became frustrated at Ry's inattention and snapped shut their notebooks. Ry glanced over the top of Furrington and Jesus Christ, who were cavorting upon his lap, and saw his mother wince at the men and touch her upper lip to reference their mustaches. The next time they came they were clean-shaven, and Ry talked. The men glanced at each other throughout the session, and when it was over one of them looked around as if what he was about to do were a lapse in protocol. He gripped Ry's shoulder, leaned in, and said, "Don't worry—the bastard's going away for a long time."

Ry nodded because he was supposed to, but he could not keep his eyes from the tiny columns of hair that were trying to push through the skin above the man's upper lip. See? Right there? The world was not to be trusted.

The subsequent days were used to wean him back to solid food; to inflict two more procedures on his frostbitten extremities; to check on the cast on his left ankle; to fit him for crutches; and to stitch, poke, frown at, salve, and rebandage the hole in his head. Numerous sets of X-rays were taken of his brain, and when the doctor traced with a pen the areas of concern, Ry wondered if he was already dead—in the X-rays, he looked like a ghost.

The results, said the doctor, were both good and bad. What was good was that his reparative abilities were top-notch. What was bad was that, as tall and strong as he was, he was still a kid, and a trauma like this one could be compared to dropping a baby on its head. Jo Beth, he said, using her name, needed to be vigilant until her son was full grown, and they needed to beware further trauma to the head, including the rattle of things like city buses or roller coasters, as well as strong magnetic forces, which could initiate relapse. This last warning worried Jo Beth because she did not know how to guard against it, but the doctor raised his hands in apology. He shouldn't have even mentioned it; in all likelihood, they would never encounter a magnetic field that powerful.

Nine days later Ry was back at home. He dug up one of his mother's old leather purses, modified it into a hip sack, stuffed in his three companions, and hobbled off to do his chores. In his mother's face he saw concern about what he supposed was his serious and dutiful manner, but she did not realize how little time there was for playing or laughing when one was fielding so many important whispers.

Jo Beth watched him line the toys alongside his supper plate, facing outward as if watching for attack. She watched him readjust their sentry positions upon the sink or tub before hand washing or bathing. Each night when she tiptoed inside his room to whisper good night, three other tiny heads poked out above the bedsheet, and soon she began to include them in the nightly ritual: "Night-night, Jesus. Sweet dreams, Mr. Furrington. Sleep well, Scowler." It was the best part of every day for Ry, a moment of directionless joy. He had the best mother in the world and no one to thank for it.

School presented a bigger problem. Was he just going to pose these figures on the edge of his desk? Jo Beth's bold, unspoken decision was why not? Upon crossing the school's concrete threshold and entering the familiar calamity, Ry felt the fear dry from his skin like perspiration. These chilly halls were no colder than Black Glade, their distances no crueler. Ry concentrated on the stab and swing of his crutches, the sheet-metal reverberation of his locker, the fifth-grade classroom's incense of ground pencil. He kept his head down during Miss Plaisted's welcome back and said nothing when Carla Green scooted her desk over to help him catch up with assignments. It was afternoon—math—when he finally succumbed to the trifecta of whispers and unzipped his hip sack. They crawled out and claimed three of the desk's four corners. He was aware of the looks; he turned his eyes to Miss Plaisted and saw that she was a bit slack-jawed herself. A moment later, though, she remembered the chalk in her hand. Ry felt his shoulders relax and began following her lecture for the first time that day.

The dolls made everyone nervous and uncomfortable. The dilemma, from an adult point of view, was that Ry had begun to excel. For years he had been the personification of the C-minus student. Now he was distinguishing *their* from *they're* and *who* from *whom* like it was second nature, and his victory at the ballyhooed fifth-grade spelling bee had juvenile oddsmakers clutching their heads in disbelief. Math, long his worst subject, had rocketed his name through the ranks until it sat among the crème de la crème of Miss Plaisted's grade chart. To Ry, though, succeeding in the class was no more notable than carrying out chores—though his amazing innovations of wood and wire all across the farm were making those tasks easier, too.

Ry knew that he wasn't really any smarter. What he was feeling must be comparable to when a kid with lousy vision looks through prescription glasses for the first time. Furrington was naturally fussy about words; his fur tickled Ry's

111

ear when he giggled their proper placement. Jesus Christ, meanwhile, had an extensive knowledge of history; writing down which president did what and when was a piece of cake. And math had become the easiest subject of all, though also the most unpleasant. Each calculation was rent with the slashes and puncture wounds of division signs and fraction bars, evidence of Scowler's impatient attack upon the helpless numerals. Ry finished each page of equations sweaty and gasping, the pencil ruptured, the paper ripped. Miss Plaisted picked up the homework, blew away the lead dust, smoothed out the ripples, and edged away. At home Ry observed the same look of uneasy pensiveness in his mother. Both adults waited for the next development.

An excuse for action came in a matter of weeks. Jo Beth was called to the school to pick up Ry, who sat placidly in Principal Teague's office with his unzipped hip sack and pristine white cast—she hadn't noticed until now that not a single student had signed it. The other boy, Teague assured her, had been in no shape to wait around for Jo Beth's appraisal. He was bleeding far too profusely and, in Teague's experience, the sooner stitches went in, the better.

Ry was aware that this was his prompt to express remorse. Yet it was hard to feel bad about trouncing a sniveling, smart-lipped little monster, which was exactly what the boy had looked like through Scowler's eyes. Ry looked at his mother's hands, clasped but shaking in her lap, and started to feel bad anyway. He swallowed and zipped his hip sack shut.

Scowler began hissing immediately, so Ry barely heard when Miss Plaisted knock-knocked, entered, and began unleashing her pent-up observations. Ry Burke was secretive.

He hid his drawings in art class so no one could see them and smashed flat his clay sculptures before the teacher could grade them. Ry Burke was crafty. After taking a hit in gym-class dodgeball, he had gotten a bathroom pass, scoured the thawing playground for dog feces, and during recess smeared the feces to the underside of his attacker's desktop. Ry Burke was highly intelligent. This, too, was true, at least according to the books, although let's be honest—weren't the books a little suspicious, given everything else? And now Ry Burke was violent. This wasn't the first incident, Miss Plaisted insisted. The ensuing pause conjured up nightmares of unspecified blacktop beatings.

Finally the school could recommend what they had wanted since day one, and Jo Beth could accept that recommendation with an air of reluctance. Psychological evaluation—that was the ticket. There were handshakes. Pats on backs. Positive progress had been made today, they were sure of it. His mother's clasped hands, Ry realized as they got up to leave, had not been shaking from fear. They had been shaking from excitement.

The first therapist, Dr. Kent Thurmond, wasted no time blaming it all on Ry. The child had survived a trauma, he said during the very first interview, and that engendered a good deal of cognitive dissonance. The long day and night in the woods had also inspired strong feelings of invincibility. To handle the runoff, the boy had instilled his toys with some of these unrealistic attributes. These invented personalities simply needed to be uninvented; from this moment on, they were to be known only as the Unnamed Three. Ry grinned because he liked the new moniker. Jo Beth, however, forced an apologetic smile and asked if it was normal for a psychiatrist to offer such conclusions with the young patient sitting right there.

He was fired. Other therapists followed, but none were up to handling the Unnamed Three. There was Paul Pulchalski, who wanted to peel back the layers of quote unquote normal ego functions. Jo Beth said that sounded painful. There was Janelle Smith-Warner, a violent-trauma survivor herself who chewed anxiously on her long blond hair while fretting about her own career and romantic orbits. There was the stoop-shouldered Monroeville doctor who declared Ry a "tasty" challenge because of how he was firmly in the latency stage, so much more interesting than those in the phallic or genital. The sole standout was an Iowa City shrink who intrigued Ry with his talk of a "death instinct." Ry bristled, though, at the man's misquoting of his companions' names as "Furryman," "Mr. Jesus," and "Frown Guy."

Just when all hope was lost, there came the butcher. Handing Jo Beth a white-papered parcel of pork loin at Sookie's Foods, the aproned man took one look at the toys poking from Ry's hip sack and decided not to let go of the parcel when Jo Beth tried to take it. The two strangers bridged the counter, connected by meat. The overhead music cut out in favor of a price check.

"My sister can help him," the butcher said.

The accuracy of this snap judgment seemed to crush her. Ry did not fully appreciate his mother's new responsibilities—he knew she spent increasing amounts of time yelling at farmhands, on the phone with bankers, and driving to the Bloughton courthouse to deliver statements—but one thing he understood was despair. He could not bear seeing a woman of this caliber defeated. Her sleeve was right there, so he tugged it.

"It's okay," he whispered. "I don't mind."

Jo Beth took her son's chin between her thumb and index finger and gave him the kind of dazed examination usually reserved for new fiancées testing the clarity and cut of their diamonds. After a while she let go, squared her shoulders, and nodded at the butcher. The man wiped his hands and used his wax pencil to write a name and number.

"Her name's Linda." He winked. "You tell her I said to give you the pork-loin special."

Linda Colson worked from a home that doubled as a floral arrangement business, which she ran with her sister. The air was syrupy and the carpet seeded with spines of baby's breath, and a clacking curtain of beads was all that separated the rest of the world from the living room where Linda met her clients. The space was brown and orange and dappled with motes of dust soaking in the ample sun. Ten or twelve crystals spun from a western pane and their associated pellets of rainbow twirled across the walls. Linda, a tall, hefty, owlish woman with braided hair all the way down her back, folded herself onto the frowsy carpet across from Ry, billowing her long skirt about her so that her lower half was concealed in a jellyfish drape.

"He thinks his dolls are real." Jo Beth seemed way up high on the sofa.

Linda Colson looked incredulous. "Who says they're not?"

Ry came to think of her as his greatest ally. The other specialists had poked at him as if they had been the butchers, each of them after the choicest cut of meat. Linda, though, displayed no similar appetite. Mostly they talked about cartoons. Ry had lost track of them but she brought him up to date: *Archie's TV Funnies, Deputy Dawg, Woody Woodpecker, The Jackson 5ive.* They also talked about toys, another topic she was well versed in: Rock 'Em Sock 'Em Robots, Erector Sets, walkie-talkies, electric football. She asked him what other toys he had, and he told her that most of them had gotten lost in the forest, but that it was okay since he had the most important three. What the hell—he introduced them. After a couple weeks, Linda asked Ry to translate their whispers and, feeling emboldened, he did. Furrington and Jesus Christ's bits of advice sounded fortune cookie-ish when spoken aloud, but Linda looked rapt. She even laughed at the right places.

When she asked to clean Jesus Christ with some rubbing alcohol and cotton balls, Ry consented. The swarthy tan of his skin buffed to a bubblegum pink, and rich stigmata resurfaced on the diminutive palms. Ry was impressed. On future visits she sewed shut Furrington's leg stump and used her own finger to tuck in the frayed ends of Scowler's skin. Ry felt Scowler's displeasure; that was no surprise. The surprise was Ry's response: He found that he *liked* ignoring Scowler. The trick was how to get away with it.

A month before the school year ended, Linda broke it down.

"They're parts of you," Linda said. "I'm not telling you that. *You* told *me* that."

"I did?"

"Why do you think Jesus Christ only quotes from the Lord's Prayer?"

Ry had never realized that before.

"Because I know it?" he ventured.

"That's right. It's the only verse you know. And the rest of what he says?" Linda flapped a dismissive hand. "It's just a big bunch of *thees* and *thys* and *thous.*"

"Oh." Ry looked at Jesus Christ. The figure was lukewarm and lightweight.

"You've told me quite a bit about Mr. Furrington, too."

"I have?"

"You've told me he's smart. He's funny. He cares about people. He has a good imagination and tells good stories. You know who else is smart and funny and creative?"

Ry felt his ears burn.

"Me," he mumbled.

"Also, I'd like to know of any real British person who says *crackers!* You find me one, I'll give you fifty bucks."

Ry laughed. He clapped a hand over his mouth.

"But, hey, look," Linda said. "You can say *crackers!* all day long if you want. That's what's so good about pretending. Anything you want to be okay is okay. You know what I mean?"

"I guess."

"And there's another really good thing about pretending too. A really important thing. When you pretend—"

"Wait!" Ry cried.

Linda stopped. For an instant she looked annoyed but her smile ingested the annoyance like a wisp of smoke. "What's up?"

"What have I told you about Scowler?"

Linda sighed and folded her hands on her skirt. "I admit that Scowler is a harder nut to crack. He's our man of mystery, isn't he?"

"Uh-huh."

Linda gathered her hair behind her head. Her knuckles fought the plastic balls of a ponytail holder for a while. Even when that was done, she spent some time taking the measure of the boy in front of her.

"Let me ask you something," she said. "This is just an idea. If you don't like it, that's cool. But do you think that the people in your family influence your personality? Because I wonder if these pretend voices that are part of you, like we were just saying, are also reflections of your family, kind of. Take, for example, our friend Mr. Furrington. Mr. Furrington sort of reminds me of your sister, Sarah. You know how much she loves you, always following you around. Not to mention that she's small! You might have noticed Mr. Furrington's rather small himself. And Jesus Christ, well, he's so smart and takes such good care of you that I wonder if he's not a little bit like your mom. Your mom's the one who helps you with schoolwork, right? And feeds you and takes you to the doctor and brings you here to see me. Now, Scowler . . . well, maybe Scowler—and like I said, this is just an idea, so it's okay with me if you don't agree with it—but Scowler is, maybe, kind of a little bit like your dad."

Ry held his breath and waited for the screams to start.

"Ry?" Linda leaned in. "You okay, buddy?"

Scowler emitted no screams, no whines, no ghastly choking noises, just a silence of colossal and damning grandeur. Ry scrapped for a distraction.

"You said," he began, replaying the conversation. "You said there was another good thing about pretending."

Linda tilted her chin and then snapped it back once the thought was recaptured. "Right," she said. "The other good thing about pretending—and this is kind of important, Ry. I want you to think about this after we're done." She raised her eyebrows importantly. "The second good thing about pretending? It's that you can *stop pretending*."

From that day forward, a heavy chain began to slide from where it had bound tight his shoulders. Increasingly he ventured forth without the Three's protection—taking breakfast alone, going to the bathroom unaccompanied, minor chores here and there. By some miracle, tragedy was kept at bay, and he experienced the naked, windblown thrill of survival. His family, too, looked better than they had in ages, more adventuresome and alive, and he began to wonder if Linda had been right, if being under the watch of Ry (and Furrington and Jesus Christ and Scowler) was not all that different from being under the watch of Marvin.

And then she betrayed him. Ry would never know what happened, if Linda had thought his independence had progressed more quickly than it had, if there had been a lapse in payment from Jo Beth, or if sabotage had been part of the plan all along. But one morning he set about his chores without the Three and when he returned an hour later, his mother was sitting idle at the kitchen table. This was not normal. Ry went straight to his bedroom where the Three had been stationed at the foot of his door and found them missing. Swaying dangerously, he used walls and furniture to drag himself back to the kitchen, expecting to have missed the key detail when he had passed by moments earlier: Scowler stuck deep into his mother's jugular, blood slurping out in hushed currents. The only flow, though, was the wash of her tears.

"I burned them." Her voice skipped around as much as her

gaze. "She told me to do it and I just did what she said." She swallowed and grimaced as if she were drunk. "Now they're all burned up."

Waves of blackness pushed from the scar in Ry's forehead. He flapped a blind hand for support and felt his knuckles fumble past the handle of the refrigerator, the coiled cord of the phone. His lungs and throat filled with the cold loam of Black Glade and he drowned in it. Next the grave overtook his mother in her kitchen chair and his sister from where she waded in from the dining room. This was their death, all of theirs; without the Unnamed Three there was no protection. Ry collapsed upon the scuffed linoleum. He heard himself bleat out seizured demands for information. How long they had burned. The location of their corpses. Surely they could salvage something—Furrington's marble eyes, a glob of melted Christ, the singed steel skeleton of Scowler—and mold them into a new being. It was their only chance.

The next thing he became aware of was the blankets of his bed tucked so tightly around him that his arms were pinned. Linda Colson—he would never forgive her. He pictured a red Iowa dusk and the fleeing outline of the woman's stocky body—no, she was *fat*, the lady was *obese*, just another one of the cowardly, secretive, sly monsters Scowler had warned him about—and how her blubber became a horrific hindrance as she was chased into the narrow corridors of Black Glade. Jo Beth, too—oh, how she had fooled him. Neither woman would last long in the wilderness.

Anger shook down to grief and he felt the mopping handkerchief of his mother and heard her sorrowful shushing. In alternation came the fretful sounds of Sarah entering and exiting, her socked feet passing over the hallowed spot where the Three had made their last stand. Ry tried to remember the final moments he had spent with them. Furrington had been positioned to the left of the door; he had been *tra-la-la*-ing a jaunty tune. Scowler, as usual, took the center spot. Jesus Christ took the right side, and had taken the longest to balance upright. His feet were too small, that was the damn problem. Ry had cursed and then felt ungrateful. Jesus Christ, who never held a grudge, had consoled him in a voice pristine and true. They were the Three's last words.

We're little now, he had said. *But we shall grow up. Just like thou.*

Ry made a full recovery. He could tell it disappointed everyone. As the school year ended, his grades acclimated to lower altitudes. Classmates went back to ignoring him, or shoving him out of the way when they got sick of him blocking the hallway with his crutches. Violence no longer heavied Ry Burke's fists—it was obvious to everyone. On the farm the motivation behind a dozen ingenious innovations dissipated, leaving behind a ten-year-old whose long legs and dangling arms looked less like the tools of a budding genius and more the manacles of a gangly dullard. On the first day of summer vacation, he abandoned his usual seat in the milking parlor and found himself shivering in the predawn darkness of the Costner Eighty. Tendrils of alfalfa hay tapped his bad ankle as if to remind him of a time when life was fearful, yes, but fearful with meaning.

Ry squinted at Black Glade, wondering if that was where she had thrown down the tiny bodies and burned them. He thought he smelled cinder; he searched closer now, the alfalfa at his feet. Had it happened in this field right here? It was pointless speculating; he knew it was time to forgive his mother, but distrust lingered. The woman's allegiances shifted too easily.

So he was alone. He accepted it as best he could. There had been comfort in knowing that he was going to one day die at the hands of his father; now he felt only uncertainty. He realized with dismay that these were the conditions under which human beings lived their lives. A mist of rain pearled Ry's face and made his clothes feel like a layer of packed clay. He looked at the darkening dirt. Death had been his anchor, but there were other posts to which he could fasten himself: the Osage-orange trees, the silos, his sister. Release one; move fast; latch onto another. It was how he would spend his next nine years. He turned his face to the sky. It was really coming down.

A Darker Shade of Violet

MONDAY, AUGUST 24, 1981

0 HRS., 1 MIN. AFTER IMPACT

The dog was missing.

"Snig?" Marvin ejected phlegm from his throat and rose to wobbly knees. No more than a minute had elapsed since impact and he was the first to move. He looked one direction and winced, then repeated the routine the other way. Ry watched from where he was implanted in the lawn. His ears were ringing and his skin felt tender. Dimly he pictured the shotgun. Where was it? Could he get to it? But he kept getting distracted by the rain of ash, so pretty, so bizarre—the snowfall of the apocalypse. There was a loud exhale and Ry twisted his neck to see his mother slouched ten feet away. One of her hands was tentatively investigating a patch of scorched hair. After a moment she looked up at the sky and Ry followed her gaze. Tree limbs above them still reeled in slow motion, while individual leaves zagged to the ground aflame. The birds had flown.

"Here, boy." Marvin sounded dazed. He had one leg planted at a ninety-degree angle and, after a mighty inhale, pushed himself to a standing position. He was after the dog, not the gun, so Ry clenched his stomach muscles and sat up. Now he could see Sarah lying five feet away and wide awake, eyes rolling cautiously as if any further motion might awake her from this dream of survival. Ry checked on his father again. He was wobbling in the direction of the McCafferty Forty, where a mist of soil clung to the air like a bruise.

Ry tore his eyes away and whispered to Sarah. "Hey. Hey. You okay?"

Sarah propped herself up with an arm. Her hair floated in a crazed net, an effect that would have been comical under other circumstances.

"I think I'm fine," she said. "I think I fell."

"We all fell," Ry said. "Listen to me: Find the gun."

Marvin was now as far as the garage. One hand dug into the termite-ridden wood for stability; the other shaded his eyes to get a better look at the northeastern field. "Do you know what this is?" he asked no one in particular. "I think I know what this is."

Ry fought his way to his feet. Both knees popped. He took a moment to sway, then extended a hand to help his sister. As she accepted the assistance, Ry turned to his mother.

"Mom," he whispered. "Mom?"

"Yes. I'm here. I'm okay. It's just . . . my ears."

"Find the gun," Ry whispered. "Right now, find it."

Jo Beth and Sarah considered the grass around them—

overgrown, Ry's fault—but they seemed foggy about the instructions. Ry cursed and took a step, and his vision rocked. Recovering, he swept his eyes across the area, hoping for a flash of wood or metal. Through the cloud of dirt the morning sun turned everything shades of yellow and purple. This strange color contrast complicated the effort, but everyone's confusion was buying him time. All he needed were a few more seconds.

Marvin turned around, his forehead lined with wonderment.

"It is a meteor," he said. "A meteor has fallen on my farm."

There was a pause, then all four of them looked to the southern sky, as if expecting to see four more fireballs bearing down. Recognizing their shared postures as belonging to the resident expert, Ry and Jo Beth turned to Sarah, who was busy tamping down her hair with the air of someone primping for an appointment. After a few moments she noticed their eyes, and then shifted her gaze uncomfortably between them and her father.

"Meteorite," she said. "That's what they're called when they land."

Ry looked to the back forty, then to his sister, who was clearly only beginning to process the madness of what had just occurred. What made him even more uneasy, though, was that she had yet to display the proper amount of fear of her father. It was entirely possible that Jo Beth had never shared with her daughter the extent of Marvin's depravity. Curiosity, then, was only natural.

Marvin nodded as if Sarah's terminology rang a distant bell, and then he began to approach. Jo Beth looked too bewildered to react one way or another. Ry's body seized with panic, and his eyes skittered across the lawn, frantic for discovery.

"A meteorite, Jo." Understanding was dawning on Marvin's face. "There was a—I don't know why I didn't think of it right off. At Bluefeather, there was a kind of . . . an event. The whole place shook. And the walls, some of them just blew apart like nothing. This—this *thing*." He pointed a thumb back at the field. "I'm telling you, this is the same exact thing. And the Professor said—I didn't tell you he got crushed. He did. One second he was relieving himself into the toilet and the next . . . But maybe six months back he said something about this, about a what do you call it, a group . . ."

"A belt," Sarah said. A familiar gleam was beginning to light up her eyes. "The Jaekel Belt."

Marvin snapped his fingers. "That's it, a belt. Poor guy. Had he only lived to see it. He said it was of real scientific interest, and if chunks from this belt found their way to the ground, the person who found them would be one lucky son of a bitch because—"

He turned and looked once more at the distant field. Instantly Ry blundered across the lawn, neck straining, eyes spinning, fingers splayed and ready to snatch the gun from its hiding place. Insects leapt from his path and blades of grass recoiled from his swiping feet. Suddenly he saw it—a darker shade of violet, a few feet away to his right, and he tumbled for it, fingers outstretched.

The shotgun lifted from the ground, but in the hands of Marvin Burke. The man rotated the staff of walnut and steel as if trying to recall its purpose. The more he held it, though, the more its weight transmitted a significance, and soon it jounced lightly within an ever more assured grip. Marvin looked up and saw his family staring at him. At first he looked surprised. Then the gap between his front teeth showed itself.

"Money." His voice took on the brisk snap of nine years past. "That's what this means, Jo. And that's why I'm sorry, but I'm going to have to take it with me. Stash it somewhere until the heat is off and then—you have no idea. You have no idea what a university will pay for something like this."

Jo Beth looked lost. "Pay?"

"Museums, too. There could be a secret auction. Not much different from fielding offers when selling off land. Doesn't matter who I am, how I'm dressed, not if I have the goods. The Professor said it's done all the time—some yokel finds a rock in his outhouse and makes a killing. You wouldn't believe the dollar amounts he bandied about. You want to take a guess?"

"No. What? *Marvin.*"

"We've got to excavate it. We've got to do it now, right now; there isn't much time. My God, don't you see it, Jo? This is a gift."

He looked at his pallid, petrified wife as if expecting reciprocation of his enthusiasm. Ry found the gleam in his eye too familiar. It was the same fervor displayed by the great farmer when discovering the first signs of life in his fields; when slapping the swollen udders of a nervous cow approaching her first milking; when stalking, pitchfork in hand, the dusty alleys of a towering new metropolis of bales. It was the greedy look of revelation: There was one crop of value yet to be harvested from his beloved soil.

Marvin Burke hitched up the shotgun and turned his gaze on each of them.

"All right, then," he said. "Let's go have us a look."

0 HRS., 16 MINS. AFTER IMPACT

The smell was unexpected. It hit them when they were still a hundred yards off, their quickly and poorly chosen shoes munching through the lunar crust of the northeast-ernmost field. It was a fragrant methane reminiscent of the muck once generated by the farm's cattle, only with a stifling undertone of hot copper. Ry tasted it at the back of his throat and tried swallowing. It burned all the way down. Five more minutes and the stench crept into the territory of the distressing. Jo Beth tented a hand over her nose and mouth and silently urged Sarah to do the same. Sarah, though, had her sights locked on their destination.

The fugitive took point; it was a kind of bravery. If Ry had been less dazed, if the ground had not been so fatally pitted, he might've gained enough speed to pounce upon the man's back. Then there was the shotgun to consider, flashing in the sun with the speed of a twirling baton. The firing mechanism might jam after so many years of disuse, but that was an outside chance given Marvin's diligence about keeping the gun well oiled. Ry let his eyes ease back to the ground and saw four, eight—no, more than he could count—giant black triangles leading to a depression in the field near the tree line of Black Glade. Seconds later Ry's shoes were crunching through the residue. They were scorch marks. The dirt itself had been toasted.

Marvin toed the edge of the crater. Sarah joined him like it was nothing, her blond hair close enough to tickle the Winchester's trigger. Jo Beth had no choice: She swept in beside her daughter, darting an arm around her shoulder and pulling her away from the weapon, but then leaving the gesture half fulfilled when she saw what lay at her feet. Ry came last, slow as old age. His hope was that his father would be wrong—a rare and delectable occurrence—and the contents of the crater would be something rather pedestrian: a weather satellite, a ball of hail, some other atmospheric burp. The truth, though, was in his family's postures: the shrinking back of an insecure species.

The hole bored through countless strata of soil. At the top, the crater spanned nearly thirty-five feet, a giant toothless mouth. The walls were smooth as charcoal from the heat that had seared them. Stray ends of root systems dangled like cauterized arteries. The crater's overall effect was dizzying, even though it was only roughly fifteen feet deep; a steaming pool of muddy water hid the precise depth of its lowest point. Peeking through the liquid was a rock of indeterminate size, a couple feet in diameter, maybe more, black and glossy and fascinatingly notched, a miniature planet of coral-reef complexity. Though only a few inches were revealed, Ry could vouch that it was like no stone he'd ever seen.

"Water," Marvin muttered. He looked sidelong at his son, droplets of steam fattening on his glasses while his beard darkened and curled. Ry's stomach cramped at the irrefutable evidence of his incompetence. This surprise vat of moisture showed that the farm's lifeblood still flowed.

"Marvin." Jo Beth's face was as blank as paper. "Is it safe?"

"It's safe, Mom," Sarah said. "Can we go get the camera?"

"No."

"Can I go down and touch it?"

"Of course not."

"We've got to," Marvin said. "Good Christ. Good *Christ*."

Marvin shifted the gun to his left hand, placed his right

on his knee, and leaned over the hole. His forehead peaked at the heightened smell. Ry could not help but be intrigued. He followed suit, leaning over, and when he sniffed it hit him like a too-cold drink, not just the overpowering smell but sheets of magnetic waves so charged they puckered the pores of his skin. He inhaled, choked, tasted salt, and expected a nosebleed.

(hello)

Ry swallowed to clear his throat of blood before responding. But there was no blood and no one had spoken. He looked to Sarah, but she showed no signs of hearing a thing. She leaned into the magnetic field as if it were a thrill ride, her lashes fluttering as vaporous forces moved each long blond hair. Ry felt it too: His eyebrows twitched like insect feelers.

"I'll do it," Sarah said. "Is anyone listening? I'll go down there."

"That smell's going to make us all sick," Jo Beth said.

"No worse than pumping diesel," Marvin said. "I pulled that duty for a month. You get used to it."

"And it's hot. Look at the steam. Let's go back. The two of us can talk. I'm sweating. *We're* sweating."

"If it was that hot there'd be fire," Sarah insisted.

Ry noticed the fresh space in his sister's teeth and felt a crazy certainty that he would find the missing tooth in the crater, its fluoride polish impervious to the volcanic glass that caked everything else.

"There's no fire," Marvin growled, "because all that's left out here is dirt."

"The whole hole is so big," Sarah said. She turned to her brother. "The whole hole. Ry—*the whole hole.*"

With her attention on him he considered asking if she had

heard that faint, ringing *hello*. But he was an older brother and with that came the responsibility of being amused by pointless wordplay. He mustered a sickly smile and a jittery wink—the best he could do.

"It's big, all right," Marvin said. He reached into the front pocket of his shirt and with practiced agility withdrew the sorriest pack of cigarettes Ry had ever seen: flat, gray, and speckled with errant flakes of tobacco. Luckies—Jeremiah's favorite. While trying to shake free a stick, Marvin raised an eyebrow and scanned the cemetery remains of the land he loved. "Makes the whole back eighty look . . . I don't know. Little. That isn't how I remember it. Not at all." The crooked cigarette went between his lips and his nimble fingers dove once more and came back with a crumpled book of matches. "You remember the night the steers got free, like they were angry about the low-grade hay, like they knew the milk cows were getting the good stuff." He tucked the shotgun under his arm and struck a match. The flame was butterscotch, weak. "And out of bed we jumped, all of us in our underwear, flying through the corn back here trying to round them up." His lip hiked, betraying real affection. Ry's mind, too, conjured snatches of the frenzied hunt, his muddy briefs, the moronic thrill of flailing unclothed through nature. "Jo, you remember. How long did it take us?"

The hand holding the lit match was trembling.

Ry concentrated on it, willed it into a symbol of hope.

"All night," Jo said. "Into morning."

"God, the mornings here. The mornings."

His voice softened in a way Ry wasn't sure he'd ever heard before.

"Things here," he said, "weren't perfect. But I did try to provide. It was all I knew how to—"

The fire died. Marvin's fingers shook even harder for a moment, a death spasm, and then snapped into a fist. There was no breeze to blame so he blamed inconvenience. Having to hold the gun under his arm while trying to ignite damp matches was too awkward, and with brusque motions he stuffed the cigarette, soft pack, and matchbook back into his shirt pocket—and there Marvin froze. Relief rinsed his face as the tips of his fingers fondled an unseen object bulging from the bottom of the pocket. Ry felt a warning in his gut that there were other secrets yet to be revealed.

"Yes, indeedy. Half the day was spent wrangling. Because loaded with crop, this here stretch was—there's no other word for it. It was *big*. Bigger than eighty acres, once you were inside it. A rock, even one like this, had it fallen from the sky back then?" He looked at them in turn: wife, daughter, son. "Why, I believe the corn would've gobbled it up. In fact . . ." He let his eyes tickle across Ry's face. "Those one or two steers we didn't find that night, I've always figured that's what happened. Corn got hungry." He jerked his eyebrows. "Chomp."

Ry jumped. He hated it, but he did.

Marvin grinned. Filaments of tobacco floated in his beard like scabs.

"Time's a-wastin'." He motioned the shotgun barrel at the crater.

Ry took a deep breath and squinted. The clouds of steam were thinner now. Sun blasted off the water, which hissed as it lapped at the rock. The lustrous ore seemed to squirm in its stew of energy like a knot of wrought-iron snakes. Ry had no business down there, none of them did. But his mother's haggard face—how easily a bullet could unsnap tendons from bone. The padding of girl-fat that swaddled Sarah's organs—how crudely a shot would yank garish colors from the paleness.

Marvin appeared to read his son's mind. His red and weary eyes examined both possible targets. Ry wasted no more time. He stepped over the edge of the crater, dug his left heel into the soot, and eyed a path that should not prove too difficult for a young man of sure footing. It wouldn't be fun, but as Marvin had said a million times, running a farm never was.

0 HRS., 42 MINS. AFTER IMPACT

Three feet down the smelly exhaust enveloped him like warm honey. He wiped it out of his eyes and flung it aside. Another step lower and he found himself emerging damp from the steam clouds. Magnetism at this level was palpable; his pulse struggled against confused gravity. With his heel he kicked a foothold into the smoldered grade, leaned back, and slid—seven feet down, eight feet, nine. He crouched and locked his arms around his knees. Less than a foot away, the pool, roughly four feet across, swayed like melted chocolate.

The meteorite was an extravaganza. Ry leaned forward, extended his neck, and held the posture breathlessly. The exposed rock gleamed with mercurial liquescence and twinkled in neon tones of pink, purple, and blue. Ry angled his head and an entire world of sparkling lace revealed itself, floating within the rock like a field of golden mushrooms. Ry longed to grip one of the rock's many outcroppings—how much like handles they looked!—and see what other dimensions there were to discover. He stretched out a hand.

The field of energy straightened the hair on his knuckles. His arm hairs rose next like flowers awakening to sun. After that his neck stubble became a garden of thorns. Then the pressure upon his skull began to build, steady as a closing vice. Ry's jaws scraped past each other with an abrupt squeak and he pushed himself back from the meteorite, clutching his ringing head between his palms. Bitter methane folded like construction paper down his throat. He gagged and his vision went black.

(hold still)

(i can't find you)

(yes, you)

Ry opened his mouth to scream that he was *HERE, RIGHT HERE!*—and with that he crested from blackness to discover a slamming headache. Long black fingers had wrapped around his legs. He gasped and kicked but they were just shadows from the people staring from fifteen feet up.

"Ry? You okay? You okay, Ry? You okay?"

The subsequent cough told him that this concern came from Sarah, not Jo Beth, and even in this crippled state the slight from his mother hurt. He nodded in response, but that was a bad idea because it widened what already felt like a gaping hole in his head. He pushed himself farther from the meteorite.

"Feels weird," he managed to say. "Real weird. I'm coming up."

Sun glared from shotgun metal. The muzzle made the scribbly motions of aiming.

"That's not necessary, Marvin." Jo Beth's voice carried well in the absence of the birds. "He'll do what you say."

"I'll judge what's necessary."

"But I can help. Just talk to me."

"Talk? Jo, I can barely *think*."

"Because you're hurt?"

"Because the situation is tense." Marvin probed the gap between his front teeth with his tongue. "And because I'm hurt."

"That's what I'm saying. Let's slow down. Let's think this through. You haven't told me a thing. How you got here, anything."

Ry took a knee and tried to reestablish a normal pattern of breathing. It was possible that these requests from his mother were a brilliant ploy. If she could draw answers of any detail from her husband, Ry might have a chance to make a move that counted. He'd just need to hang on to his slippery powers of judgment.

"There's nothing to tell," Marvin said. "I got out."

"Because one of these things fell?"

"That's right."

"And it knocked down some walls?"

"Knocked down? It turned the east end of my cell to chalk."

"And you climbed out?"

"What else? Only it was up, Jo. I climbed up."

"Up?"

Ry stood and turned toward the crater wall. He winced as the heel of his shoe crunched through the glasslike surface. It was the kind of noise Sarah would jump at, if her attention wasn't fixed upon her parents.

"The ceiling's what fell in," Marvin explained. "That's what buried the Professor. If I'd used the toilet first, it would've been me."

"Well, I'm grateful."

"No, you're not."

"I am," Jo Beth insisted. "That's not what I would have wanted."

"Please don't say that."

"I'm sorry. But weren't there any guards to stop you?"

"Guards? Christ, yes. They were everywhere."

"Then how . . . ?"

Marvin at last deigned to look at her. The gun dipped and its bead slid from Ry's forehead like a drop of sweat. "How. How." Marvin's lips flattened strangely, and it took Ry a moment to identify the emotion as amusement. "Jo, the questions you ask." He was pleased, though, and symmetrical patches of beard thickened with the twists of a wry grin. As a master of the kitchen-table soliloquy, the only thing Marvin Burke might crave more than revenge was a chance to bask in his own ingenuity.

Ry crouched, prepared his muscles to move.

"There was a game room," Marvin said. "Directly above my cell."

"A game room?"

"Pool, shuffleboard, darts. You know, rewards for good behavior."

"It was above your cell?"

Ry moved on all fours up the side of the crater. His parents seemed to leap closer.

Marvin's whiskers twitched with his grin. "The noises would drive the Professor crazy. Me, I came to like it. Little men and their little games. When the ceiling opened up, all of it just sort of . . . slid."

"Even the pool table?"

136

"Fell right into my cell. Christ if it wasn't a sight. Balanced up there on the edge, big as a whale. Then it was lumber."

"And you used it to get out somehow?"

The climbing noises of Ry's hands and feet, even those of his labored breathing, were too loud. He froze, held his breath. Somewhere above his head he could hear his father swallow, how the subsequent inhale peeled his tongue from the roof of his mouth.

"Men on the inside," he said, "that's all they talk about. What they'll do if God reaches down and rips open a hole. You know me well enough. You know I'd have a plan. And a contingency plan. And a plan three, a plan four."

"I do know that. Or I should've known. I'm sorry if I forgot."

"Darts. Billiard balls. A pool cue. Maybe I picked up other things too, I don't remember. But in the right hands, these objects are not toys."

"Did you hurt anyone? Tell me."

Ry was practically within arm's reach of Marvin's ankle, but Ry looked at his shaking wrists and locked elbows and found that he could not move another inch until he heard the man's response. Because before grappling with his father it would be wise to know exactly what he'd become.

"Did I hurt . . ." Marvin laughed once, a sandpaper sound. "I don't know, Jo. To get out of that place I had to do some things, and some of those things were surely bad. But I'm telling you—it was like it wasn't me. It was like someone else was doing them. I don't remember the half of it; I wish I did. You don't have to believe me, but it's the truth."

"I believe you, Marvin. Honest, I do."

Perhaps it was the word *honest*—used too often inside

137

penitentiaries by men who were anything but—that riled him. Marvin gave his head a shake and dug a thumb into his temple, drawing blood and smearing soot. Ry rubbed his own thrumming skull and shut his eyes. Words, when they next came, sizzled.

"You think I like this spot I'm in, you're crazy. But you put me here, Jo. You and the boy. I'm not putting this gun down if that's what you're hoping. I can't. The Bluefeather folks might think I'm under rubble at the moment, but that moment will pass. And then they'll come. They'll come *here*, and then I'm done for. That's the situation and nothing in the world can change it except this rock."

Ry slit open his eyes to find Jo Beth, her arm graceful upon emergence from the nightgown, reaching out to touch her husband's chest with tentative fingers. The prison-issue shirt above Marvin's heart was crusted into a brown, immovable snarl.

"You have to let me look at that."

"No time, Jo."

"You'll drip. They'll find you."

The unjust dead ends of life momentarily appeared to overcome the man. His eyes wandered across the perishing plain, the infected air, his own damaged body. "It does hurt. No doubt you could work wonders. If things could be different, I'd say something else. You'd say something else. You'd be proud of me, even. God, who knows."

He winced from more than one kind of pain and, as if for cover, he reached again for his pack of Luckies. Only this time Jo Beth's fingers slipped in and plucked the pack and matches from his pocket. She withdrew a cigarette, inserted it into her mouth, struck the match, and then cupped her hands around the flame like someone who knew what she was doing. She took a hard puff, a gray veil lifted in front of her face, and then she held the cigarette out to her husband. He touched his shirt pocket, making sure the secret object still lay untroubled, and then took the cigarette, putting his lips where hers had been.

Ry could blame it on the heat or the meteorite's haze, but what he saw in Jo Beth's expression was no illusion. Ry knew that look. He had seen it for years in department store check-out lanes as Jo Beth eyed the stacked cart of a woman with a thicker pocketbook, or during sewing deliveries as she stole glances at some woman's new car or backyard pool. Though Jo Beth hadn't had access to the Burke savings account in those days, it had been far from empty.

Marvin's sins were serious but rarely had he erred in business matters.

"Your hair," Jo Beth said, venturing to touch the thick black tufts. "Your beard."

Marvin looked at his feet. "You shave by their rules in prison."

"I like it," she said. "I do."

Ry could not bear another word. The time for crawling was over, and he shot to his feet on the uneven grade and hurled himself up the final few feet, at the same time altering his angle so that his body was in line with the meteorite. If Marvin shot, at least some of the buckshot would fragment the miraculously unfragmented rock. Ry wondered who would cry the loudest at this damage, husband or wife.

There was no chance to grab his father's ankle. All things dreamy drained from Marvin's face and the gun sprang.

"What are you doing?" Marvin demanded.

Ry raised his arms in surrender.

"Sarah, run." He had to believe in the power of chaos.

"What?" Jo Beth was aghast. "Ry, no."

"I don't want to run," Sarah said. "I want to see it."

"Don't cause trouble," Marvin warned. "Either of you."

"Sarah, do it." Ry believed his own voice had never sounded so tired. "Run."

He closed his eyes. He hoped to hear the gunshot. Even more, he hoped to hear the diminishing claps of his sister's escaping feet.

Instead, he heard the voice.

(oh, no)

(do not lose faith)

(dear boy)

These words distracted him and by the time he heard his sister's footfalls, closer instead of farther away, it was too late. The first thing he saw was the stunned faces of Marvin and Jo Beth. Turning around, blinking and twisting, finally he found Sarah, who was skidding down the embankment in pajamas. When he reached for her all he got was a quick, cool slide of blond hair across his palm. He spun, hit the incline, and lost his wind. Jo Beth's shouting—*Sarah!*—brought him right back. His sister was trying to make good on her begging and go touch the damn thing, and he saw her slip down the fired slickness of the crater, her little thighs flexing in a brave attempt to stop her momentum. Her arms helicoptered and then flew forward to pad her fall, and though one of her arms caught beneath her chest, the other landed right where she had wanted, directly upon the meteorite. Her fingers wrapped around one of the black nodes like five tiny pink whips.

Sarah for a moment oriented herself in silence, taking note of her body and appendages. Her face, smudged and stupefied, at last discovered her right hand curled around the beautiful, glistening rock, and she shouted out long before taking any physical action.

"It's hot," she said. "It's hot! It's *hot!*"

"Sarah!" Jo Beth shouted. "Help her!"

Ry's heart hopped into his mouth, fat and bleeding and choking off air. Sarah's legs pedaled and her body jerked, and an instant later her fingers ripped free and skimmed through the mud, and were tucked into her gut before Ry could see their condition. Sarah, her pale lips quivering, shouldered up the bank as if she were armless. Ry's paralysis broke and he fell over his sister like a cage, wanting to embrace her but afraid to touch because of the whimpering and weeping and now, quite suddenly, the coughing.

"She's hurt! I'm bringing her up!"

Hearing genuine alarm in his voice was gasoline to the fire of Sarah's panic, and on cue her whine amplified into a scream. Ry slid one of his arms under her knees and told himself that the rise in volume was not—was *not*—to be taken as an accurate gauge of her injury. He put his other arm beneath her shoulders, stood, and began the process of lifting and planting feet, recalling school film strips of astronauts, their boots crashing to the pale moon with arduous slowness.

Jo Beth's arms tangled with his, sharp nails scraping at his wrists and biceps. Ry resisted—what right did she have to help now? Sarah, though, rolled toward her mother. Ry let it happen, unexpectedly furious, and dropped to his knees as Jo Beth stumbled from the crater with her new, thrashing burden. Ry planted his elbows over the lip of the crater; he sucked for air, in, out, and watched the corresponding flit of a weed that had survived the interplanetary clash.

"Sarah, let me see." How many times had Ry himself given in to that smooth, motherly firmness? "Let me see. It's all right, let me see."

"It hurts! It huuuuurts!"

"I know, sweetie, just let me see so I can make it better."

Ry's neck creaked when he moved it. Marvin was still there, the gun held inches from Ry's temple but with only half of its former authority. A bead of sweat puckered from his father's eyebrow, crept down the rim of his nose, and clung to the bulbous tip.

"We're going back to the house," Jo Beth said.

"Hold on," Marvin said.

"That hole's not going anywhere. Please."

Marvin took a step away from the crater, folding the shotgun back against his shoulder. Jo Beth hoisted the girl's fetal, twisting body. She could not hold her daughter indefinitely, and this more than anything tilted the entire afternoon onto its edge. Marvin spat his cigarette and held a fist to his injured heart.

"Fine, we all go. But we come right back and that's not up for—"

Jo Beth staggered forth. Black, brown, then white dust enfolded her legs. Marvin watched for a long moment, then looked at Ry, the sweltering silence both accentuating the father's failure in getting his prize and challenging the son to go ahead and do something about it. Ry sagged into his elbows; he was rid of energy, out of breath, and literally at his father's feet, though he could not help but feel a small victory had been won.

Marvin's voice crackled like flame. "You think there aren't worse things than sewing someone to a mattress?"

Ry screwed his fingers into the dirt and brought himself to shaky knees. Before long he found himself eye to eye with his father. They were the same height, look at that. Ry let a heedless smile exit through his mouth like a whisper. In the distance, Jo Beth was making fine time, already to the shed where they used to store commercial feed.

Marvin stepped aside and motioned with the gun. Blurred by Ry's squint, the barrel took on a red hue and became the bat—it would always be the bat—and Ry wondered and feared, as he always did, if he would ever be brave enough to use it. He took a step toward the house and passed through a perimeter of the meteorite's voltage; an elastic tension snapped away from his skin like latex. There was a matching throb at the center of his head, where the darkest of things had always filed their claws.

(so much light)

(how pretty)

(are you gone away?)

(hello?)

1 HR., 32 MINS. AFTER IMPACT

The universal dinginess that made everything the same color, the foot-worn stripes that marked a lifetime of short-cuts, the silos standing like once-fearsome kings with shoulders rounded by defeat—it was easy to believe the farm was unchanged. The only clues otherwise were the few charred leaves still drifting across the back lawn. Ry managed to find one and stamp it before climbing the back steps on his way inside. The shotgun nicked his shoulder blade and the reedy wheezes coming from behind him made it evident that Marvin's injuries were flaring. The house reacted to their weight; it tsked as if disapproving.

Jo Beth was at the sink filling a glass with water. Ry went no farther than the pantry door. Marvin stopped, too, as if they had intruded upon some private feminine ritual. She lifted her eyes only to make the quickest of identifications and then went about topping off the glass, setting it on the counter, and opening a cabinet.

"Well?" Marvin asked.

"Well, she's burnt." She withdrew a bottle of aspirin and shook it once before clapping it to the counter. "I don't know. I think she'll be all right. It's hard to say. You know burns. There's not much you can do for them. It's pink—who knows what that means."

"Rub freshly chopped onion on it," Marvin said.

Jo Beth shook two aspirin into her palm. "Nothing's fresh here."

"Vinegar, then," Marvin said. "It'll take the edge off."

"No home remedies," Jo Beth said. "She's got ice in a rag."

The lid was half screwed on before the threads slipped and made a plastic grinding noise. Jo Beth threw the lid into the sink. She turned around and looked at her husband. Her eyes were expectant. Marvin inhaled noisily but said nothing.

"You should take a few of these yourself," she said.

"I might," he said. "But we've got to get back out there."

144

Her lips went pale with pressure. Slowly she shifted her gaze to Ry.

"Would you take these to your sister?"

He glanced at his father, who was busy inspecting his wife for signs of treason. Cautiously Ry moved around the table, lifted the glass of water, and held out his hand. Jo Beth opened her hand over his and for a second he was convinced of a secret maneuver, that what would drop into his palm would be a small paring knife—just like that, reuniting them on the same team. Instead two white pills bounced across his palm. He closed his fingers and felt the aspirin soften and stick.

Ry moved away from the sink and toward the dining room. Below his feet a surreal glimpse of a past life: a scrap of holiday wrapping paper stuck to a splotch of maple syrup. Next he looked upon the limp needles of the makeshift Christmas tree, and that's where the reverie ended, because above that was the phone, their savior. He paused just long enough to recall the utter destruction of the telephone pole across the road. There would be no more calls made from this house, maybe ever.

Sarah was curled up on the sofa. Piled on the floor, sent there by her cycling legs, was a piece of in-progress sewing. Ry flung it behind the chair before kneeling; Marvin hardly needed more evidence of the ways in which his wife had moved on without him. Ry set his elbow on the cushion next to Sarah, and her moan crescendoed.

"Shhh." Ry opened his palm and looked at the aspirin. It was the first still moment of the day, and it provided unexpected space for Ry to acknowledge the morning's enormities. Water sloshed from the glass. His shoulders were shaking.

With Ry mute and Sarah's sobs reduced to a drone, their parents' voices carried.

"We should get her to the hospital."

"There's no use asking that."

"We don't know anything about that thing out there. It could be radioactive. Just being near it might have done something to her."

"We don't know that."

"That's exactly right—we don't know. How are *you* feeling?"

"I told you."

"Not that. I'll dress that. I mean your head. You're going to tell me you don't have the worst headache of your life right now?"

"I don't know what you're talking about."

"Seriously? You're seriously going to tell me that?"

"I am."

Such a coarsening of voice typically forewarned hitting. Ry closed his eyes and waited for the meaty smack. Instead there was a drowsy silence in which nothing happened, though when Jo Beth next spoke her tone was less strident.

"Then you're the only one, Marvin."

"I've never felt better in my life and that's the God's honest truth."

Sarah whimpered and Ry's eyes shot open. He glanced at the door, thought about closing it, and judged it an unnecessary risk. They'd just have to keep their voices down.

"Hey. Sarah. Hey."

Her feet did a little dance of pain.

He tried another tack. "Hey, shitburger."

At this she turned, gasping as if woken from a nightmare.

146

The salty residue of tears striped her face pink and white. Water dripped steadily from the cloth around her injured right hand, darkening the sofa cushion, the pillow, and her pajamas.

"I'm sorry I didn't run when you said."

"It's okay. Everything will be okay."

"Ry, it hurts. I'm not lying."

"I know." He held out the glass and the pills. "Take these."

Even suffering, she took the time to look skeptical. "What is it?"

"Arsenic. Take it."

"Ry."

"Go on."

Teeth bared bravely, she propped herself up on one elbow, pinching an aspirin aloft in front of her face. She had been swallowing pills for only a few months now, and never in a situation this dire. But lodes of strength ran deep in this girl. A little line dimpled her forehead. She placed the pill on her tongue and with impulsive speed slopped water into her mouth and rocked her head backward in the same alarming style of pill-swallowing as their mother.

"Good girl. One more."

She coughed, the aftereffect of having done something vaguely medical, but it caught in her lungs, wet and crackling and more resonant than any sound that had ever originated from that tender chest. It might have been the same cough she had been nurturing since yesterday. Ry grimaced—it might not. Thirty brutal seconds passed with her spine curled and wretched. Finally she leaned back, taking hold of her injured appendage just above the wrist and settling it in her lap.

"I have a question," she whispered.

147

"One down the hatch," he urged softly. "How about another?"

"He's going to take it? The meteorite? And sell it?"

Ry shrugged. "I guess so."

Sarah frowned. "That's a bad plan. It doesn't make sense."

Ry thought for a moment. "I guess not."

"And it falling here in the first place—that's crazy, right? That's crazy that it happened."

Ry nodded. "It is."

"Okay, I have another question."

"All right."

"Is he going to shoot us?"

"No."

"Ry, be truthful."

"I am. No."

"Is he going to shoot *you*?"

It was a trap well set. He massaged his head. "I don't know. I hope not."

"You have a headache?"

"Yes."

She extended a tiny pale hand, touched the bottom of his cupped palm, and lifted it so that the remaining aspirin was elevated to the level of his lip. They did not make girls any finer. Holding back tears, Ry took the pill and placed it on his tongue. She handed over the sweating glass. He tipped it back, swearing to himself that he'd get his sister out of this mess no matter what kind of sacrifice it took.

The pill was in his mouth when there came a knock at the front door.

2 HRS., 11 MINS. AFTER IMPACT

Ry swung into the dining room. Marvin and Jo Beth crowded there, faces broadcasting their fear that Ry might shout for help, because who had any idea what might happen after that. Five heavy raps upon the door—and then a silence in which none of them moved or breathed.

Then of course came more knocks, harder this time, and six of them; Ry now had an idea of what being shot felt like. People did not make idle sojourns to the Burke farm—it was on the way to nowhere—so this visitor had some good reason to be there, and knowing how farms operated the visitor might amble around back to hunt for them in the barns or fields. They had to face this right now.

"Anybody home?" boomed the voice. "You folks there?"

Phinny—oh, Christ, it was Phinny. Ry's heart skipped and he gaped at his mother, guilt and heroism swirling in his throat, and she transferred his paralyzed appeal to Marvin. He bit his lip with such force that beard hairs shot outward like quills. He made a motion at his wife with the shotgun.

"Answer it," he whispered. "Get him out of here."

Jo Beth looked at her husband as if he had asked her to host an impromptu dinner party. Her eyes pleaded but he kept white-knuckling the gun, and the way the old parts rattled, agitating the loaded shell, made everyone nervous. Seconds, swollen with fear, dripping with torture, ticked by. At last Jo Beth moved her head in loose circles; maybe it was a nod, though it looked more like her neck had snapped.

She moved toward the door as if reeled by fish line. Marvin snatched a fistful of Ry's shirt and pulled him against the dining room wall so that the two of them hid only a few feet from the front door, mere inches from Phinny's view, the muzzle of the shotgun pushed into the back of Ry's skull. There was a noise behind them, and both of them twisted their necks to see Sarah standing slack-jawed, the damp cloth draping from her forgotten injury. She might talk, she might scream—Marvin opened his mouth to deliver a warning but there was no time.

Locks snickered open and the door mewled like a cat.

"Why, Phinny." Ry winced; the *why* was too much. He heard the rusted springs of the screen door push wide. "Good morning. Or is it later than that already?"

"You know you got live wires out here?"

Phinny was livid. As gregarious as the man was, he had no patience for incompetence, and the front yard writhing with downed wires had set him on edge. Ry pressed his eyes shut and told himself to stay quiet, stay quiet, stay quiet.

"Yes," Jo Beth said. "I know. I'm sorry."

"Lightning hit that thing? Sweet Jesus. Dangerous as hell. You're keeping that girl of yours away?"

"I am. And I'll call the phone company and get them to take care of it."

"You'll call them? With what?"

"With the . . ." Jo Beth's voice was louder because she had turned to point a finger at the kitchen, where the dead phone swung like a man hanged. "Oh. Of course. I can't call, can I?" She giggled; it was over the line of normalcy and Ry held his breath.

"How about I call for you when I get back?"

"Oh, Phinny, that would be wonderful. I'm sorry I'm scatterbrained, I just—"

"Now, look." The shake of a box of spark plugs brought

back to Ry the sweet, safe memories of motor oil and uncooperative engines. "I know these are late. Mary came back from a weekend at the lake with her fellow hoodlums and told me she's dropping out of school, so I had to dish out all kinds of hell. That had my attention for a couple days, I admit. Then I backed over my mailbox. I know this isn't a great excuse. But dammit if I wasn't distracted by all this nonsense with Mary and I guess I wasn't looking where I was going because I steamrolled that thing, and it gave my back axle a talking to. So there's a day lost right there. Worst thing of it was my mailman refused to deliver a single piece of paper so long as that mailbox was down. Said it wasn't regulation. So I had to fix that axle and get myself to town to pick up my mail. Long story short, here's your plugs, and I hope to God they work because they're a different brand and I didn't have time to double-check compatibility."

"Thank you. Thank you, Phinny. This is wonderful. I'll let Ry know."

"Where is he? I better show him myself."

"I . . . ah . . ."

Everyone in the house sweated.

"Ry," Phinny repeated. "He here?"

Ry did not need to see his mother to picture the tics of her lie: the false, faltering smile, the eyes rounded and blinking as if somehow offended. They were red flags for anyone with half a brain and Phinny was as sharp as they came. Jo Beth's silence became a thing too hot to touch, and then the gun was jabbing into Ry's back, prodding him into the hallway.

"Fix this." Marvin's threat was clammy against Ry's ear.

Ry snatched the briefest of looks at Sarah, planted in the center of the dining room and at her father's mercy, before a shove sent him into the hall. Shoe rubber squeaked across tile and instantly four eyes were on him: Jo Beth's childlike in naked distress, Phinny's peering from the shade of the porch. Ry straightened and pushed himself down the hall. He arrived to find his mother holding open the screen door and looking ridiculous—nightgowned and aggrieved in the midday sun. Nothing felt right and Phinny would sense it.

Ry tried anyway: "Howdy."

Phinny held up the box. Ry saw right off that the spark plugs were just what he needed and parted his lips to say it. But he paused. There was a chance here. If he was careful, if he was clever. He settled in next to his mother and gave Phinny a once-over: frayed cap with the seed manufacturer logo subsisting on two or three threads, waterfall beard pouring over the chest, thick neck and thicker torso giving the man the dimensions of a grizzly. It was the bleached overalls Ry was most interested in; often the pouches and loops held screwdrivers and hammers, any of which might be handy if Marvin decided to attack.

"Hiya," Phinny said. There was no doubt that he was giving Ry the eye. "Better late than never, I hope."

What Ry needed was to send a signal. There was a crazy man hiding six feet away. A gun. Something in the field. They were hostages. Sarah was hurt. Back off, Phinny, drive away, fetch help. But Ry could not risk mouthing any of these words, because if Marvin was peeking he would see everything, and there was Sarah to think about. Ry dug his fingernails into the soft wood of the doorframe and let his mind spin. Then: a delirious flash of inspiration.

"We don't need them," Ry said.

Jo Beth turned her face to her son in disbelief.

152

Phinny's frown deepened.

"You don't need them."

"Nope."

"Huh. You don't say."

Ry looked at Jo Beth for backup. She withheld reaction, perhaps thinking of that trip to the emergency room she wanted for Sarah, but what else could she do? She nodded to Phinny as if passing along wonderful news. Ry's nerve endings tingled with the audacity of the gambit: Marvin's escape plan surely hinged upon the car, and the car would not run without the spark plugs, and Ry, following his father's directions, was going to send those spark plugs away. It was a thicket of risks and rewards, a minefield of dangerous outcomes, but once spoken there was no option besides total commitment.

"Yeah, we got them already," Ry said. "Sorry about that. Found them in town."

"That right?" Phinny was unnaturally still. "Whereabouts?"

Ry shrugged. "Oh, let's see." His voice was all over the place. "Riley's Gas. I think that's right. Yeah, that's it. He just happened to have them on hand. Sorry I didn't mention it. I was going to call this morning, but . . ."

"The phone pole. Went kablooey."

Ry forced a laugh. "You should've heard it."

Phinny took his time switching feet. A funny smile emerged beneath his beard, one that said: *You can't fool me, you little shit.* Ry intensified his stare to send his own message: *Back the fuck off.* Controlling facial muscles, however, proved tricky—his head was pounding and the sweat rolled heavy as blood.

Phinny's sigh was theatrical. "Well, I hate to do this to

you, pal. But I'm going to have to ask for payment anyhow. Two whole boxes and whatnot. You know how it is."

Ry turned to his mother with a slowness that he hoped communicated the caution with which she needed to respond. Jo Beth looked down at her body and found that not only did she not have a purse, she had no proper clothes, either. Her forearms twitched as if longing to cover the areas where lace packaged her skin. Phinny looked apologetic, just for a moment.

"I don't know that we have it," Jo Beth said. "Ry?"

"No," Ry said. "I don't think we do. Tomorrow, though. How's that? No reason to waste your time. I'll bring it by."

"I'm in no hurry." Phinny spoke with such calm that Ry expected a yawn. "How about I come inside and you see what you can dig up? Even a buck or two would be great. I'm thinking about grabbing a bite and could use a little tip money."

Jo Beth's naked arm rattled the screen door chain. Despite Marvin, the gun, the meteorite, everything, Ry could tell that she was seconds away from letting the mechanic inside. Phinny saw the same thing and lifted a foot to take advantage. Ry shoved himself into the man's intended path.

"Don't," Ry said.

"Smells out here," Phinny said. "You burning something?"

"It's the wires."

"Doesn't smell electrical." He planted his foot in a new direction.

"Come on—don't."

"At least let me in out of the sun so we can talk."

Honor among men was strong. Ry never knew how strong

until he had to betray it. He summoned all of his bile, his hatred, his frustration, and redirected it at this man who even now was proving the definition of friendship.

"I don't appreciate what you're doing," Ry said. "You were late. *Very* late. This is always how it is with you. It's a disgusting way of doing business, and if you honestly expect me to pay for that kind of service, then I don't know what to say. Making my mom feel bad? Making demands? She's here in her *nightgown*. Can't you tell she's not feeling well? And you're trying to push your way in? I'm glad this happened because now I know never to deal with you again. Get the"—and here his voice snagged and faltered—"get the hell off our property."

Phinny Rochester drew himself up to full wilderness height. No one dared address him this way, at least not since Marvin Burke had left the scene. His eyes drained of their cunning and went flat as pavement. Ry raised his chin and chest, a paltry defense.

It was Jo Beth who played the deciding card. She gestured at the world beyond the front porch and said, softly, "Please go."

Phinny bared his teeth and looked from Jo Beth to Ry and back again. No matter his instincts, there was a deeper code imprinted into him regarding the requests of women. He inhaled.

"All right."

He pulled his cap down so that it pushed out his ears, the only parts of him that were undersized. The boxes of spark plugs were palmed; Ry felt a pang of loss. Phinny patted his other pockets out of habit and turned, ducking his head to fit beneath the motionless chimes, the hanging fern. Ry followed his progress down the steps and path but did not see any truck; the hazard of the live wires must have forced Phinny to park down the road. He began to wander off the path and Ry craned his head to watch. Then, mercifully, Jo Beth pulled the storm door shut, doing it so quickly the screen seemed to capture the entire world like a butterfly in a net.

2 HRS., 32 MINS. AFTER IMPACT

Marvin's sooty paw snatched the front door and pushed it shut. There was a clatter as the shotgun barrel traded parries with dead bolt and knob. For a moment the objects seemed locked together, and Ry, backed against the staircase, saw a way to the gun if he could only move fast enough. But of course he couldn't—if he had learned anything at age ten with the red bat, the sewing shears, and Scowler, it was that he could not, when the shit came down, finish the job.

The locks thrown, Marvin backpedaled. He was noticeably sweatier. His prison-issue shirt was ready to tear like tissue paper. His arms and hands seemed inferior to the insurgence of the gun, which jerked about with such force that it threatened to go airborne. The hallway had never felt so small.

"No car." His voice crackled. "And no one was going to say a thing."

"I didn't think of it," Jo Beth said. "So much was happening."

"And I suppose you sold off the tractors." Marvin kept creeping backward. "And the combine and the baler and the mower, too. You've sold off everything. You've sold off yourselves, too—you're just too stupid to see it. And look how rich it's made you. Just look."

"You're right. You're absolutely right."

"Neither of you considered that we might need the car to drag out that rock? That I might need it to take that rock with me? Those things didn't cross your minds? Or did you just decide you'd try being clever?"

"That's not it at all," Jo Beth protested. "Phinny was coming inside; we had to say something."

"You're not nearly clever enough," Marvin growled. "Not by half. You know what this changes? Nothing. I'm still taking that rock with me. Doesn't matter to me one bit how we bring it up. Bare hands? Fine. We've all got a pair of those. We'll bring it out with our bare hands."

"You're shaking," Jo Beth said. "You're tired and hungry. Breakfast—I can make cheese eggs just like you like them. Or lunch, anything you want."

"Food? Jo. You play your cards so quickly."

"What? No. You misunderstand."

"How much time can we kill? How long until the sirens show up?"

"Marvin! Stop it! You're hungry! That's it! We're all hungry!"

"I hate that you think me so underhanded, Jo."

"I hate that *you* think it of *me*! It's food, Marvin. I'm not going to force it."

"Force?" He held out the Winchester. "See this? This does not mean nothing, Jo."

"It means—" She closed her mouth. No one could bury a glare like Jo Beth Burke. She spoke more softly. "I don't know what it means."

"Thank God I'm here, then," Marvin said. "I'll tell you what it means. And pay attention, both of you, because there is to be no more of this cheap purchasing of time. We have a car, we don't have a car. We need to go to the hospital when something's just a burn, just a regular burn. Enough of it. This is the end. Here's how it's going to go. Listen up."

Phinny slung an arm around Marvin's throat. He had come from the dining room, the kitchen, the back porch, the unlocked doors that were country habit. Marvin's arms went ramrod straight, the shotgun held vertical like a staff, while his features squeezed down to rodent proportion. Ry's body made the smallest of hypnogogic jerks. The struggle, so sudden, featured almost no sound or motion. The men bent like wet wood. Phinny shortened—evidence of bearing down—and veins shot up Marvin's neck, his skin flushing purple. Both men held a Vitruvian pose, filling the doorway, until Marvin whipped back with the shotgun and struck Phinny in the forehead.

He toppled into the dining room while Marvin stood gasping for air and spewing stringy liquid. Ry thought one word—*Sarah*—and tried to get a fix on her. Marvin's neck ballooned with a great, pink inhale, and he spat in Ry's direction with a whistling rage. Ry felt Jo Beth press herself into the front door. But then there was the squeak of wet flesh against tile and Marvin turned, allowing Ry a better glimpse into the darkened dining room. No Sarah that he could see, but there was Phinny on all fours, big as furniture, taking deep breaths and watching marbles of blood drop from his brow and crack against the floor.

Marvin stepped bowlegged into the dining room as if

to sneak up on a willful horse. Phinny's verdant eyebrows popped up and he darted his left arm outward. It snapped around Marvin's calf like a whip and an instant later Marvin was on his back, a whoosh of air blasting from his chest. At that very moment Ry shouted, "Sarah, run!" but the cry was lost when the gun landed flat on its side with Marvin's outstretched hand on top of it, the metal crash unlike anything that had ever before disturbed the house. Phinny made a lurching crawl at Marvin, but his right knee scrawled through the blood puddle and he dropped to the floor. Phinny gave his first cry of pain and pressed a hand to his hip.

It had been seconds, no more than fifteen, for all of this to happen. Fantasies of entering into battle and delivering a heroic kick seized Ry, but just as he swayed in that direction his mother began fussing with the locks, and Ry paused because this, after all, was what Phinny was fighting for—the chance for them to escape. The first lock was thrown and it rang like gunshot; Ry instinctively ducked and saw Marvin, spread-eagled, push a hand into Phinny's face. The larger man clasped his paws around Marvin's wrist and wrenched it. Marvin fought to a knee but Phinny kept twisting the arm, and Marvin, making a series of quick grunts, found himself tumbling over his own legs into a full roll. He hit the deck and for one second the men lay opposite, head to feet.

Ry cringed at a sudden hot smack of sunshine and an inrush of aching fumes. The front door was open. Jo Beth shoved at the screen door but then stopped and looked at her son; the door, meanwhile, swung wide, singing, and then inched back as if offering second, third, and fourth chances. Ry tried to guess what she was thinking: Could she get away without her daughter? Could she get away *with* her daughter? Or was it that valuable chunk of rock waiting in the back field that gave her pause?

Bones clacked—clavicle, elbow, jaw, tailbone, heel—as the men went at each other. Their grappling had a sloppy playground quality. The shotgun was still there, grabbed and slapped with hands and feet, its steel reverberation punctuating the soft *whump* of clothing and flesh. Ry took a step toward the dining room to intervene because he had to, even if failure was assured, but Jo Beth snagged his shirt. Her lips pursed, about to call out for Sarah, waiting for a single second's pause in the bedlam. Then, with one accidental thrust, things changed.

Ry was not sure he saw it right. The barrier of Phinny's shoulder appeared to slide just enough to allow Marvin's elbow to shoot forward. It was a rubber-band movement, and the result was the muzzle of the rifle jumping at Phinny's face and punching into his left eye. It withdrew just as fast, and Marvin, jarred by the quick and confusing event, scuttled away and backed himself against the far wall next to the kitchen.

Phinny was frozen, his mouth agape, his hands rigid as if holding a basketball between them. An endless moment ended: He released a howl of acid fright. Ry gulped a breath—he too had been breathless. Marvin did not move from his seated slump; in fact, he held the shotgun away from him as if fearful of its malice. Phinny held out his arms as if totally blind instead of halfway there and pushed himself to his feet, giant but trembling. His fingers patted delicately at his cheek. They did not like what they felt—they pulled away and Phinny screamed.

His walk into the hallway was ungainly. Ry and Jo Beth backed onto the first steps of the staircase and cowered there. It was an awful thing, and they knew it—a friend grievously injured and *this* was their response. But Marvin was only a few yards behind and looking unhinged. Phinny slumped into the hallway, a skyline of blood drawn across the wallpaper by his fingers. Two more steps and he was in the sunlight's warmth. Ry shuddered at the sight. The shotgun muzzle, when it had entered the socket, had squeezed the eyeball to one side and, unable to contain itself, the vitreous humor had ruptured and now jiggled against Phinny's cheek like smeared egg. He kept moving, though, his arms outstretched in toddler fashion, staggering past Ry and Jo Beth. He kicked the screen door wide.

They listened to his heavy steps pound across the porch cement. Marvin appeared at the end of the hallway, back bent, the twelve-gauge gripped tightly by both hands. He looked after the injured man with an expression of numb exhaustion. He sniffed forcefully, trying to imbue himself with power, and shuffled down the hall and out the door without giving his wife and son, the miserable bystanders, a single look.

The ache in Ry's head doubled. Feeling a sudden need to move, he lifted his feet until he found himself on the front porch several feet behind his father. The porch was an unfrequented place and had become, in the years since Marvin's incarceration, a purgatory for the doomed: four wicker chairs with moldy cushions, an expired pair of heavy old lamps shaped like owls, and an ineptly rolled tarp that now only bred mosquitoes. Jo Beth joined her son in this graveyard, acting reverent. A moment later Sarah emerged and took hold of Ry's left elbow with a hand still wrapped in damp cloth. They could run, but they would never make it, not the three of them together.

Phinny had fallen to his knees near the tree. One strap had slipped and his overalls hung at half-mast, revealing the muggy mat of an old T-shirt. Moles and hair were exposed near his hip, and Phinny's realness gripped Ry with ferocity.

Marvin considered the shotgun, then scanned the horizon. A gun blast was a thing that could arouse interest, especially in a community put on edge by the local prison disaster. His hand strayed to his shirt pocket, drawing strength from the object that hid there. Then he turned around and gave the porch junk a regretful perusal. He reached over, still too far for Ry to make a play for the gun, and took up one of the owl lamps. Marvin shook off the shade and tested the lamp's heft by bouncing it in his palm.

With the air of one carrying out distasteful orders, Marvin relegated the shotgun to his left hand, took hold of the lamp with his right, and crossed over to stand beside Phinny, whose polite, seated posture suggested one awaiting a picnic. After a few seconds, Phinny lifted his face to the sun and smiled.

"The headache." Phinny's tone was beseeching. "I can't concentrate. I'm sorry. I'm . ... Can any of you think? I can't think. You ought to. I lost my thought. The telephone wires, you ought . . . You ought to. I'm sorry. I meant . . . I tried to—the smell distracted me and I lost my . . . I couldn't get . . . I couldn't get my . . ." He turned to Marvin with a trusting, hapless look that showed off a set of blood-spattered teeth. Phinny's one good eye blinked hopefully. "I'm going now. One second. I'm . . . I'll—"

The base of the lamp cracked against Phinny's head with remarkable finality. Somehow Phinny did not fall; his arms waggled as if emulating a chicken, and this accidentally joyous dance continued while Marvin drew back the lamp for another blow. Ry reached out for a porch pillar to keep himself upright but it was too far; his swipe caught air and he landed with his hands on his knees. Marvin's whine, canine in its register, was what got Ry to look again, though what he saw was murky: that golden owl diving for the kill, a dark dart of blood, a large carcass slumping, a patty of pink meat and white bone where a man's face used to be.

Ry's hands found Sarah's shoulders and turned her around to face the house, and he began saying things in cheery tones, hoping his voice would block out whatever sickening snaps and moist thumps came next. And came they did, and it was as if each blow sent jets of magnetized air up his nose and into his—

Smack.

(oh, there is you)

Smack.

(lookie lee, lookie loo)

Smack.

(lookie you, lookie me)

Smack.

(and oh how happy we will be)

Then it was over, though Ry did not know how many seconds had passed. He was just inside the door, huddled against the banister, Sarah beneath him. Her eyelash brushed his cheek and Ry became aware that she was looking outside and so he did the same. Marvin stood hunched on the back porch, the gun in one hand, in the other the busted murder implement, which rained blood onto the cement. The lamp was half destroyed and Ry choked in disgust. Its cheap production, its novelty shape—an insufficient tool to have taken the life of such a man.

Marvin's feet dragged across cement.

"No, don't," Jo Beth said from somewhere.

His dark shape printed itself into the white rectangle of the open door.

"You." Marvin's voice was gored, saliva and bone. "You did this to me."

Ry shoved Sarah out of the way. He heard the dual knock of her knees as she went tumbling to the floor. Jo Beth yelled her husband's name, already sounding defeated because she knew that she was. Marvin shuddered as if throwing these distractions off like a cloak, and then those ropy arms of Ry's nightmares uncurled with the owl as their malformed bludgeon. He, Ry, was more suitable prey, he admitted it. Not full speed, though still plenty fast, the bird splayed its claws and attacked.

(Ry,
Oh, Ry,
Here's your hug,
Don't cry—)

The Hole Was Deeper

MONDAY, AUGUST 24–
TUESDAY, AUGUST 25, 1981

9 HRS., 49 MINS. AFTER IMPACT

Eccentric architecture awaited him when he returned: stair-cased ceilings, floors sprouting hanging lamps like sun-flowers. He was upside down. He rolled across the hard edges of the stairs and propped himself against the exoskeleton of the radiator. There was a tunneling of vision and muting of sound. Carefully he crawled his gaze down the wallpaper and across the eastern window that his mother had always wished were stained glass. He became satisfied that it was the same old hallway. Nevertheless he was lost, if not in the house then inside his own head, and he felt the solid certainty that he would never be found again. But almost instantly, he was.

"You're not how I expected." The voice came from above. "Old chum."

The staircase swooped upward from Ry's feet. He traced

its route with utmost care and even then almost missed in the darkness the huge turquoise teddy bear sitting upon a middle step.

"Mr. Furrington." Ry was both awed and heartbroken. "You're big."

Furrington's head was easily the size of a kickball, his torso the dimensions of a bulging sack of laundry. His stiff outspread limbs, cute on a small stuffed toy, looked cadaverous on someone roughly the size of Sarah. Ry anticipated a tickle of joy but instead felt only wariness. Furrington looked—Ry hated to even think it—*used*. Perhaps he had been just as dirty nine years ago. If so, his smallness had hidden the grime. Now slick lines of filth shone along outliers of the washrag fur, while thicker whorls of plush sharpened into greasy points.

Though he had no neck, Furrington's head rotated in Ry's direction. Daylight glinted off the dusty marble eyes.

"Aye. So I am." The British accent was still melodic. Ry watched the bear's mouth for movement, but the sewed dashes remained fixed. Furrington raised an arm and looked at it. "Truth is," he said, "I liked it when you were the only big 'un. Now that I'm big, too—well, I don't much know what to do with meself. Not sure how it all came to pass. You?"

Ry had trouble finding breath. He nodded.

"Oh, yes? Bully, then. Want to let a bloke in on it? Who's to blame for this awful mess?"

Ry opened his mouth and found it keening with sobs. He knew the answer, of course he did, but it was one too cruel to put into words. What he needed to do was turn away; this apparition was something to be sold off at a garage sale with no more than a twinge of nostalgia. But my God, how

166

could he deny his teddy bear, built to be squeezed, designed to comfort? He owed Furrington. Didn't he? Love was love. Wasn't it?

Ry contained his tears.

"It was time," he replied. "Time did it."

"Time, eh?" With a creak of fabric, Furrington's head turned left, then right. Ry took these motions as evidence of deliberation, and when they stopped, he was sure that the bear was dead, and it had been he, Ry, who had murdered him with callous words.

A flicker of movement. The marble eyes caught the sun.

"Can't say me old bean knows nuffing about time." An edge of playfulness lifted the end of the sentence. "All's I know is about friends. You and me, we're still friends? Righty-right?"

Happiness happened so fast. Ry's eyes watered and dripped into his reckless grin.

"Yes," he said. "We're friends. Of course we are!"

"Oh, aces." Furrington's voice trembled too. "Brilliant."

With a little pig-snort of effort, Furrington rose from where he sat. Resting a fingerless paw on the banister for balance, he began to hop. One hop, pause; another hop, pause—the whole operation as silent as a sheet. Ry was distressed until he understood: Furrington's left leg, the one Ry had chewed off in Black Glade to use for kindling, had not magically grown back, and Linda Colson's sewing of the wound, so impressive when Ry had been ten, now looked like the crude X patterns of a budget surgeon.

Evidence of burning, though, was nowhere to be seen. It was a miracle Ry chose not to question—this was a second chance and he would take it. He went from seated to kneeling, and found himself at an equal height to Furrington, or less so if you counted the bear's dusty bowler. Ry turned his guilty eyes to his knees. A second passed, a fat and painful one, and then Ry felt a paw, light as wind, caress his neck.

"It's been a long time," Furrington whispered. "A long time spent in the dark."

Part of Ry had known all along that the voice from the crater had been Furrington, yet he had brazenly ignored the teddy bear's calls. Ry was and had always been a terrible friend.

"I'm sorry," Ry said. "I didn't know—"

"That I was down there? Oh, yes. And what a black and quiet place it was to be."

Ry touched his forehead. The old wound had reopened.

"But you're out now?"

"Indeed."

"And can I—" Ry choked on the word.

"Yes, friend?"

"Can I . . ."

"Ask," Furrington said. "You've nothing to fear from me." Tears washed down Ry's cheeks.

"Can I hug you?" he cried. "Can we hug?"

"Dear boy." Furrington's voice was hoarse with emotion. "Why else do you think I'm here?"

Ry sobbed and threw his arms around the bear. Furrington rocked with the force of the embrace, but his cotton innards absorbed the worst of it. Face buried in the matted plush, Ry inhaled the sweat of decades. He cried and laughed and had a fleeting awareness that the harder he sunk his fingers into this being of cloth and thread, the more he became unstuck from the real world. But how little he cared!

"I've waited oh so long," Furrington said.

"I thought I'd never see you again," Ry said.

"I as well. Oh, it's so good—"

"Yes—"

"It's like a dream—"

"Is it? Is it a dream?" Ry heard his own rising panic.

Dousing anxious fires was Furrington's specialty. The bear pulled gently from the hug, and with his soft arms still tickling Ry's ears, he gave the young master the full consideration of his unblinking brown orbs.

"Maybe that's up to you, friend." Furrington's voice carried the warmness of a smile. "If it *is* a dream, I hope never to awake."

"Me too. Me too."

"My, my. Look at you. Just look at how you've grown."

Then the world reasserted itself with a smash from the dining room. Ry snapped to attention and noticed for the first time the afternoon sun, how much time had passed since he had been struck unconscious. More sounds rang out, these from Marvin Burke, though only three lone escapees pierced the warm cocoon of the hallway: "fault—traitors—disobedience—"

This was enough to begin the unraveling. What he was doing here was shameful. His family was fending off execution and he was *hugging*. Ry could blame Marvin, but he could also blame himself—he was the one who had sat next to a galactic magnet while it took parts of his brain and loosened them like baby teeth. This was fact, this was science; Furrington was but a manifestation of his weakness.

"You," Ry accused, pulling away.

Furrington's marble eyes were unblinking.

169

"There's little time, chap. I want to help."

Ry held his head in his hands. "You want to confuse me."

"Bloody hell I do. You're me mate. I want what's best, I do."

"What's best," Ry moaned. "What's best is you go away."

"Go away? Why, I've a mind to pop you one."

From the other room came a hollow crack like a fist or foot put through wood. Ry strained to see into the dining room but the angle of the door kept things hidden. There was blood on the floor, though, and that was real. Ry followed its drips and smears. A man had been killed. A real person, not a fantasy being, and he was lying on the front lawn, dead. Ry moved toward the dining room.

Furrington's soft paw touched Ry's arm. It was enough to stop him.

"Oh, friend. I helped you in the past, did I not?"

Reluctantly Ry nodded; the movement caused a few more repugnant drops of history to thicken between his eyebrows.

"There's a bloke." Furrington's eyes glinted with dead constellations. "Now, I know I was never the smart one. But do as I say and get her out."

It was vague, confusing. Ry pressed a palm to his aching head. "Who?"

As if in answer, Sarah slid her narrow body through the hallway door.

Furrington flew into the shadows as if lashed to a parasail. Ry assessed his sister, an awesome combination of twitching, flexing flesh when compared with an inanimate lump of cloth and stuffing. She came forward, her naked white toes dodging every single spot of blood. A cloth was still wrapped around her right hand, but that infirmity had been superseded by her overall sickness. Her skin had a chalky pallor and her lips were scarlet. She held out her hands to grab hold of her brother for stability, but they floated upward. Ry reached, encircled a wrist, and brought it home.

This woke her with a gasp. Her body pitched.

"It's scary," she said. "I'm scared."

"What's happening?" Ry whispered.

"He's yelling. He's being really loud. Mom wants to take us to the doctor but he keeps saying no. Ry, I don't want to go. I hate the doctor. But Mom wants me to. He says he'll let me stay here inside while he takes you and Mom back to the field. That's fine with me because I hate the doctor. Also, I threw up and he yelled. Ry, what happened to Phinny?"

"Nothing. Slow down. He's fine."

"He's lying under the tree. I can see it from the living room."

"He's sleeping."

"Ry! Don't lie!"

What pain there was in adulthood, the chisel scrape of truth.

"Don't think about it. I need you to listen."

"He's not *moving*."

"Sarah. Look at me. Not the door. Me."

Her eyes spun like pennies about to fall flat from their narrowing loops. Ry nodded quickly so as to set the hook of attention. When he spoke he was disheartened to hear a voice desperate for validation.

"I want you to look at the staircase."

"Ry, no games."

"Fuck. Sarah. Do as I fucking say. Look at the fucking staircase and tell me what you see."

Her white cheeks and red lips pouted in silent suffering. But she did what he asked, turning her head all the way to her left. Ry did not follow her gaze. Instead he monitored her eyes as they tracked right, left, up, down.

"Now tell me what you see."

"Stairs."

"Nothing else?"

"Ry."

"Nothing hiding on the stairs?"

"Please! Ry!" Tears sparkled at the corners of her eyes.

Ry gripped her shoulders and shook.

"You don't see him? You don't see a bear? A big blue bear with a hat and bow tie? He's not there?"

A curtain of pity, heartbreaking for its subtlety, slid across Sarah's face. Her tears stopped and the weak smile she conjured was almost motherly. When she spoke it was with a gentle reassurance.

"Oh," she said. "There he is."

Ry's heart stopped. He squeezed his sister harder.

"You see him? You really see him?"

"Yes."

"You really see the bear?"

"Yes! I see the stupid bear!"

He nearly laughed in mad glory. But then doubt asserted itself. How the hell was he to know if she was telling the truth? He could not force it, not from a girl smart enough to know that the one thing grown-ups wanted to hear more than anything else was a happy lie.

"That's fine. That's great. Thank you." Ry smiled in a way

he hoped was soothing. "Now pay attention. I need you to get out of here. I need you to run and this time I mean it."

Her face crumpled along lines of genuine fear.

"We can't," she whined. "Phinny tried and he's still out there on the lawn."

A shout from the other room killed an argument. Then footsteps; Marvin was coming. Ry held Sarah tighter and put his face inches from hers. From the darkness of the staircase he could see the twinkle of marble eyes, and he felt a bolt of nerve. His spine straightened in a way that it had not since fifth grade, during those few months that he had been the smartest, craftiest kid in the entire class if not the whole school. It was a feeling he had missed.

The footsteps snapped across the dining room tile.

"You wait until we're in the back forty and then you run." Ry's own voice stunned him, so cold and strong. He remembered the blood spatters all over the front porch. "Go out the back. Cut across the lawn, get on the road, go southwest. Go to the Stricklands'. Got it?"

He almost made one more demand: Take White Special Dress with you. But it was impossible for any number of reasons, not the least of which was that, once she had it, she would never let it go, not even if Marvin was bearing down on her and the dress was impeding her every step.

"No, Ry, I'm dizzy. I'm sick. My hand."

A shadow fell through the crack in the door, an array of lines: legs, arm, shotgun.

"You can do it." The four words just came to him, and he placed them gently before his sister. It was verbatim what Furrington had said to save Ry from certain death in Black Glade, and Ry was not surprised to find that the words still

173

worked. Shining through Sarah's gummy eyes was a glint of the absolute faith she had in her brother. Then the hallway door opened, the gust lifting strands of her tear-heavied hair.

Marvin's skin was patterned in streaks of war paint, evidence of hurried efforts to wipe away blood. His beard was snarled into bright thatches of coagulation; even his glasses were tinted pink. Finding Ry up and moving appeared to be something of a surprise, and he paused to give his son an appraisal.

"Thought you'd never get off your ass," he grunted. He noticed Sarah, and his swollen eyes bulged. "Why aren't you lying down?"

Ry stole a glance at the stairs. Furrington remained crouched and watchful.

"Water," Sarah croaked.

Ry thrilled to the cunning falsehood coming from this angel face.

"Then ask your mother. No, get back on the couch. No more getting up."

Sarah glanced at her brother once more, a bit of a risk, but what heart-stopping valor Ry sensed within those clouded eyes. She turned and stumbled back the way she had come. Before disappearing around the corner, her entire body tilted, and Ry wondered if she might be laying it on a little thick. If so, what a girl. He started to turn to Furrington to see if he'd noticed.

Marvin fit the butt of the shotgun into his armpit so that the muzzle pointed at Ry's shoulder. There was something victorious in the black gap of teeth visible over the man's curling lip. Marvin lifted his bloodstained right hand. In it was a brand-new box of spark plugs. Marvin shook it once and it rattled like shotgun shells. Everything they needed, it turned out, was in the palm of one huge and hairy hand.

10 HRS., 22 MINS. AFTER IMPACT

The spark plugs were difficult to remove from their cardboard packaging. "I killed a man," he kept saying. "With my bare hands I did it. And now I can't get these stupid things out of a stupid box." None of them had ever heard such insecurity from Marvin Burke, and each new failure was linked to what he had done to Phinny Rochester. "No one can pilot a tin can like this," he said while crashing the Beetle across the brutal ditches and sudden shoulders of the McCafferty Forty. "Not even me, and I've killed." The car got stuck twice, the wheels spun in place, and it took orchestrated rocking—with Ry at the back bumper pushing—to continue their nightmare momentum. It took three times as long to drive to the crater than it took to walk. "The farm is mine and that means the rock is mine. Understand? That's why more than anything I had to kill." Ry and Jo Beth sat silent, he in the passenger seat and she in the back. They wanted nothing more than to forget Phinny's grotesque demise, but Marvin's obsession filled the air of the car with a slaughterous stink. When they finally reached the crater's edge and turned the car around, Ry was the first to scramble into the blistering white sun. Marvin followed, mumbling murder, as if the only way to minimize the violent boundary he had crossed was to talk it to death.

Sarah was not with them. She had been left nearly catatonic on the living room sofa, new ice bundled to her right hand, a fresh glass of water perspiring on the end table.

Marvin had repeated instructions about what she was not allowed do, which was everything, the reason being, of course, *that he had killed a man,* and that meant there would be no more fooling around. Jo Beth, who had finally traded her nightgown for a sad and threadbare dress, took a moment to restate her husband's instructions in kinder tones. The words fell ineffectually against pillows and blankets. Sarah's eyes had long since slid away from her parents' faces. She did not look capable of sitting up, much less escaping. Ry prayed that she was faking.

Jo Beth was the last one out of the car, carrying the rope and hooks and gloves that Marvin had plucked from the garage walls. Her cameo features surrendered nothing and Ry swallowed an unbearable frustration. He didn't begrudge her plots—plots were anyone's prerogative. What burned was her refusal to share them. Her son's involvement in subterfuge, it was clear, guaranteed failure. Ry stepped up to the crater edge with humiliation storming in his ears. What Jo Beth thought of him was absolutely true. He was the one, after all, who spoke to teddy bears.

The fumes were terrible: fat, immobile, yellow.

"We've got to hook it." Marvin unknotted the rope. "Hmmmm it and drag it."

Ry stopped cold.

"What?" he asked. "*What* it and drag it?"

"Hook it and drag it. Hook. Drag."

"Yeah, I know," Ry said. "But—"

"I'd do it myself. The speed, the efficiency, your jaw would drop. You've probably forgotten what efficiency looks like. But I can't be the one. Someone's got to hold the gun and I'm the one who took a man's life."

Ry pulled on the gloves and displayed his ready fingers. Sarah's best chance of escape came if everyone was busy staring into the crater. So safety be damned—downward he would go. He nabbed the rope from his father's hands and with three brisk shakes untangled it. The hooks, black and almost invisible against the charred dirt, were knotted to either end of the rope. He gathered the slack rope around the bracket of his forearm and started toward the crater. He chanced one more glance at the farm to see if Sarah had emerged.

Instead he saw Furrington skirting the edge of the field. Portly, gallingly limbed, and down a leg, any movement was hardship, but perhaps he too had heard the humming soak through Marvin's words like blood through bandages. Ry recalled a time when he had been just as loyal, refusing to go anywhere without his teddy bear. Only children knew devotion; it gave him hope for Sarah. As he took his first step into the crater and punched through the skin of the magnetic field, he told himself to go ahead, breathe deep and swallow, be a connoisseur of poison—both Sarah and Furrington deserved it.

Crouched at the bottom two minutes later, he leaned over the muddy water, inches from the meteorite's surface, and examined the silky contours, the fantastic terrain, the obsidian brilliance. He lifted the hooked rope, ready for the plunge, but before committing he stole one more upward glance. He had to squint; the fumes were thick enough to dull colors. There was Marvin, bisected by a blade of yellow—the shotgun in the sun—and Jo Beth, red hair snapping like flames. *Good*, thought Ry. *Run, Sarah. Now, now, now.*

Ry looked to the opposite side of the crater's edge.

A bowler hat peeked over, black as the meteorite against the clear blue sky.

"Giving it the old college try, eh?" Furrington asked.

"Didn't go to college," Ry said.

"Willikers," Furrington said. "Well, heave ho and all that."

Ry nodded and drove one arm into the water. Sunk to his bicep it was warm; to his forearm, warmer; where his gloved fingers touched bottom, the water was simmering. The hole was deeper than Ry had estimated. He twisted his neck to keep his ear from submerging, and the slight readjustment sent the water sloshing. A droplet hit his lip and it burned. Contorted and sputtering, Ry made another unhappy observation: His sweat went unbothered. There were no bugs, no mosquitoes. And still no birds—not a single one had returned.

"Don't much care for it," Furrington said. "Being back out here, that is."

Ry went at it blind, jabbing the hook beneath the chocolate swirls of water, hoping it would snag onto one of the many protuberances so that the rock could be hauled up the bank like a ball and chain. Clanking noises reverberated through water, but the hook did not catch. Shouts came from above, and though the splashing kept Ry from understanding, he sensed impatience and wondered if now might be the moment Marvin's chatter about his first murder gave way to his second, and the last thing Ry would see would be his own brains splattered colorfully across glossy black stone—

The hook caught with a satisfying tug. Ry gasped in surprise, pulled the rope to keep it taut, and flopped to his back like a fish.

"Got it," he called, panting. "Got it, got it."

Up above the gun lowered. The heads of husband and wife touched as they peered.

"Blimey," Furrington said. "Upsy-daisy time?"

The pain in his skull tugged at the scar on his forehead. He nodded at Furrington. It was time to get out. On all fours he climbed. At the top Marvin was there to twist the rope around his own arm and run it to the car. Ry collapsed over the edge of the crater, seeing multiple Marvins whip the rope in figure-eight patterns around the bumper. The rope remained tight—Ry could see dust thrum from the strained fibers. The engine coughed to life. Ry refocused and saw Marvin behind the wheel, the driver's-side door open, the gun sticking up like a headless scarecrow in the passenger seat.

"Tee-hee," Furrington laughed. "Tee-hee."

Ry raised his chin from the hard black dirt.

"What?"

"Don't you see? In the car? Tee-hee."

"See what?"

"The shotgun," Furrington giggled. "The shotgun's riding shotgun."

Ry chuckled. Jo Beth looked down at him as if he were urinating on her shoe.

"Stop laughing." Her eyes shone. "It's going to work."

The Beetle gunned, a peevish bee drone that was pretty funny too. Ry tucked in his lips to muffle his laughter and heard the hiss of the rope slicing through dirt, though it was the second noise that shut him up: a heavy, wet slurp coming from the bottom of the crater. Ry froze, his face still caught in an arrangement of hilarity.

"It's out?" The cry was coming from the front seat of the car. "It's out?"

Jo Beth peered over the edge. Ry scuttled until he was standing upright and facing the hole. Marvin's plan had worked. The lower portion of the crater was slathered in gooey mud ejected during the meteorite's dislodging, and the rock itself now rested on the incline. A layer of ooze hid much of its majesty, but even as they watched, mud slopped off to reveal tantalizing glimpses. Roughly two feet in diameter, it was a shimmering infinity of tunnels and mazes.

"It's so black," Ry said.

"It's so gold," Jo Beth responded.

"I do not like it here," Furrington added. "Like it here I do not."

The car horn honked and Jo Beth turned around and waved enthusiastically, nodding that yes, yes, the rock was out. Ry waved too, feeling the unaccountable desire to cheer this fabulous accomplishment. Marvin's right arm braced itself against the passenger seat as he looked backward at the crater. The front wheels turned, and dust began to rise as if the field were being cooked. Ry and his mother turned to watch the progress of the meteorite. The rope stretched to sewing-thread thickness and the rock budged. It waggled in a way that suggested it was surprisingly lightweight; it was the embankment itself that was the problem. With painstaking slowness, the rock shaved through six inches of scorched clay. The engine whined, and then came another magnificent three-foot surge.

The rock abruptly stopped its progress. Mother and son gasped in perfect unison. Ry turned and saw the Beetle, several car lengths away now, shuddering within a gray and swirling fog. The back wheels, trapped in a gulley, whirred with unchecked speed. The engine cried out and then receded to a putter. Brake lights strained weakly in the sun, and the shotgun was plucked from its shotgun position—Ry felt a twinge of humor, even now—and Marvin bolted from the car.

Both Jo Beth and Ry shrank back. Marvin leaned over the edge of the crater, his knotted face loosening upon seeing the object of his desire at such close range. He held out a hand as if needing to touch it. The rock's whale skin winked wetly in the summer glare. He had to shake his head to clear it, and there, standing in his vision, were his wife and son.

"We're stuck," he reported.

"I'll push," Ry said.

"We're *stuck*." Marvin scratched his beard as if it were a colony of ticks that had taken root on his face. "Pushing won't do any good. We need to tamp down the . . . if that will even . . . we need a . . ." He peered into the crater gingerly and Ry followed suit. The hole at the bottom was like an open throat. "We need a hm hm."

Ry looked at his mother. Her lips were parted, the picture of caution.

Jo Beth ventured forth. "A what?"

"A hm hm. If we're going to get this out."

Marvin took in his family's feeble bewilderment. His knuckles shook, rattling together wood and steel parts of the gun. Ry opened his mouth to say anything at all.

"Good gracious me," Furrington declared. "Away she goes."

Ry knew at once what he meant: Sarah. He shifted his gaze and saw his sister exiting through the back door of the house just as instructed. Even at this distance her dizziness was evident. Her arms were aloft as if pinching a dress to curtsy and she gawked at the buildings around her. Ry experienced the awful certainty that she would start stumbling toward the McCafferty Forty, just like Furrington, but then she banked toward the road.

"You're not listening," Marvin seethed. Ry flicked his eyes back to his father, who was staring at Jo Beth with a knowing intensity. "We can get this thing. There's a path to success. It's the same path as always: Pay attention, follow orders."

"I am, Marvin," Jo Beth said. "But you said. . . . I can't understand. . . ."

Sarah stumbled. Something like a sob rose through Ry's chest.

"Your thoughts are elsewhere." Marvin tore at his cheek; flecks of stripped skin littered the beard like dandruff. "You think I don't still know your mind? You think I didn't notice the boxes?"

Sarah kept moving, beneath the clothesline, past the ruins of the old milk house.

"Boxes? What boxes?"

"In the car, Jo. The backseat, Jo. Boxes, packed and taped. You were that close to leaving this farm."

Sarah, halfway across the lawn, paused to touch a tree's lowest leaves. Ry's urge to yell at her conflicted with an awe for her youthful grace.

"I was . . . ," Jo Beth said. "Those boxes have been . . ."

"You're handing a death sentence to a place that has given you so much, if only you'd take a step back and see it."

"We had to." Jo Beth's tone was steady. "At some point we had to."

Sarah snapped from her trance and resumed her waddle. Ry sketched the best path across the lawn, forty-five degrees southwest, and how the dairy barn would hide her in less than sixty seconds, thirty if she picked up her damn feet. He pretended to look at his father, but could not help but follow the white light of hope: Sarah's white nightgown, the white

182

cloth on her hand, her white-blond hair, the white skin everywhere else. She was going to make it.

And then the barking began.

Marvin's jaw snapped shut and his chin lifted. Ry almost screamed—*Run! Run! Run!*—because Sarah was just standing there, staring at the dog loping at her from the east, the direction of the old Horvath Property, the dog who had been hiding since the blast from the sky and was now deliriously happy to find a friendly human. The barking ratcheted in volume. Marvin mouthed a word—*Snig*—and turned toward the house.

The deadliness of the moment made some kind of sense to Sarah and she pulled herself behind the same tree she had been fondling. It was too small for the job, and if you knew where to look, there were her arms stuck out to either side. But Marvin was watching Sniggety, who lingered beside the concrete block shed on the eastern side of the house to lift a leg.

"Sniggety." Marvin licked raw lips and shouted. "Snig! Here, boy!"

The dog disappeared behind the house but would re-emerge in mere moments to reveal Sarah's location. Ry had no time. He opened his mouth but no brilliant words of distraction emerged. Then inspiration hit: Furrington would help! A few panicked seconds later, Ry located the bow-tied bear, but he was drunkenly hopping away from the crater, his paws paddling before his muzzle as if dispelling a swarm of bees.

"Snig!" Marvin was manic. "Here, boy! Sniggy!"

The dog appeared on the western side of the house, doing his best trot, oblivious to his master and focused on Sarah.

Marvin followed the action. Sarah would be discovered in seconds. The weight of grief planted itself on Ry as a yoke.

"The dog's deaf," Jo Beth said. "He can't hear you."

Father and son both turned to look at Jo Beth. For Ry the realization was a punch to the gut: She *knew*. She knew her daughter was out of the house; she knew the tree behind which her daughter was hiding; she knew the handful of seconds Sarah needed to make her escape. Jo Beth favored Ry with a glance, and with torrential force Ry's heart ripped open to make space for this storied protector, this queen of saving graces—damn him forever for his doubt.

Marvin gave his wife a disgusted frown. Somehow the dog's deafness was her fault. Sarah was psychic: At this instant she scrambled, exposing herself for five seconds before ducking behind the toolshed. At that point, Marvin looked back to see Sniggety moving in the shed's direction, his barking hoarse and adamant. Nine years had affected Old Snig in many ways but some things did not change: This was not a dog that barked for no reason, and Marvin knew it. He took a step in the direction of the house.

Less than ten feet from the shed, for no reason that was apparent, Sniggety stopped. The red drama of dusk felt sudden, and all three of the watchers leaned forward and squinted. Sniggety lowered an investigative muzzle and nosed something on the ground. He pawed. His tail swayed in uncertain patterns. Then his tongue emerged to lap.

Marvin turned away first.

"He's hmmmm. He's hmmmm."

Jo Beth was the next to turn away, averting her eyes to Ry, and when that proved too disgraceful she lowered them to the incinerated dirt at her feet. Ry squinted at the front lawn for another moment. Sniggety's loins were braced, his teeth low and busy. A primordial part of Ry recognized what was happening and his stomach contracted. The old dog had always had a taste for dead flesh.

"Hold the line." Marvin's voice was unsteady. Through his shirt pocket he drew strength from the hidden object. He pointed to where the rope angled over the edge of the crater. "I'm going to rock the car. Don't let that rope go slack. You do *not* let it go slack."

Ry nodded and kneeled. Even through gloves the rope felt alive. He longed to somehow avert Sarah's eyes from the sight of Phinny's desecration, just as he had done during the man's final moments of life. Sarah, though, was nothing if not a starer and would undoubtedly get her fill.

Marvin got into the car and Jo Beth lost control. Her hips made weak ovals and her eyes cast high over Ry's head and into the wilds of Black Glade. She concentrated in the opposite direction of Sarah's path and that took strength. Ry, prisoner to his heart, could only look to the toolshed, where Sarah resumed picking her way across the lawn.

The car horn honked, and instinctively Ry took the rope with both hands. The tenor of the engine changed and he felt in his palms the backward sway of the car as it tried to rock from the pit. But it was Sarah he watched. She approached the downed telephone wires like the pythons they were, her nightgowned arms stretched like sails, her body displaying unexpected acrobatic prowess. Errant electric sparks drew yellow lines across blue air; it was nearly evening, a perfect though dangerous time for escape.

The rope slithered through his gloves and the heat of the meteorite doubled. Ry blinked—Marvin had done it, had maneuvered the car from its pit. The rope creaked as it adjusted to the car's new direction. This was not good. Ry looked at the car and saw that it now directly faced Sarah, who was making a spectacle of herself by hopping around. Marvin would see her. Ry panicked and turned to Furrington for guidance, because he had just had the most dangerous idea of his life.

He set his boot alongside the hook latched to the rock's guts.

"Furrington? Furrington!"

"Quiet," Jo Beth pleaded.

The bear, meanwhile, tilted toward silos.

"Heading back, methinks." He was far away now. "Not feeling tip-top."

The car chewed dirt. The line snaked. The meteorite, huge and bleeding mud, propped upon the lip of the crater. In the car, Marvin turned to face forward, aiming himself right at Sarah. No time, no time—Ry's toe dug at the hook.

"What do I do?" he cried. "Please! Furrington!"

"Shut up!" Jo Beth hissed.

The bear's bowler hat moved across the dying sun and his voice dwindled to nothing.

Ry could wait no longer. He kicked at the rock and his aim was true. The hook fired from the meteorite with a glassy shatter. A foot-long ebony shard spun through the air like a vampire bat, and the rope flung back at the car with such force that it blasted the field with a cough of gray. The Beetle, suddenly lighter, spun out and ended crooked with a startled Marvin punching the brakes. Almost playfully, the meteorite tumbled down the crater and seconds later splashed back home in the puddle of mud. Ry did not see it, though, because he was staring at his sister as she reached the road. A second later she turned right and disappeared.

Marvin opened the car door and considered the spilled rope.

Ry found himself laughing—great big wheezes. Jo Beth looked at her son, her lips twitching with a silent question. Ry nodded through his convulsions. She lifted a hand to touch her lips, and when she confirmed to herself that she was still there, she accepted the truth: Her youngest child was free. She sobbed once, hard. Ry saw daylight sparkling through the old holes of her ears and between her fingers, and he could see every other tiny scar on her body—an illusion brought on by squinting, but one he liked.

Marvin approached until he was close enough to read the relief on their faces, which told him everything he needed to know. They had conspired against him. His *family*. He faced south and perhaps for a moment entertained the fantasy of a pursuit complete with bullets blazing from the window of the Beetle. But there were a dozen reasons why the idea was worthless—Sarah's head start; which way she went; the way tires caught in ditches. This fight was lost.

Marvin nudged his shoe at the single dagger of meteorite remaining topside.

Verse: "Hmmmm."

"That's right," Ry laughed.

Chorus: "Hm hm."

Verse again, though this time Ry took it: "Hmmmmmmmmm."

He did not witness any impact; the man had speed. Air left Ry's body in a crush, and the sweat, dirt, and blood he tasted was from his father's shirt, wadded against his tongue as the two of them twisted through the first embrace of their life—kind of euphoric, really—until Ry recognized that they were airborne, then rolling down an embankment, then crashing alongside the meteorite in a single package of noisy bones. The shotgun made a chintzy chime as it glanced off the top of the rock. Marvin dropped a fist into Ry, twice, in no particular location. Ry coughed and saw another blow coming, and though he braced against it, it landed with much more success, a brick to his cheekbone. His hair was sopping, not with blood as he first feared but with the greasy mud of the meteorite's pool. There were hands around his throat now, but they were slippery, and Ry wiggled, believing that his father could not maintain that kind of grip for long.

The grip, however, changed. Marvin's fingers laced through his son's hair and drove his skull into the meteorite. Ry heard a crystalline crunch. For an instant his eyes were pressed to the rock's labyrinth and he was lost in its folds, then Marvin's arms plunged Ry's head underwater. His entry into liquid was like a slap to naked baby flesh; his eyes, already open, adjusted to the dim brown world. Each time he whipped his head to find air it struck the rock, expelling a glittering fog of sediment. He was total, pure awareness, especially in those seconds before blackout: Marvin's screams, smeared by fluid; the noise melody of his mother wailing and making her way down the bank; and a third voice right there in his head, deep and steady, having been fed on the vitamins of stars.

"—WORTHLESS—"

(rarer than gold, frankincense, myrrh)

"—BETRAYED—"

(beloved)

"—SEND YOU TO HELL—"
(heaven awaits)
"—FOREVER—"
(and ever, amen)

11 HRS., 54 MINS. AFTER IMPACT

Night crept across her skin like wet cement. It was pleasantly cold, pleasantly heavy, even as it threatened to fix both legs into a statue position. Sarah kept her legs turning, though, because those were her brother's instructions. She hugged her elbows, being careful of her throbbing palm, and wished that she were wearing her long underwear instead of her nightgown. Long undies made her look like a baby, but they were a heck of a lot warmer.

It was scary how darkness bore down from all sides, but also electrifying. If only she felt better so that she could fully appreciate it. She thought, as she often did, of Ry's journey through Black Glade, accomplished when he had been but a year younger than she was now, and as usual she felt two burns: one of pride, and one of fear that she would never measure up to such greatness. Every year at school kids came up to her and asked if Ry Burke was her brother. She used to relish the attention, but now she dodged it. At some point in her life, she would have to take the risks that would define her.

Sarah peered across the field to the north. Far away was Black Glade's grasping horizon. Maybe she wouldn't cut through those particular woods, but why not another shortcut? Rescuing her brother and mother was a lot more helpful than pretending to see imaginary bears, and it would reap a greater reward than any tooth-fairy payout. Future school-mates, when whispering about brave deeds, might mention Sarah Burke, too.

She stopped walking. Her defenseless soles stung from the gravel. Dead ahead—west—was the way to the Stricklands'. Technically, though, the Crowleys were closer. Ry had sent her along the simplest—not the quickest—route, and she felt a little affronted. Especially after the way she'd dodged those power lines and dealt with what was happening between Sniggety and Phinny. She'd earned the right to make her own decisions.

Sarah aligned herself with the waning moon. If she was right, the Crowley farm was a straight trip through this corn-field, over a hill of soy, and down into a dandelion-filled valley that Sarah had always envied. There were scads of Crowleys, seven or eight of them, including daughters older than Ry and younger than Sarah, and as she took her first step into the ditch she imagined being in their company, not the littlest or the biggest but just one of the gang, with fine and varied examples of womanhood everywhere she looked.

The yellow stalks lapped her skin like cold, dry tongues. Even in their post-harvest state the plants outstretched her, and within seconds she lost her sense of direction. That was okay—just follow the row. For a time the only sounds were the rustling of leaves and her whispered counting of paces, but after a while she noticed the stray chirping of one or two birds. That was a good sign and she brightened her step. This trip should take no more than half an hour.

Soon she came to an area where a number of stalks had been flattened. Her pause was brief. Someone had been here before her and that was another good sign, because if it had been one of the Crowleys then she must be close to their farm. Sarah smiled. She couldn't wait to see their faces when she showed up at their door. Those Burke kids, they were capable of anything.

Mostly she wondered if Esther Crowley would be there. She liked Esther, not because Esther had ever been especially nice to her but because she was dauntless and quick-tongued and big-breasted and made up her eyes with unparalleled artistry—and best of all she was still young enough for Sarah to exercise her own aspirations. Ry hated when Sarah teased him about Esther, and Sarah felt bad about that. But she knew—she *knew*—that Esther was exactly what her brother needed. Ry was not a normal boy. Sarah would know that even if kids at school weren't constantly saying it. But a girlfriend, a bold one, who'd show him that there was more to life than the mazes he'd made in his mind, would work magic.

The row she was following got uglier. Stalks were smashed in great volume and furrows had been kicked through the dirt. Goose bumps erupted across her arms and neck but she told herself it was just a nighttime chill. Esther—she concentrated on Esther.

They had nearly had sex, Ry and Esther. Everyone knew this. Sarah herself had found out from Tina, one of Esther's little sisters, who relayed the whole upsetting tale one morning on the bus. Tina's references to anatomy and maneuvers were cryptic to Sarah, but one thing was for sure: Ry had failed tragically in his quest for romance. Sarah had sat silent for the rest of the bus ride, hands folded atop her Holly Hobbie lunch box, knowing that she should think less of Esther for spreading this story but instead resolving to redouble her efforts in bringing the two teens together. One day Ry, too, would have the confidence to gossip about sex like it was no big deal. If that meant he had to become a little meaner, a little shallower, well, then—

Sarah stopped with such abruptness that her torso pitched. She grasped a cornstalk for stabilization, but it had no weight and snapped in two. One of her knees hit the dirt and her lips curled in disgust because she had almost touched it, this dead animal strewn across the path in front of her. It was probably a squirrel, though the pulped mass of fur and skin rendered it beyond identification. A much larger animal had been here and done this. In fact the bigger animal probably beat down this very path. Sarah told herself to keep moving and sidestepped the carnage.

Her courageous mood was spoiled. She was frightened now and that was unfair; tears welled and she tried to outrun them. Her arms were spread wide to help with balance and all at once she became aware of a slickness across her fingers. Without stopping she checked her palm and discovered a dark splotch, and she wondered if her burn had blistered. But there, on the stalks, was more of it.

The moonlight was sheepish but Sarah knew blood when she saw it. Now it wasn't Esther that she wanted, it was Mr. Crowley, any adult. For a crazed second she even wished to see her father with that rusty old shotgun. More than anything she wanted to turn back without looking at what came next, but she knew very well that she didn't possess that kind of discipline.

Blood was everywhere—sparkling from corn silk, winking from purple mud, gleaming in beads strung across spider-webs. Crumpled in the center of it all was a corpse, the body heaped like bonfire wood awaiting the match. Next thing Sarah knew, she was inching closer, her naked toes picking through the surrounding viscera as if they were every bit as dangerous as live wires, until she was at an angle where she could see the man's face. Even before that moment details were sinking in, items of clothing she recognized. Those shoes that belonged to her brother, how unspeakably horrible to find them, of all places, here.

It was Jeremiah. He was dead; she'd never seen anything deader. She made the positive ID from the clothes Jo Beth had gifted him and from those malformed hands, not from his face, because his face was only partially there, having been ripped off along with the uppermost part of his head. Sarah realized with a sick, cold sensation that the twist of flesh she had encountered earlier in the corn had not been a squirrel at all.

18 HRS., 35 MINS. AFTER IMPACT

Jesus Christ was eight feet tall. Ry did not recall this fact from years of bone-dry sermons or the Sunday school storybooks with their depictions of interchangeable men in slovenly robes. But Jesus Christ filled the bathtub in which he stood, the bumps of his rubber hair smearing the ceiling mold. The hair was painted brown, though much of it had flaked off, revealing an underlayer the dull-gray color of exposed brains. Similar patches of gray poked through elsewhere: two spots like nipples upon his pink chest; a palm dot like an extra stigmata; and, worst of all, along his kneeless legs, chipped paint like leprous welts. Ry knew that it was his carelessness that had done this to Jesus Christ. He remembered knotting the long limbs to his belt as he fled through Black Glade. He parted his numb lips to apologize.

"Sorrow not, child." Resonant yet gentle, the voice came from everywhere at once. "I am resurrected."

An ache fit over Ry's head like a helmet, and he judged it not as the flare of injury but as the sensation of the saved. He took a moment to get his bearings. The bathroom air was foggy and dimly lit. He was crumpled at the front end of the empty but humid tub, one leg tossed over the edge, his head resting just beneath the faucet. Realizing this, he braced, expecting water, the continuation of his drowning.

"Thou remember the last words I spoketh?" The oval head titled but there was no emotion in the line-dash mouth or white-dot eyes. Steam gave rise to perspiration upon the rudimentary features and the moisture fell like taciturn tears. "I toldest thou that we would grow up. Have we not?"

"Yes," Ry said. "Oh, yes."

"Gentle Furrington is here too. He missed thou greatly."

"I missed . . . both of you, I—"

"And we thou."

"But what about . . . ." Ry's mouth hung open. "Am I going to see—"

"Hush," Jesus Christ said. "We shall not call upon that one. His is the world of Revelations."

Like a series of still photos, events began to fill in the blanks of Ry's memory: his father, the gun, the crater, his sister's escape. Rather than being left to smother in the mud, he had been deposited in this tub, but he was quick to remind himself that such a lucky break did not mean that he was out of danger.

He gave Jesus Christ an important look. "We have to be careful. We need to—"

"Son." His father's voice was as brilliant as orchestral music compared with the soft sighs of the shower conversation. "Time to get up."

Ry craned his neck and found Marvin no more than an arm's length away, cloaked in steam, hunched over a sink whistling with hot water. Resting behind the knobs of hot and cold was the Winchester, bejeweled with moisture. The mirror, cloudy and drizzled, concealed Marvin's face, and he was shirtless—his torso an unsightly knot of prison muscles—and he held in one hand a razor. Ry recognized it as his own and lifted a hand from the slimy floor of the tub to touch his face. The pimple alongside his nose was the only variation from the smoothness.

The razor rattled against porcelain. Marvin used no cream but put the blade directly to cheek. Ry looked away and saw, next to the shotgun, the foot-long shard that had broken free of the meteorite, its dazzling topography magnified by tense little beads of water. Marvin's hand strayed and caressed its countless edges. He lifted the fingertips to his nose, where he sniffed; to his lips, where he daubed whatever slick magic he had wiped from the shard's surface; to his tongue, which licked at the fingers like a child goes after runners of ice cream.

"We can't see, we can't work." The razor repositioned itself, the blade cutting across cheekbone. "We can't work, why, then, we'll just wait for dawn. I'm not happy about what you did, son, but I can't do anything about it. That's a lesson in itself: You make the best of what you've got. I've been wanting a go at a shave anyway. Maybe some supper. We'll

195

have another chance, you and I, you bet your life. And soon. Dawn comes early this time a year."

"Let me take him." Jo Beth's voice came from the bathroom doorway. "I don't want to hear him choking again."

"Father-son time, Jo. You have to respect it."

"He swallowed too much. . . . Can't you just let me have him?"

Marvin rotated the blade in the stream of water. "Women will worry, son, but don't hold that against them. Their fate is not their own. Worry is understandable. When it becomes too much, well, you nip it in the bud."

Jo Beth inhaled. But she held her words.

Ry was riveted by familiar notes from his childhood: the wet rip of hair removal, the *ting* of cheap metal to porcelain sink, the gurgle of water thickened with hair, his father's luxuriant sigh.

"Most fellows consider shaving as a chore. That's the wrong way to look at it. Think of it instead as one of life's sustaining rituals. There's so many on a farm. There's the alarm clock; there's chickens; there's things to be done before sunrise, before the rain, before winter. Same thing here. It's a task to be done before things go too far. It also answers everyone's first question: Can you operate on the schedule of manhood? Yes. We can. It is a ritual we *love*."

The razor rattled. Ry thought he could hear individual hairs hit the sink.

"Jesus Christ, it feels good."

Ry looked to Jesus Christ at the mention of his name. The towering rubber figure did not move. Beads of water worked their way down his luminous body.

"They're not real enthusiastic about handing out razors in

prison. Shaving's not a ritual they appreciate and, believe me, they have plenty of rituals of their own. Except theirs don't make a man, no sir. Theirs pull the manhood out of you like deboning a fish. Until all that's left is the worst of impulses. Things you want to possess, people you want to hurt, women you want to have forceful intercourse with. No good. None of these feelings serve you any damn good at all. But I won't sugarcoat it. Bad impulses can be useful if you can hang on to yourself, your true self. They can act as cheap fuel for an engine that wants to quit. You think we're miles apart, son, but it isn't so. We're closer than you think."

The razor glided right past extended jugulars, a jutting Adam's apple, the final patch of matted neck fur. Steam rolled in torpid clouds like a manifestation of Marvin's wisdom allowed to fatten in a way not permitted in nearly a decade.

Marvin placed the blade to his forehead, right at the hairline.

"Oh, no," Jo Beth said. "No, don't."

"It feels," Marvin breathed, "like spring."

The razor went back. A long strip of fur peeled off and plopped to the sink like a dead rodent. The bulb above the mirror shone off the segment of newly exposed scalp. Ry thought it must be nearly impossible to shave a head with a safety razor; though, on the other hand, no one wielded a blade like Marvin Burke. Back and forth it went—*shick, shick, shick*—and great volumes of hair were sliced away, much of it floating like bugs in the heavy fog. Ry blinked his father's hair from his lashes and spat it from his lips. Only the dagger of meteorite went unaffected—black strands jitterbugged inches away like shavings of magnetized metal.

Marvin's interlocked back muscles fattened as he twisted

around. The pink, puckered scar on his neck where Scowler had drilled for blood was now hideously revealed. Before Ry could look away light splashed off his father's skull, so expertly shorn that it gleamed like a balloon. His chest hair was thick and matted with blood over his heart, and upon his flushed face was a surprise that should have been predictable: a mustache, thick and soaking. He held up the dripping razor.

"Your turn," he said. "Up and at 'em."

Ry turned to the figure hiding in the shadow of the shower curtain.

"What do I do?" Ry whispered.

Jesus Christ said nothing but twisted to the side, becoming a helix. The action made sense to Ry: Turn the other cheek. He nodded enthusiastically and gripped the edge of the tub. He could and would turn his cheek, both of them quite literally, if that's what Marvin wanted.

"Thank you, Jesus," he said.

Marvin's mustache crawled upward. "You speaking to someone?"

"It's his friends," Jo Beth said.

Ry, halfway to his feet, threw a harassed look at his mother, who still hovered at the bathroom door, her skin like parchment. She gave him a glance that suggested she knew what she was doing. Ry doubted that viscerally—the Unnamed Three were to remain unnamed, especially by their murderess.

Marvin's eyes traveled from wife to son. "Friends? How's that?"

Jo Beth nodded so vigorously the hot clouds in the bathroom eddied. "Imaginary friends. Toys. Things he had as a boy." She lifted a palm attached to a weary, dead-weight arm. "It's what I was saying earlier. He's not okay. He's been damaged—as a *child*. And now today, everything's that's happened today? At least let him go lie down."

Horror crawled across his skin. How long had his mother felt this way? Who else shared her opinion? Did Sarah follow him around only because her mother insisted upon it? Maybe Jo Beth even paid Sarah for her pretend devotion? God knows Sarah would do anything for money. Or Esther Crowley—what about her? Had their sexual encounter been intended as no more than what kids called a mercy fuck?

Marvin's mustache worked in circles before he responded. "Here's an idea, Jo. How about supper."

"Food?"

"Father-son time. What did I say?"

Jo Beth was shaking her head. "You're not listening—"

"Jo." This was firmer. "Late as it is, we'd all be grateful to sit down to some supper."

Her shoulders held their height for a few more seconds before relenting. Ry looked away from her because he did not want to witness further evidence of her forfeit. Instead, he heard it: the creak of the floorboards that confirmed her following orders. Marvin's eyes trailed her for a moment. The kitchen was in line with the bathroom and they both knew that she could not escape his watch. The light was brighter once she had departed and Ry squinted, almost missing his father's beckoning gesture: *To your feet, soldier.*

Ry did not check with Jesus Christ this time. Soon he was on shaky legs before the mirror, grasping the warm porcelain with one hand and taking up the razor with the other. His knuckles grazed the shard of meteorite and his brain burned as if it had been scratched. He tried to focus on the metal blade; it vibrated, became two or three. Marvin took hold of his son's flagging wrist and worked the razor from Ry's fingers. Without a word, Marvin pounded it against the sink to void the clotted hair and with a breathtakingly specialized grip placed the blade to his son's cheek. It felt blunt and cold and Ry experienced a twinge of doubt.

A thumb and forefinger angled Ry's head just so.

"You cling to your mother," Marvin said. Noises from the kitchen, as if in response: a pot banging, water blasting; Ry knew all too well the sound of the colander striking the countertop. "That's partly my fault and I know it. Growing up's the hardest thing there is, and you've had to do it without a father."

The blade began to pluck hairs, one by one, from Ry's sideburn. It did not take long. Soon the irate edge of the blade was nicking along his jawline. There was a pop of pain as the razor claimed a ribbon of chin, but Ry was glad when the hot bullet of blood ran free. Injuries of men were not injuries at all—hadn't Marvin been the one to say that? They were but the building of braver skin. A thumb set upon Ry's cheek to push for a more advantageous angle and Ry found himself wishing a strange thing, that Sarah would take her time in bringing help so that this scene, so long in the coming, could continue.

"I'm going to share something with you. It's not for your mother, not for your sister. It's just for you." Marvin kept his voice low and his eyes on his work. "When I was your age, I had toys, too. Yes, me. Not the fancy stuff you grew up with, with all those moving parts. Wooden toys, mostly, army men with guns painted on. They were gifts, from my grandmother almost without exception, because my father—well, my father was like me. It pained him, I believe, to see an able-bodied boy messing with dolls when there was a whole mountain of work to be done. It's fine for girl children. Girl children will have their own children one day and will need to know how to use toys to distract them. Little boys are different. You have to take those toys away. It's the taking, in fact, that is so important."

The blade nudged the fair hairs of Ry's upper lip and hovered there.

But it did not claim those hairs; the razor left the fledgling mustache untouched. Instead, Marvin's fingers spidered across the top of his son's head and pushed until Ry bowed. There was a soupy moment where nothing happened. Ry listened to the spoon-to-pot clattering from the kitchen, the bathroom sink's throaty choke, the liquid dripping from Jesus Christ's extremities. Then the sensation of sharpness returned like fire against the nape of his neck. The razor began to glide up the back of his head.

"I even had a favorite toy," Marvin said. "See, I had me a cowboy and Indian set. Little cowboys with their guns, little redskins with their tomahawks and bows. I knew who you were supposed to root for. I grew up listening to *Lone Ranger* shows just like everybody else. But I had a secret, and I'm telling it to you now, man to man."

The razor alighted and cracked against the sink. Goose bumps raced across Ry's scalp where there was no more hair. He felt two runners of hot blood streak down the side of his face, splitting paths around the ear and converging into a single stream along his jaw. It stung, but the bruising push of the meteorite fragment dulled everything.

"I was for the Indians." The razor was back at the nape,

cresting, peeling off more hair. "They seemed better to me. Stronger, more efficient, more spirited. No matter the cowboys' numbers, the superiority of their weapons, the Indians just kept on coming." Marvin shrugged. "I suppose I also liked how the Indians cut their hair."

The razor went too far, past Ry's hairline, and sunk like fangs into his forehead. Marvin had to wiggle the blade to dislodge it, and blood crept like tar past Ry's starburst scar, down the bridge of his nose.

"The one I liked best was Scalper Jim. He was taller than any of them, taller than the cowboys, too, if you didn't count their hats. Muscles out to here, a headdress to beat the band. A face braver than the bravest white man's, lantern jaw, nose like a hawk, and no eyes you could see because of that avalanche of a forehead. Scalper Jim always won. Always. Even when he was the last surviving member of his tribe, he'd bide his time and pick off the cowboys one by one. Scalper Jim left no prisoners. He lived up to his name."

Marvin's voice was dreamier than Ry had ever heard it. It was no wonder that the shaving was getting sloppier, bloodier. Each new runner of blood grew cold against his skin as magnetic waves beset it.

"One day my father boxed up my toys and gave them away. But he didn't get Scalper Jim because I kept Scalper Jim under my pillow. Scalper Jim never accepts defeat—with him it's victory or death. Fathers, though, they know best, they really do. And when my dad found me playing with him, he sat me on the stump out back, put Scalper Jim in one of my hands and his whittling knife in the other. And I—"

Marvin coughed, cleared his throat. The breath was a cool tingle somewhere in the vicinity of Ry's ear. Marvin reached for the object hidden in his shirt pocket but the shirt was folded atop the toilet. Instead his fingernails closed to a fist over his wounded heart.

"I was the one who put the knife to Scalper Jim's throat," he said. "He didn't flinch. Sharp as that knife was, it could barely chip the surface. Took me twenty minutes to whittle off the chin, another ten for the nose. A whole hour to take off his face. And I . . . I'll tell you the truth. I cried like a baby. But Dad waited me out. He knew it was my last cry; I think I knew it, too. Took me all afternoon to turn Scalper Jim to sawdust but by the end I was out of tears. I grew up that day. Yes, I did."

This time the tapping against the porcelain had a climactic finality. Ry felt two hands take his shoulders and redirect them to face the mirror. One of Marvin's palms reached out and squeaked across the glass. Layers of gray gave way to a fleshy blob. Ry gripped the sink and pulled himself closer. The face he saw was Marvin Burke's. But when Ry moved his head, the head in the mirror moved too. The shock of his new baldness was mesmerizing. Long stripes of blood dried to his face like watermelon markings. He swiveled his neck so much that vertebrae began to crunch. With a jolt of exhilaration, he felt that he understood his father: The man cut hair like he whittled wood, poorly but with total commitment.

Marvin's face, another pink blob, joined his in the mirror. The mustache hairs fluttered, the voice beneath them softer and quicker than ever as if rushing to say something he had never planned to admit.

"Scalper Jim was with me in prison. He was. It's true. Every day I pictured his moment of execution, the way he faced it. I tried to emulate it. It kept me alive. So I understand, I do, toys and what they can mean. But you know what it says in the Good Book. There comes a time when we must put away childish things."

The silverware clash they heard from the kitchen had an emphasis.

"Supper's ready!" Jo Beth sounded desperate.

Ry stared at himself, his father, himself, his father.

"Just a few more hours. And then we work together. Right?"

Ry couldn't tell which pink blob those words had come from.

He tried out the last word for himself: "Right?" He wasn't sure about it and craved third-party confirmation. "Jesus Christ? Is it all right?"

There was no response. Ry endured a moment or two of anxiety, then suspicion, then exasperation. These supposed friends of his, what good were they? They recoiled from any gesture that counted. Marvin was right when it came to childish things.

"Supper's getting cold!" Jo Beth cried. "Please."

Marvin looked into the sink, extended his index finger, and ran it through the damp layer of hair that coated the basin. The finger came back up fully furred. Slowly he reached over and spread the tiny, prickling hairs across Ry's upper lip. He withdrew his hand and both father and son checked the mirror. The makeshift mustache was patchy and asymmetrical but served its purpose. The similarity was now uncanny.

"Supper." Jo Beth's pleading was softer now.

"You hungry?" Marvin asked.

Ry shook his head no. Some of his mustache flaked away. Marvin raised an eyebrow. Trust was being offered here and Ry felt a desire to earn it. After all, his newly shorn head looked so clean, so efficient. Was becoming like his father the worst thing that could happen? It would at least give Ry the authority to bend the wills of the stubborn and salvage something from his squandered life. Marvin picked up the dagger of rock, wrapped his fingers around it, and weighed it in his hand. He nodded, his shiny head winking in the bulb's hazy gleam.

"Well, you take a load off, then. Rest up. Dawn's practically here."

19 HRS., 44 MINS. AFTER IMPACT

They kept singing, which, first of all, wasn't very polite. Ry was lying facedown on his bed, fully clothed, each thread of the quilt poking like wire into his sensitized skin, none more so than his bare scalp. He was in no mood for sing-alongs. But having their playmate back in their midst had spurred Furrington and Jesus Christ into heights of celebration. They looked past his comatose behavior. This was the most joyous of reunions and they gave it their truest voices.

Ry's initial concern was the music's volume, but after renditions of both "Angels We Have Heard on High" and "Holy, Holy, Holy," Ry accepted that his friends' voices were not pitched for adult ears. Not far from the half-closed bedroom door, in the kitchen Marvin and Jo Beth were sharing the least punctual supper of their lives—it had to be just a couple hours before morning. Occasionally Ry could hear Marvin's remarks about the number of minutes till sunup and finding Sniggety before then, and he could hear a good deal of humming, too, but this discernment came only in the pause between each bellowed round of singing. After six hymns Ry could bear no more and scrambled to a seated position.

Furrington was perched upon the foot of the bed, wagging his single leg in time with the music, while Jesus Christ towered above, undulating his elbowless arms like a conductor. Both figures were stunningly real: Motes of dust clung to Furrington's glass eyes and shreds of cobweb swung between Jesus Christ's head and the ceiling lamp. They were finishing up the fifth and final verse of "Shall We Gather at the River," Furrington on a melody that was sharp but enthusiastic, Jesus Christ making harmony with his magniloquent bass.

"Yes, we'll gather at the river, / the beautiful, beautiful river; / Gather with the saints at the river, / that flows by the throne of God!"

Furrington bounced. The bedsprings zinged.

"Smashing! Simply smashing!"

"Heavenly," Jesus Christ concurred. "Blessings upon this house of worship."

"Why . . ." The word slid from between Ry's lips, tasting sour. He reminded himself to keep his voice down and tried again. "Why are you two so *happy*?"

The pair of shining marbles and the pair of white dots both oscillated his way.

It was hard not to squirm within their blank, merry stares.

"Our joy soundeth like thine," Jesus Christ said. "Does it not?"

Ry rubbed his oozing forehead scar. "What joy?"

The pink face tilted in his direction. "We have traveled o'er a long road, bore the hammers of much misfortune. Yet bells shall ring, for we are home. Hark!"

"Hark!" Furrington parroted. "Hark, hark! Oh, that's fun. Give it a try, old boy!"

"No," Ry said. "I won't."

The stitches of Furrington's mouth seemed to turn downward. "Just one hark?"

Ry drove the heels of his hands into his temples. Dried blood from his lacerated scalp crumbled into brown sand.

"The sun's going to come up." He spoke with utmost control. "I'm going to go help my dad get his meteorite. Then he's going to go away. And then you're going to go away, too. Both of you."

The teddy bear and plastic savior were frighteningly still.

"You think he'll leave, do you?" Furrington's voice was innocence itself. "Once he's got what he wants?"

"Yes," Ry said. "I believe so. Yes."

"True belief," spoke Jesus Christ, "is man's rarest quality."

"No." Ry's throat tasted raw after so many words. "It's loyalty. That's what's rare."

"Bollocks," Furrington scoffed. "I've been loyal as a knight! Look at me leg!"

"Then why'd you leave me? In the back field? Right when I needed you?" Ry turned savagely upon Jesus Christ. "And you didn't have much to say in the shower, did you?" He pressed his hands over his throbbing eyes. "I'm too old now. I'm too old. No more fooling around. No more playing."

"But," Furrington said, "playing is what we *do*."

"And we have waited so long," Jesus Christ said, "to return to the promised land."

Ry felt a twinge of guilt, then thought of his father and that twinge evaporated. The land was Marvin's. The land was

Ry's. These beings that emerged from its depths were trespassers.

"I know you waited," he said. "And I'm glad you got out, I am. But—"

"'Twas a star shining on high," Jesus Christ said, "that guided our way."

"Oh, the brightest, shiniest, beautifulest star!" Furrington cried. "And when I saw it—crackers! I knew it was true! It meant we were—"

"And, yea, the star led us—"

They finished together: "home."

It *was* a star, the meteorite, that had freed them, whether from the McCafferty Forty or from the recesses of Ry's brain was the question. He pressed his face into greasy palms and felt the prickly smear of his bogus mustache.

"Ry," whispered a voice from the window.

Past the fantastic shapes of Furrington and Jesus Christ, between the orange of bedroom and the black of night, whips of blond hair flickered in the space between the window and the sill. It was possible that nothing else in the world could have distracted Ry from making this choice between father and friends.

It was Sarah.

19 HRS., 33 MINS. AFTER IMPACT

By the time he had raised the screen and was lifting his sister through the window, the room's other occupants had melted themselves into opposite corners with a deftness either impressive or chickenhearted. Sarah had put her arms around Ry's neck for the ride and kept them there once her feet were planted, assailing him with a physical realness—noisy, quivering, smelling of night. He closed the window to shut out whatever had scared her and she folded into him like dough.

Ry laced his fingers behind her scrawny back and caught her. He sensed a thinning of noise from the kitchen, dialogue becoming one-sided, utensils with less to scrape, and muscled Sarah to an arm's length. Her face was a spectral gray. Her feet were black with mud. Though the rag on her right hand was gone, the skin of that hand was sallow and rubbery.

"He's . . . he's—"

"Shhh. Real quiet."

Sarah gulped down some air and then took on steadiness as one puts on a suit, one limb at a time. Ry adjusted his squat so he could look straight at her. She rubbed her bleary eyes and blinked. And blinked again. And again.

"Ry," she gasped. "Your hair."

He forced a little laugh. His lips felt to him like wax.

"You don't like it?"

She shook her head with such force that the dam broke and the tears came full force. It was loud. Ry shook her shoulder with one hand, made a serious face, and with his other hand pressed a finger to his lips. With curt movements of distaste, she extracted herself from his clutch and pushed herself against the window. Ry grimaced, took two long steps to the bedroom door, swung it mostly shut, and came back across the room. The look she was leveling was unfamiliar: forehead pinched, eyes wary, lips withholding. When he recognized it, he was taken aback. It was the look of distrust.

He affected sternness. "You better have some excuse."

"I'm scared," she said stubbornly.

"That's no excuse. I told you where to go."

"But I saw him."

"Who? Our dad?"

She shook her head.

"Mr. Strickland?"

She shook her head.

"Who else is there?"

Her lips went white as she deliberated the potential pitfalls of honesty.

"Jeremiah," she blurted. "He's dead."

It was a sucker punch. Ry reached out for her in retaliation. She dodged and instead he found solid wood and so leaned into it, taking a moment to process the sadness—and then the outrage. Jeremiah had not served his full sentence, but anyone who had seen the old man's ravaged physique or suffered his lumbering speech could tell that his debt to society had been paid and would, in fact, forever accrue interest. That he had died at the exact moment he might have tasted a bit of freedom was unjust.

Ry coughed out a platitude: "He was old."

"No," Sarah said. "There was blood. Lots of it."

"What do you mean?"

"I don't know."

"What happened?"

"I don't know!"

He inhaled sharply through flared nostrils. *Little bitch*, he thought.

He'd never thought such a thing of his sister.

Part of him, a new part, rather liked it.

"Was it his own blood?" He enunciated the words with precision.

"Yes."

"How do you know that?"

"His hair," Sarah said. "His hair was gone."

Ry touched his pate. "Like mine?"

"No," she said. "It was gone. The whole top of his head."

"You're not making any sense," Ry said, but it was a lie. He palmed his skull and felt how the veins pulsed with their freights of blood. The stuff would gush, he figured, if your weapon was more serious than a five-dollar razor.

"It was an accident," he heard himself say. "He fell. Or jumped to hide from a truck. There's concrete in those culverts."

Sarah was shaking her head miserably.

"There was skin," she sobbed, "in the corn."

Ry punched the wall; Sarah's flinch made him punch it again. Why did she find it appropriate to poison others with her personal nightmares? Ry realized that his father had been right about one thing: Sometimes the man of the house needed to curtail female misbehavior. He moved forward to do just that when a chair in the kitchen screeched back as someone stood.

Sarah forgot her injuries and traumas—*See*, Ry thought, *the faker!*—and pawed at his shirt, seeking protection. Ry held her in check and grinned at her hysteria. When she noticed, her mouth fell open in horror. Ry had the strongest hunch of his life; he leaned in and found exactly what he suspected.

A tendril grew from the red recess of her empty tooth socket. It was delicate and green and topped with a waxen bulb. Sarah jerked away but he snatched her jaw with his hand and dug in a thumb to prevent her mouth from closing. She yelped and twisted. He liked the feel of her bones trembling beneath his fingers. He peered more closely and saw the

211

tendril sway with the intelligent caution of an octopus tentacle. Sarah appeared oblivious to its existence, which made perfect sense, because when is a monster aware of its own monstrosity? Ry bet that if he pulled down her bottom lip he would find gums squirming with subcutaneous invaders.

"Ry," she whimpered.

In swept Furrington and Jesus Christ. Their cascade of disapproving whispers tried to remind him of other people of flesh and blood that he'd mistaken for demons. Marvin Burke, emerging from the throat of Black Glade as a prehistoric beast? Linda Colson, transformed into a rippling blob? Ry admitted that it was tough to be totally certain. The safe thing to do, he figured, just to be sure, was reach into Sarah's mouth, grab the tendril, and pull, and, if he was lucky, reel it from her jaw, yard after yard, like the tapeworm it was. But that outcome would take luck, and his father had always advocated making your own luck with swift, definitive action. What Ry needed was to simply close the tooth hole. What he needed was a needle and thread.

He aimed his free hand at her teeth.

"Easy, chap!" Furrington said.

"Shut up," Ry muttered.

Sarah ducked, tossed her shoulders, and tried to pull away. Ry clamped his hand harder around her jaw. His thumbnail sunk into her lip. He could see the risen half-moon of blood.

"All thy beasts are reflections!" Jesus Christ cried. "Know ye this!"

"Shut up, shut up!" Ry shouted.

In the kitchen a dish clattered down, followed by the squeak of a shoe turning on linoleum. These tangible sounds broke his concentration for a moment. That was all Furrington and Jesus Christ needed to cut through his delirium with soothing overtures of understanding and love. In a quick but blinding flash, Ry recognized his sister's injuries, exhaustion, and terror. These things comprised a handy catalogue of a brother's failure; they also represented the best opportunity for redemption. He withdrew his hand from her jaw. She needed to get away from him, right now, before he could change his mind.

"The attic," he gasped.

"Yes, hidest thou in thine attic!"

"Hurry, lassie, hurry!"

Even as she was stumbling away and rubbing the fingernail indents from her cheek, relief washed over her face: Her brother, horridly as he was behaving, had not ordered her back into a night haunted by dead repairmen and massacred convicts. She bolted. Ry had a last-second impulse to reach out, snare that sparrow wrist, and call out to his father: *I've got her!*

But she was just a flutter of white nightgown trailing into the dining room. Ry closed his eyes and counted off *one Mississippi, two Mississippi*. That was all it took. Footsteps pounded their way to his bedroom, and he stepped back so as not to be struck by a fist or gun. The swinging of the door blew a gust of air into his eyes. He squinted, wondering if he would be able to lie to his father's face. But the eyes that locked onto his own did not belong to Marvin.

19 HRS., 48 MINS. AFTER IMPACT

Jo Beth pushed him with her hand and hissed.
"Where is she?"

213

The prepared lie came out anyway: "Who?"

Her glare of callous impatience was a brand-new one.

"I know my own daughter when I hear her."

He tried to look over her shoulder. "Is he . . . Did he—"

"Did he hear her? I don't think so. He's out there on the porch steps, calling for the dog."

She widened her eyes like Ry was stupid. He cocked his head and sure enough heard a distant cry from the backyard, the patriarch trying to bring in line the one family member still delinquent: *Snig! Snig! Here, ol' Sniggety boy!*

Jo Beth shook Ry by his shirt.

"Where is she?"

"Upstairs. Don't worry—"

She leaned closer, spraying spittle.

"My God. How could you let her inside?"

"What? She came back. She—"

"She does what you say, Ry. You could've told her to hide out in the field, one of the barns, anywhere. She'd be safer in Black Glade."

Ry felt a stab of insult. The woman knew not of which she spoke.

"Where are the police?" She paced a tight circle. "Where the hell are the police?"

"Is he coming back inside?" Ry asked.

"Yes, any second, and now your sister's trapped upstairs."

"Mom—"

"It's that piece of rock you broke off." She stepped over to the door, threw a worried glance at the kitchen from which Marvin would emerge. "He can't stop fooling with it. He's obsessed. Like he used to get at harvest time. He keeps . . . touching it. He even started—I mean, we were eating and he used the point like you would a *toothpick*. He claims it's not affecting him, but how can that be? I haven't even touched it and my head hurts so bad it's going to explode."

She paused again to make sure the calls for Sniggety were ongoing.

"Now listen to me," she said. "This obsession? It gives us opportunities. We need to take them. I had him there in the kitchen with me for a half hour. A *half hour*, Ry. I distracted him in a million different ways and you were in here with a window. Ry. Wake up. That's the kind of opportunity we cannot pass up again."

"Mom—"

The complaint was interrupted by a howl in the night—Sniggety. No, it was Marvin. They sounded so similar.

Jo Beth snapped her fingers in Ry's face.

"Hey. *Hey*. Look at me. He keeps fooling with that piece of rock, there's going to be more chances, and soon. I've gotten close to the shotgun four or five times. This is what I'm talking about. I spilled water on the gun while we were eating, pretended I was clumsy. I thought maybe if the shells got wet—well, who knows? And aspirin. I crushed an entire bottle's worth of aspirin while I was making supper and wasn't able to get it into a glass without him seeing but it's right there on the counter, right by the sugar bowl so he'd think it was spilled sugar if he saw it, and Ry, if we get the chance we have to get him to drink that stuff down."

"But," Ry said, "he said he doesn't have a headache."

Jo Beth's lips parted in astonishment. "Ry, I'm begging you: Focus. It's very simple. He ingests that much aspirin, he'll bleed like crazy when we cut him."

Through the window they heard Marvin's victorious

215

mutter, the slap of his free hand upon canine flank, and then an odd clanking noise that took Ry a moment to place. It was the old dog chain, which had not seen use in over fifteen years. There was no key to the open padlock, but the idea nevertheless had an appeal. This was how a man asserted control over his home: locks and chains. The cocksure swagger Ry had felt during his shaving began to return. By now Marvin had discovered the uselessness of the padlock and would be, right this moment, on his way back indoors. That did not leave Ry much time to show his dad what he could do.

Jo Beth sped up her instruction. "Don't trigger him to do anything. Indecision, discussion, that's what we want. Every minute that goes by is a minute closer to the police showing up. And don't talk about Sarah. Don't even mention her name."

Her chin crumpled. Ry inspected it for monstrous parts.

"You're her brother," Jo Beth said. "Her big brother. I need you to think what you're doing."

"I know," he said. "I'm trying."

"Try harder," she said. "This is not a game."

The back porch door squalled and there was a final shouted command for Sniggety to stay before Marvin's footsteps pounded into the kitchen and paused upon acknowledgment of his wife's absence. Then they picked up again, fast. *Game*—Jo Beth had used the word to compare her son to his worthless toys, hadn't she? Well, Ry would show her a game.

He stepped up to his mother and slapped her in the face.

There were three seconds of ice-water shock. Even Furrington and Jesus Christ were speechless as the red imprint of a palm materialized on Jo Beth's cheek. Ry flushed with pride at his handiwork; he had confidence that both of his parents would recognize their son's behavior as that of a fully realized man. He waited for his mother to touch the welt with the same wonder he'd seen junior high girls pet their first hickeys.

Instead she struck him. Ry's head rocketed to his shoulder and burst with pain. He cradled his cheek with a hand, imagining loosened teeth, wondering if it was possible that a thatch of tendrils might start pushing out of *his* mouth. Maybe the seeds of monstrosity were sowed in his body, not his mother's and sister's, and that zit on the side of his nose was suppurating with mutant slugs. He sniveled at his mother through watery eyes.

Eyes blazing, Jo Beth flung back her arm for a second blow. But Marvin was there to catch her elbow at its highest point. Jo Beth did not gasp or turn; rather, she strained harder, surging toward the ingrate boy, and when she realized that her right arm was going nowhere she lashed out with the less-experienced but just as motivated left, landing a series of fumbling smacks even more demeaning.

Ry scurried out of range and looked to his father for the familiar frown of disappointment. Instead he found a man emblazoned with energy. Gray residue from the splinter of meteorite hid like damp ash under his fingernails. His mustache looked as if it had been dipped in gray paint. When he grinned Ry had to avert his eyes—the front teeth were like mirrors, plated with shavings. The shard itself was clamped by his left hand so that it rested alongside the barrel of the shotgun like a second magazine. He wet his lips with a molten tongue.

"Whoa, Nelly," he said.

Marvin seemed invigorated by the freshness of physical

217

struggle. Ry straightened. Possibly he had not performed poorly after all. Now all he had to do was get rid of these embarrassing, unwanted toys before his dad spotted them. Ry was not like these playthings, not anymore, and that was something they needed to accept.

He hissed at them from the side of his mouth.

"Go away."

"Away?" Furrington blustered. "Oh, rubbish!"

"I don't want you here!"

"That's grown-up folderol, is what that is."

"Enough!" Ry's volume was growing. "No more time for playing!"

"Each man lives," Jesus Christ intoned, "to experience joy."

Ry could bear this foolishness no longer.

"Don't tell me what to think! Don't you dare! A what? A giant stuffed animal? A Jesus the size of a basketball hoop? You're going to tell me what to think or what I'm supposed to do with my life? Are you serious?"

Gradually he became aware that his parents had gone motionless.

A tree limb tapped gently on the side of the house, the only sound.

"Ry." Jo Beth controlled her tone. "I'm . . . let's . . . how about we all go have some tea? I can make tea."

"All of us?" Ry demanded. "The whole family?"

She looked hesitant.

"Your father and you and me," she said carefully.

Ry waved an arm at Furrington and Jesus Christ.

"Not them, though. Not the liars."

Jo Beth moved her head in an uncertain pattern.

"No," she said. "Not them."

"And Sarah?" Her verboten name tasted as good as cigarettes.

"Tea," Jo Beth said. "Let's go make some."

"Sarah," Marvin echoed. "What about her?"

"Let's go," Jo Beth said. "Let's all go now for tea."

Marvin watched his son with interest, and Ry blushed.

"You saw her," Marvin surmised. "Where?"

"I . . ."

"Ry!" Jo Beth barked. "Stop this! Please stop this!"

"Mum's the word, mate," Furrington hissed.

"Stop talking to me!" Ry shouted. "Stop telling me what to do!"

"Thou findest conflict where there is peace," Jesus Christ said.

Marvin took a step closer to his son and asked again. "Where?"

Ry looked from his father to his mother. Was he supposed to tell or not?

"Calm thyself," Jesus Christ said. "Never shall they suspect the attic."

Ry gasped and flapped a finger at Jesus Christ.

"You said it! Attic! You said *attic*!"

"Ry! Please shut up! We'll drink tea! Now! Please!"

"The attic," Marvin mused. "I had forgotten about the attic."

Jo Beth threw herself at Ry and rained punches. He folded himself onto his bed, curled inward to absorb the impacts, and told himself that the blows were nothing but the courteous knuckle bumps of a table full of gentle people passing around teacups on saucers. It was ever so pleasant; he could taste the slice of lemon, feel the dribble of tea on his chin, hear the polite chuckles at his harmless foible.

It was only when Marvin peeled Jo Beth away from his son that Ry's humiliation blossomed anew under the helpless, ineffectual, impotent gazes of his so-called friends.

His words made furious splatters.

"Go away! I hate you! I never want to see you again!"

Beloved Mr. Furrington blanched as if all color were being squeezed from his fur in tight fingerfuls. Noble Jesus Christ stiffened as if his rubber had hardened to a substance that would shatter if dropped. They were once again murdered and yet managed to sorrowfully bend their strange corpses into the room's narrowest realms of shadow. That was not enough for Ry. Though his hands were busy protecting his ears from the final scraps of Jo Beth's onslaught, they itched for matches and kerosene. If he could, he would do as his mother had done years ago and burn these monsters to ash.

20 HRS., 35 MINS. AFTER IMPACT

They went upward but it felt like a descent. The roomy dining room and high-ceilinged stairwell gave way to the cramped hallway and tomb-sized anteroom outside Sarah's and Jo Beth's bedrooms. Ry pulled the attic door down from the ceiling and unfolded the ladder, and the three of them took a minute to stare into the mausoleum darkness. No one wanted to be first. But Ry knew that his father was monitoring his progress, so up he went.

Moonlight glowed through the pulled shade of a window at the far end of the room. Otherwise it was pitch-black. Ry swatted for the first light cord and his fingers brushed through Sarah's hair. His heart stopped and then he realized it was only a cobweb. Jo Beth's head poked through the opening near his feet and Ry offered her a paltry smile. She refused to look at him. She ascended at the urging of the shotgun; Ry leaned and saw Marvin bringing up the rear. Ry steadied himself, waved his arm around, found the flyspecked plastic at the end of the light string, and pulled it.

The mechanism clicked and the bulb winked awake. Ry shaded his eyes. He had not been up here since before Jo Beth had begun packing for their exodus, and he had imagined it as partly cleared. However, the room was exactly as he had remembered: a claustrophobic tunnel between two walls of boxes that rose like the steps of Mayan temples. Sarah could be anywhere. There were recesses dark enough to contain hideaways—certainly secrets—and crests topped with pieces of junk perched like gargoyles. Ry inched forward to give his mother room and the floor squealed in agony.

The butt of the gun thunked against the floor as Marvin completed his entrance. He held the Winchester in one hand, the dagger of meteorite in the other. His excitement was betrayed by how both items shook.

"Is there another hmmmm?"

It was Ry's job as son to know this shorthand. He frowned.

Jo Beth offered a monotone interpretation. "Is there another light, he asked."

"Hm hm see."

"He can't see," Jo Beth said.

Ry pointed to the far window.

"Well, hmmmm," Marvin said. "Hm hm hmmmm."

221

"Go turn it on, he said."

Ry addressed the passageway. The room was fifteen feet long at most. Sarah had to be within touching distance, taunting them with her silence. Well, he would flush her out. Reluctant to feel a rat throe beneath one of his landing feet, he moved by sliding his shoes. The floor hissed like it was salted.

The dimmest moonlight reigned at the far end. The knotted end of the second light's pull cord batted Ry's lips. It tasted sour. He caught it and hoped that, when he yanked it, he did not see Sarah right away propped among the boxes— it would be like seeing a corpse. Let it be gradual, he prayed. He counted out a deep breath.

"Sarah," he croaked. "Come out, now."

He pulled the cord.

Sarah was right next to him and she was headless.

Ry would never understand how he held in the scream. He stumbled back, landed his heel wrong, and tripped. And in that weightless instant he experienced the true horror of re- gret, because he should have listened to her about Jeremiah, about the top of his head being gone, because here she was, victim to the same decapitation. By accident he caught him- self against the box their TV had come in a million years ago, and through the updraft of dust he made out Sarah's lack of arms, the pole that stood in place of her legs, the zippered body bag that already encased her torso.

It was the dressmaker's dummy, standing in its regular place next to the window. Ry could almost hear Marvin's piti- less laugh. Ry flung his head left, right, to the rafters, to the floor, at cardboard, wood, wicker, plastic, glass, the whole il- logical puzzle constructed from their lives' castoffs.

"She's," Ry panted, "not here."

Marvin shoved his chest into a wall of boxes like he wanted to fight it. It did not respond and he turned the threat upon his son. "She's here. You *said*."

Ry tasted panic. "I thought she was."

Marvin kicked lightly at a lower crate. The stacks above wobbled.

"She hm hm."

"She *is* here," Jo Beth interpreted.

"She hm."

"She *is*."

"Hmmmm."

"She—"

"Hmmmm-mmmm-mmmm."

"She . . . she . . ." Jo Beth shook her head, lost. "Ry, *isn't* she . . . ?"

The room was torn apart; it happened in what seemed like seconds. Marvin brought down boxes on both sides of him with powerful drives of his arms, and before the packages split against the floor he was flailing at the next layer. The landslide ejected payloads of newspapers, tax forms, long-forgotten correspondence that took off on white wings. His feet hammered at a wooden crate until it buckled and bled the spangled shards of holiday decorations. Ry slipped on a busted garbage bag and fell into the dummy's armless hug.

By now Marvin was chest-deep in the innermost layers. His neck swelled with the effort of extracting the staple-and-tape spines from obstinate containers. Pewter figures, old table-ware, and outdated purses slopped to the floor like slaughter-house entrails. No central thoroughfare remained; the room was postearthquake.

Marvin's eyes, speedy and black as bees, found Ry and stung.

"That." He pointed. "*That.*"

Ry looked at the mess in his lap. It was the contents of one of his mother's sewing baskets scattered in a roadkill smear, complete with spool skull, pincushion heart, button blood, and scrap-cloth skin. Marvin kicked through the rubbish and pointed again, this time with the shotgun and at the dressmaker's dummy. Ry ducked the invisible bullet and snatched the hem of the dustcover, eager to prove to his father that the dummy was not Sarah.

He stood, lifted off the cover, and dropped it to the floor. It took a while for him to notice his mother's strangled whine. Marvin closed in on Ry, his feet grinding through the clutter with the same bored crunch of Sniggety chewing through a bone. The shotgun muzzle touched Ry's shoulder and moved him aside.

There was no question about it: White Special Dress outshone the shard of meteorite, had just as many facets, was just as hypnotic. Marvin held his breath and reached out to touch it, but his fingers hesitated inches away as if weighing the possibility of electrocution. Finally they pounced, pinching the ivory taffeta. Ry could almost feel how the texture melted like lotion into his father's coarse skin.

Marvin's voice was muffled. "What is this?"

"It's nothing," Jo Beth said. "A hobby. Junk."

"It's not nothing."

"That's why it's up here. It's just an old—"

"*It's not nothing!*"

Marvin snatched a handful of the dress, right at the neckline. Jo Beth shuddered at the crude molestation. He pulled, trying to tear the delicate fabric from the model, but whatever laces or clasps Jo Beth had invented were impressive. He snorted in frustration, then moved toward Jo Beth, pulling the dummy by its clothes in the manner of a caveman. The headless thing came obediently, its circular metal base clucking across the garbage-strewn floor.

Jo Beth had both hands palm up as if eager to take back her baby.

"Look at it," Marvin said. "What is it? What is it really? It's a few goddamn buttons. Goddamn thread. Little goddamn bits of hm. It shouldn't mean anything. Should it? But this crap is what ruined us, Jo. Ruined our hmmmm."

"That's true," she pleaded. "That's absolutely true."

"And still you flaunt it."

"I don't." To cover her bases she tried again. "I do."

Marvin planted the dummy with enough emphasis to make a point, and Jo Beth's knees jarred as if it had happened to her. The base snapped from the pole, wobbled a few feet, and came to rest against Ry's shoe. With nothing to stand on the dummy dove but did not hit the floor—it was caught in the sling of the dress, which was still snared in Marvin's fist. Ry heard individual threads give way: *Ping! Ping!*

"They told me you were trouble," Marvin said. "Everyone said hmmmm some other girl."

"I am trouble," Jo Beth said.

"*She sews*, is what they said. They said it like it mattered."

"It shouldn't have. It's my fault that it did."

He shook the dummy by the bodice, and through some fluke of angle and motion the dress, rippling as gorgeously as a tiered wedding cake, slipped free of the breasts and shoulders with a satin sigh. The naked wooden torso clunked to

225

the ground. Marvin teetered with the sudden loss of counter-weight, then lifted the dress in a surprised fist. It puddled over his forearm like a dollop of frosting. They all felt it: Marvin had taken away the dress's feminine shape, robbing it of much of its power. Emboldened, he kneeled and dug past the needle threader, tape measure, and tracing wheel, sifted through the scatterings of pins and needles, until he plucked from the mess a pair of pinking shears. He held the blunt little instrument in the same large paw as the dress and stood.

Marvin offered both items to his terrified wife.

"Please cut this up."

Jo Beth's eyelids fluttered as if pelted by a funnel of gnats. Her lips worked in silent syllables, struggling to come up with an alternate way to interpret this command. She ventured a little laugh, just soft enough, perhaps, to whisk the idea away.

He shook the dress and stared at the floor.

"Makes me uncomfortable to repeat it."

"But I told you. . . ."

"Don't do that. Don't cajole, don't hm hm hmmmm."

"And . . . and . . ." Her smile was busted and wild. "And why would I do this?"

"To change. For things to change. You want things to change, don't you?"

Ry saw doubt touch his mother's expression. Because she did want things to change. That was the whole point of leaving the farm.

"Then this is a symbol," Marvin said.

Jo Beth's lines of doubt deepened and Ry could not help but be awed. It *was* a symbol. How did his father know?

Marvin nodded. "You know what you have to hm."

He extended the dress and shears. They hovered at a level

where all Jo Beth needed to do was lift her arms and the dress would be in her possession once more. She considered it, blinking drowsily. For so many years this object had soothed the rage and depression in her blood just through contact with her skin. Maybe it would do the same now, calm these stormy waters, make everything all right.

Ry realized he hadn't breathed in forever. He sucked down a mouthful of dust.

At last Jo Beth spoke.

"No."

Marvin angled his head. "No?"

"Shoot me if you want," she said.

Marvin steadied himself. "You forget. I killed a man."

"So? Think you can kill a woman?"

He readjusted his stance unhappily. "I can do other things, Jo."

"What? Stick needles in me? Try it—you'll have to kill me. Or you're going to threaten to shoot one of my children? Do it. Do it and you'll either end up dead or I will. Either way is fine. You've got that gun you keep waving around. It has to go off at some point, doesn't it?"

Marvin's shoulders began to tighten.

"You speak out of turn," he said. "Hmmmm."

"No, you do. *You* do. This is not your farm, Marvin. It's mine. It's been mine for nine years. And what I did to it was I killed it. You say you killed a *man*? Big deal."

"I've got a plan, Jo Beth. I'm not going to let you ruin it."

"Your plan is shit. Come here and kill us? That hasn't worked. Take our money? Best of luck. Take that rock with you? You can't even get it out of the hole. And then what? You're going to waltz into some museum with it in a

227

wheelbarrow? Or what, a Polaroid picture? It's laughable. It's the most ridiculous plan I've ever heard. Prison ruined you, Marvin. I'm afraid you've lost your touch."

Marvin slotted the wedge of meteorite into the Winchester's grooves.

"Doesn't matter," he said. "I don't have to sell it. I'll *have* it. That's worth something right there. By itself. Isn't it? Just having it?"

Jo Beth's face was wickedly drawn.

Marvin turned to Ry. The stew of rubbish around his feet rattled and clacked.

"Isn't it? Son?"

Ry nodded. He had to.

Marvin's silver grin dashed across his face like a knife. He lurched forward, the gap between his teeth like a great black curtain dropping over Ry's world. Ry did not feel the fabric being bunched into his left hand; he did not see the stiff fingers of his right positioned around the child-friendly handles of the pinking shears. The black curtain lifted and there was Marvin, swooping backward to give his son space. Ry caressed the dress and fondled the shears. It was as if he held both of his parents in either hand.

"It's what I was saying, son." Marvin's bare head was bouncing in approval. "Men do the real work. There's nothing fair about it."

"Don't," Jo Beth said. "You don't have to."

"He knows what he has to do," Marvin said. "He's my hm."

Ry lifted the shears and practiced their operation. The soft noise sounded like a secret. He shook out the dress so that its full length touched the floor; its secret was even softer. He angled the tool toward the fabric, expecting the dress to scream. It did not, not even when he fit the blades over the first thick fold of material.

The act of cutting detonated something at the back of his head; he felt his brain thud against the plates of his skull. Magnetized dust from his father's hands might have rubbed off on the shears—would that mean Ry was absolved from responsibility? His thumb and forefinger pumped and the stubby jaws of the shears squeaked, and the two sabers of silver began munching through the lace trim. The pivot of the shears jammed and Ry felt stupidly happy—two inches of damage, that was all he'd done. But then the skirt went taut and the shears tore across it as if it were paper. A huge swath was flayed. From somewhere to his right came unbearable moans. Like a natural immune response, the blare in his head amplified to block them out. Both noises were distracting and he found himself having to double back, make a serious effort at chewing lamé to gristle, ribbon to confetti. Work: It was the one thing he knew he was good at.

22 HRS., 6 MINS. AFTER IMPACT

By the time his hand cramped, daybreak was smoldering through the window shade. Ry yawned and let the pinking shears drop. He noticed that his feet were gone, buried in the dress's remains. He kicked his right foot and white silk butterflies and golden lint mosquitoes briefly spotted the air. Two pearls rolled across the floor like sad white drops of blood. White Special Dress, the result of nine years of toil, was no more than a pile of cold guts, and he had acted as butcher.

He lifted his chin. There would be a proud smile waiting for him from his father, there had to be. But the man he found was a wracked ghoul, bent with the passage of hours. Over in the corner was Jo Beth, slouched and silent. There was a smell like bile. Had someone thrown up? As he sniffed, the stench became the embodiment of his parents' disgust. Hate was everywhere, shared between and directed at everyone.

Marvin's eyes crawled across the attic wreck, brave enough to dwell upon the shredded gown for only a few seconds. He dragged an unsteady palm over his shaved head, through his sweaty mustache. His glasses were left askew.

"My house," he whispered, "is a mess."

He turned with a slowness reminiscent of Jeremiah. His first step was uncharacteristic, a stumble upon some unseen piece of miscellany. Both arms went out to buffer his fall and the gun tumbled to the floor, briefly free. No one went for it. Marvin took it back in his hands and trudged forward, gesturing the barrel at his wife in a vague way but never getting close to meeting her eyes. Jo Beth took a breath that shook her whole body.

A spark of insight flared somewhere inside Ry. He remembered waking up after being attacked with the owl lamp and realizing how many hours had passed, how the next time he'd seen his mother she was wearing a set of new clothes. Marvin had not touched a woman in nine years and she had known that; there was no telling how far she'd gone to distract him from hurting her children. Now it was all wasted effort. She moved listlessly toward the door and began to lower herself onto the ladder. Her knees popped. Marvin's did, too. Their feet made rat noises as they left behind their son.

Ry stood there wheezing. He swept his eyes over the entire attic but could not bear to land them anywhere for long. The devastation was a larger reflection of the unspeakable thing he had done to the dress, itself only the latest example of his lifelong cowardice. It would have been better for everyone if Black Glade had sunk in its root teeth, pulled him into its stone belly, and spent nine years over his digestion.

He'd fit nicely up here amid the debris. All he had to do was fall. His knees had begun their weakening when, like the lit end of a cigarette in a darkened theater, a small red container caught his eye from across the room. Barely peeking through the upheaval, the container was roughly the size of a shoebox, though the flaked paint of a long-lost commercial logo betrayed its age. Marvin's tornado must have dislodged it; Ry was certain that he'd never seen it before. His knees siphoned strength from curiosity and he found himself climbing over the refuse, reaching for the container, bringing it into his arms.

Ry discovered that his palms were swampy and his wrists sore with the force of his racing pulse. The container weighed very little. The wood was flimsy, the lid fitted like a cigar box. And yet this small capsule was important. He could feel its undeniable energy in his fingertips, his eyeballs, the crack of his forehead. He walked over to the attic door, closed it, and sat on top of it—this gift unwrapping was private. He placed the box on the floor, took hold of the lid from both sides, and began to shake it free. Wood squeaked in protest. Finally the lid separated and the box itself fell to the floor, blowing out a rectangle of dust. Ry licked the air, recognized the taste. He set the lid aside.

There, not burned, not buried, lay the Unnamed Three.

22 HRS., 34 MINS. AFTER IMPACT

Jo Beth and Marvin came down the back steps connected so closely by the shotgun that the arrangement could have been mistaken as arm in arm. It was dawn, and a warm one, and yet both of them wore gloves. Marvin's pockets jingled with car keys. The sequence of events was clearly outlined and the McCafferty Forty was the preordained destination. Jo Beth slanted toward it.

But Marvin caught her elbow with the shotgun and tapped her in a different direction. She wavered but soon enough caught the drift: the doghouse. Sniggety was part of this final chapter too, she had forgotten, and she recalled hearing Marvin slap the canine's hind end while she had been inside trying to talk sense into her son. That effort had failed spectacularly. Marvin, however, had succeeded in rounding up his dog.

They stopped at the dirt patch just outside the small yellow house. Inside Jo Beth discerned the fussy rearranging of a crouched animal. It was fitting, she thought, that Sniggety had so readily turned his back on those who had taken care of him for the past nine years. Betrayal was all around.

"Snig," Marvin muttered. "Hm."

The animal shifted about but did not emerge.

Marvin knocked the heel of the gun against the roof.

"Snig. Hm hm."

The breaths emitting from the darkness were thin and rapid. Jo Beth was surprised by her instinctive concern; perhaps the mutt's master had punished him for his earlier delinquency and that friendly slap she'd heard was actually the breaking of old bones. Marvin reared back with a foot and kicked the wall sharply, once, twice, thrice. Jo Beth's heart, weakened by hour after hour of fresh shock, fluttered with each crack.

"Sniggety," she said. "Now."

Marvin looked askance at her as if annoyed that she would think her contribution necessary. But, in fact, it worked. They both heard the throat whine of a pleased dog. Except it came from off to their right. They looked to the east and saw, over by the machine shed, wagging his tail, Old Snig.

Their reaction took an extra beat. The low sun obscured their vision and exhaustion had made them both sluggish. That was all the time it took for a small hand to dart from the doghouse, run the long-dormant dog chain around Marvin's ankle, cinch it tight, and swiftly insert and clamp the antique padlock.

Deep in Jo Beth's heavy chest, life stirred.

"Sarah!"

Marvin jerked back as if he had been bitten, and within two backpedaling steps the chain pulled tight and his arms pinwheeled as he lost his balance. Without warning Jo Beth was taken with the conviction that her entire life had led to this moment, this single instance of physical contact where she—not he—was the aggressor. Her arms shot out and pushed. It was more than his equilibrium could withstand, and he fell. His back hit the ground perfectly flat and his breath expelled in one loud burst. Jo Beth was already moving away when her eyes landed upon her daughter's wide-eyed face poking out from inside the doghouse.

Marvin was coughing, orienting himself, and Sarah was frozen.

"Here!" Jo Beth screamed. "*Here!*"

Sarah wiggled through the small opening. Her bare feet danced right over Marvin's empty left hand, which shot up by instinct, the fingers scratching at her ankle, fumbling with her dirty skin. But she was too speedy and she tripped out of his clutches and went pirouetting.

Jo Beth caught her. They spun for a moment with the girl's momentum and by the time they found their footing, Marvin was sitting up and pulling on the chain and finding it difficult to slide past the bones of his ankle. He began to tussle with his shoe to remove it before registering the heaving breaths of his wife and daughter. He twisted himself around on the dirt patch and brought up the shotgun. The muzzle caught a tuft of grass and gave Marvin a moment's trouble.

Jo Beth pushed Sarah at the house. One second later she was carrying her by the armpits. They hit the steps with their shins and elbows, and though pain was everywhere she somehow flung the screen door wide, putting an obstruction between them and Marvin that would at least make it harder for him to aim, but then it didn't matter because the two of them were rolling into the enclosed back porch, Sarah smothered into her mother's chest, Jo Beth choking on her daughter's hair, and they were alive—they could feel it and taste it—at least for a few more wonderful seconds.

22 HRS., 49 MINS. AFTER IMPACT

Ry knew that every piece of advice his mother had ever received regarding these ugly, squalid, shameful dolls had been the same: Destroy them. Yet she had not. It was as if she had known that one day Ry would need them again and so secreted them here in the attic. Up here was so much more than was offered by the endless, laggard suspense of the farm's soil. Packed away in these boxes, and now haphazardly spilled, were his very memories, emotions, hopes, and fears. They were here for the choosing.

Ry withdrew Mr. Furrington. He was gray with filth and small enough to sit in the palm of a nineteen-year-old boy. Next he removed Jesus Christ, a crusty nub of rubber whose edges looked gnawed upon—by attic mice or by a nervous boy nine years earlier? At the very bottom of the box was a hollow of sharp white teeth. Ry addressed the scurvy ogre with utmost caution. His fingertips sunk into the grubby cloth and made indents into the cornmeal belly, while the stiff outer layer of skin segmented like a hardened glaze of mucus. The exposed metal leg had acquired a dull brown sheen and Ry could not help but appreciate how this frosting of rust made it all the more lethal.

Scowler was still tiny, still eyeless, still starving.

The doll convulsed hard enough to shake Ry's entire body. No, it was the door beneath him rattling. Beneath his tailbone he felt the hammering of fists and he heard his mother shouting all kinds of demands: *Open up, hurry! He's going to get free and we have to leave!* Beneath that was Sarah's voice, crying her brother's name over and over. Jo Beth gave a valiant shove and Ry lifted an inch, but then he readjusted and pushed downward. He needed a moment; he needed to think.

The amazing thing was that he could. His mind had shifted into a more fluid gear, shuttling ideas around with a clarity that was astounding after so many years in the fog. Troublesome tasks became easy. For example, he plucked an umbrella from a nearby pile, jammed the pointed end beneath a heavy crate, and brought the hooked end across the attic door. Like that, Jo Beth's leverage was gone. She withdrew with a weepy moan. Courage, long absent, flooded Ry's body, stirring to a froth other long-lost stimulants: creativity, intelligence, ruthlessness.

Scowler wormed. He wanted out. He wanted *big*. That's what Ry wanted, too, though from within the bones of the house came the ghostly protests of whatever remained of Furrington and Jesus Christ. Their whining instructions were all too familiar: Find your family and run. Yet again, run. It appealed to Ry in a way, the idea of flight, the return once more to the Black Glade of his youth.

But the vibration of the doll's razored metal was as strong as the electric fences Ry had taken hold of a half-dozen times in his stupid life. He unwrapped his fingers to find the beast huge-mouthed and laughing, because this was exactly the point that Scowler wanted to make: There were certain things you could not run from.

The memory swept in like a fetid gust: Ry toting the tidy package of sewing from his mom and Esther Crowley taking it from him and letting him inside and pouring them both tall glasses of iced tea. Ry's revulsion was instant. Why was Scowler screening this horror film at the very moment he was feeling, for the first time in a decade, the stirrings of strength? Scowler's giggle was a million children's fingernails tickling an infinite chalkboard. More details than Ry had ever cared to remember came into focus. He heard Esther's small talk, stuff about teachers and classes. He saw her body stretch to open the refrigerator and then, a few minutes later, the living room door, how her summer clothes made no secret of the plump lavishness of her legs, the drama of her waist.

Next came the comfortable music cues, hick narration,

and car-chase blurs of *The Dukes of Hazzard* and Esther declaring how she liked Luke but not Bo and Ry saying he agreed and Esther just about dying with laughter. Wait—was that Scowler behind the TV, laughing too? He wanted out of that room, out of this memory, and so was thankful when Esther invited him upstairs to see her room. They had yet to touch. It was only when he was seated on her bed did she lean over and do everything at once: matched her lips to his, swiped her tongue across his teeth, scrunched his hair with one hand, found an exposed stretch of his back with the other, and drew up her left knee so that it hooked over his right hip. Everything was in motion. He held on.

The kissing was fast and resolute; when she moved her lips to his neck or ear it felt to Ry as if she were crossing off items from a checklist. Ry followed suit and ran his thumbs over those swooped hips until she wiggled in a way that made him think he was rubbing her raw. It turned out she was just pulling her legs out from under her so that she could take off her pants and panties. Unsure if it was custom or what, he paused to take off his own jeans and underwear and then, as if by legal agreement, they both moved to recumbent positions.

Uncoiled, everything was in reach. His hands grew brave. She sat up to wrestle her arms out of her shirtsleeves and he saw moles on her back, a dozen of them, and he looked away, feeling as if he had seen something even more private than what had already been revealed. She helped him take off his own shirt. There were no moles on his torso and he felt unexpectedly perfect. She sealed her bare skin to his. They had not looked into each other's eyes since about the time that Luke Duke was telling Daisy how they had to go help Bo.

He was marveling at the spice of unfamiliar sweat when she lodged her hands in his armpits and began to raise him into position for penetration. She did it with an effortless savvy. Their sexes nudged. Something felt wrong. He checked the point of contact. The organs themselves became abstract shapes, and then it was all over. What he saw down there was the red bat—his mom had always said that someday the true ownership of it would revert to him.

Ry tried to push himself away but one palm ended up crushing her stomach and the subsequent groan of pain made it worse: The bat that had done things to Jo Beth Burke was now taking aim at Esther Crowley. Ry paddled to get out of the way. Textures crossed his palms that might have been nose, lips, or nipple, and the next thing he knew he was bent over the edge of the bed and gasping for air. He waited for tea, no longer iced, to come pouring out of his gullet, but he got all mixed up and felt the expansion of wetness around his crotch. The wrong stuff, the wrong time—he had wet himself.

He moved from the bed on arms and legs and found he was still peeing. His hands got trapped in her inside-out jeans and down he went. Her hot skin sidled up next to his and she set a tentative hand at his back. He coughed and felt pinpoints of tears jab the corners of his eyes. She was already whispering soothing things, she was being wonderful, and it sliced like hemming pins into Ry's skull. Boys didn't usually urinate at the sight of her nudity; Esther knew sure as shit that this was the handiwork of Marvin Burke. Ry found his underwear, wet and stinking. But his pants and shirt were dry and he gathered them on his way to the door. She was apologizing. He was apologizing too, not for his sexual failure but because of the bat. It was his. His own mother had sworn it.

Ry exited the Crowley house with laughter ringing from the dark worlds of the barns and sheds, from the hidden parts of the trees. It followed him all the way home, into his bed where he cowered beneath the covers and cried for hours. He would not recognize that laughter for years, until right this second alone in the attic. It came from none other than Scowler, the one friend who never shrank from dispensing the toughest of love.

Never, ever again.

Ry realized he was muttering these words aloud, over and over.

This was the lesson Scowler was teaching: Ry might be able to outrun his past but the episode with Esther Crowley represented his miserable future. Life would be a series of heinous failures, an endless procession of beds to be pissed, if he did not stand up, right now, bare his teeth, and bite.

All Ry had to do was provide Scowler an exit.

Ideas flowed with such ease! He knew just how to do it. His proximity to the meteorite had hastened the arrival of Furrington and Jesus Christ. But he could not forget the beatings that had directly preceded each of their appearances in the real world: Marvin striking him with the owl lamp and the drowning attempt in the crater water. It was just the recipe Ry required to bring forth Scowler—a little space dust and just the right kind of physical trauma. A tall order, except for what Ry found lying only a few feet away.

It was the shard of meteorite. Marvin must have dropped it when he had fumbled the shotgun on his way out. Ry shoved aside a broken sewing machine, kicked away a rubber-banded roll of Sarah's kindergarten drawings, and carefully removed a ruffle that had once graced the most beautiful dress in the world. Uncovered, the shard gleamed in the bulb light like a starry night sky across a still pond.

Ry took a moment to consider the best place on his body to do it, but it was a silly debate. There was only one spot. He lifted the dagger with both hands and fit the point into the starburst scar between his eyebrows. It slotted into the crevice like a screwdriver into a screw, as if this were what it had been built for eons ago. He felt the sharpened edge squish through flesh and chip against solid bone. His fist settled upon the opposite end as he tried to remember the hundreds of nails he had pounded in his lifetime. Often he'd sunk them in a single blow. It was possible that he'd get that lucky this time, too, though he was prepared for this nail to be much more stubborn.

Scowler waited on his lap, mouth wide to catch the delicious blood.

Ry hesitated. He prayed. He told his family to hold on, just one more minute.

What Monsters Did

22 HRS., 50 MINS. AFTER IMPACT

If he were flexible enough to gnaw off his own foot, he'd do it.

So much had gone right: the impact event at Bluefeather; his skyward escape; his journey through backyards and alleys and ditches, cropland and timber; finding the Winchester 1200 and a box of shells right behind the generator where he'd left them in 1972; and the meteorite, that thing from the Jaekel Belt if the girl was to be believed, a gift for which he had no satisfactory words of thanks. It was a new life served up to him on one hell of a silver platter.

So much since then had gone wrong. There was the killing of a man and the loss of control over his family, but those failings did not measure up to being chained by a child to the doghouse. *The doghouse.* Fates did not get more wretched.

Marvin had tried to uproot the post to which the chain was affixed, but he himself had set that post in cement seventeen years ago and his work, as always, was impressive. There was no way out except for unlocking the padlock and none of the keys on Jo Beth's keychain matched.

Sniggety sat next to him, his tail whipping contentedly, delighted about his surprise guest. Marvin looked away in disgust. Hardly any time had passed since his wife and daughter had disappeared inside and already he felt a despair the likes of which he hadn't felt since entering his first cell at Pennington. He was stuck here, either to be arrested when the cops got wise or to starve to death if they didn't.

From inside the house he heard his wife's shouts, the little girl's screams. They were trying to gather the worthless boy. Marvin throttled the gun. He knew his son was mentally deranged; he knew the little girl was genuinely sick; he knew Jo Beth suffered from the same debilitating headaches that were afflicting her children. Marvin knew this because he had them too. He had not admitted this to Jo Beth because what good did it ever do to admit weakness? But the truth was that his spine rang with a throb nearly musical; the chord it struck was true all the way down to his toes. It troubled his vision and impaired his judgment. But what it agitated most was his desire. That rock was his because this land was his, no matter what that woman said. He made another futile check of his pockets for the meteorite shard and his palms throbbed with loneliness.

He sat up against the doghouse, extended his legs perfectly straight, and laid the shotgun along his thigh. He squinted past the action bar, straight down the muzzle, and lined the bead with the knob of his left ankle. If he could keep his hands steady, a single shot ought to turn his foot into ground meat. The chain would slip off as easily as one of those dandelion bracelets he saw little girls giving their dads in prison visiting rooms. He grinned. He tasted salt. Was he crying? He wasn't sure. He couldn't even remember what the hell tears tasted like. He tried to laugh and heard his jaws squeal as he braced for pain.

A shadow fell over his leg, making his target go dark.

Marvin sputtered. He was trying to get a clean shot here! He pulled his eyes into focus and found himself looking at a pair of bare feet twice the size of his own and so strong that they did not bother with details like ankles or toes. Marvin's eyes crept over the tree-trunk legs, the loinclothed groin, the vast chest, the hawkish face, the anaconda arm with its trademark tomahawk. Each of these features was blunt to the point of ambiguity, but that's what you got when carving a man from wood.

"Scalper Jim," Marvin said. "Good to see you."

The Indian's brow loomed over the triangular notches of his eyes.

"I know," Marvin said. "I take full responsibility. But I'm going to get out. Just give me one second to show you." Marvin flashed a desperate grin and displayed his left leg. "I'm going to shoot the damn thing off. How's that, huh? It'll make a mess." Marvin laughed, a strange yipping bark. "Oh, it'll make a mess all right."

Scalper Jim glowered from his foothill shoulders.

"What? This chain? I put it here for Old Snig."

Hearing his name brought into it, Sniggety withdrew on his belly.

Scalper Jim's boulder fist tightened around the tomahawk.

"A key?" Marvin shrugged. "Sure, there was a key, but no one's used it for—huh? Well, yes. Yes, in fact. I *do* recall. I put the key right inside the doghouse here, up on a little ledge. That's how you keep a farm: You put things in their logical places. I put it there, what, twenty years ago? And I'm proud, Jim, to still remember it. Why, I could tell you—"

Scalper Jim asserted all ten feet of his height.

Marvin lowered his head like the mutt he was. "I . . . I don't know, Jim. It could be that you're right. Now that you mention it, it makes a lot of sense. Why would they move it? Why would they even know it's there?" Marvin laughed. "You're smart, Jim. I always believed that. Much smarter than me. I couldn't have—look, Jim, this is the God's honest truth. I could not have done half of what I've done in my life without you."

No response came so Marvin bowed and scuffled away on all fours until he could reach an arm inside the doghouse. He explored thick cobweb and tore past what felt like a wasp's nest until he found the familiar beam and the tiny piece of metal. Years of corrosion had glued the key to the wood and Marvin set to ripping it free. One of his fingernails bent back. A moment later, another split down the center. Marvin grinned—this was progress. A moment later he reined in his arm. There it was, the padlock key, and he displayed it proudly.

Scalper Jim indicated the new sun, the minutes that were passing.

"Right, yes," Marvin said, nodding, jamming the key at the padlock, then filing it against concrete when the rust proved prohibitive. "What's that? Ha! You're right about that,

Jim. You're always right. The best hunting, it *is* always at day-break."

23 HRS., 1 MIN. AFTER IMPACT

White Special Dress did not launch a new life as they all had hoped, but it did save one. Ry would have bled to death if not for the proximity of its soft white folds. Tugging himself back from a dangerous void of total silence, he found his clothes tarred with the blood that was still slurping from his face, and so he crawled on his belly until he was able to take two handfuls of the shredded dress. Smaller bits were used to plug the hole, while longer strips were wrapped around his forehead, tighter and tighter, to staunch the flow. The cloth heavied almost at once but held heroically. *Just a little while longer,* he urged it.

Scowler was born. He popped his head from beneath what remained of the skirt's hem, his underdeveloped limbs wriggling, his fetal face split wide. He took his first steps on wobbly legs, one bestial, one sharpened steel, two feet tall at the tallest. His head, that cone of flaking rot, tipped back and the white seashell teeth, accented with Ry's red blood, filed past one another with the sound of shifting cutlery.

Ry became aware that his own mouth hung open. He closed it, if only to shut out the hot brown reek that he recognized but could not quite place. Oh, yes, he could: It was the bilious stench of the newly dehorned steers that marched through his nightmares, the mud underfoot boggy with their terrified piss and shit and blood, the air soured by the slather of wrath and the sniff of panic.

245

Scowler's jaw snapped at a speck of dress, his first solid food. He shivered, his tumors jiggling, and continued to advance. The exposed metal pipe scritched across the floorboards, shaking an orgasmic quiver all the way into the cysts of Scowler's face. When his pipe leg crossed the metal base of the dummy, there was a celebration of sparks. Ry found himself wishing that one would land on Scowler and ignite.

"Hkk-law."

How blissfully Ry had forgotten the ecstatic, asphyxiated gobble.

"Hkk-law, law-hkk!"

Scowler tottered closer and Ry drew up his feet so as to delay physical contact a moment longer. The head swept this way, then that, bringing to light the most obvious thing: Scowler, with those shallow depressions for eyes, was blind. A blast of hope galvanized Ry. It wasn't too late! He could tiptoe away, fold up the ladder, close the attic door, nail it shut. But Scowler navigated well enough with his teeth. He gnawed at the dummy's belly, pulling up tiny cotton hernias. He swung left, burying his teeth into a stack of magazines, uncovering typeface innards. He corrected his course and toothed the floor, flecks of pure white chipping the stained hardwood.

"Hkk-law, hk'a, tk'a, tk-tk!"

If Ry did not speak, Scowler might chew himself right up Ry's leg.

"Hello," Ry blurted.

Scowler went still and silent.

The head circulated like a satellite dish until the hollow eyes locked onto the voice's origin. There came a sound like the plinking of the highest piano keys and Ry recognized it immediately. It was a hundred sharp teeth adjusting all at once—it was a grin. Scowler had been waiting so long for this conversation.

"Kt—kl, va, va, tk-tk, hr'wo-gep-gep-gep. Sk-t! Crrrr, sk, sk, lu—zu, zu. Ak! Kr'uh-kr-zni—uf. Hk! Hk! Zw, i, lok-a-tik-tik. Hwa'fwa. D'str, pk-a-pk—quish! Dak! Ssa, sstra, p-p-p-p-p-pluk! Dak! H'wosh. Ka, sa, ma—hm. A-a. Tk! Sk-t! La, raaa. Tk!"

"Please, I . . ."

"Hzch-st fet p'n, d-d-d. Meb, bem, eb, em—tk! Wz? Fa. Zep—zep, rep, de'cat-at-at-at-at! Chwok h'h'hd, swa beh ar-mar, ssa. Tk, hud. Nya-da-hoo, hoo. Yer n'ning seh—seh-nin! Nin! Seh-nin! Dsss. G've, hm, uh sus ta-ta-ta, bol! Wah; hss'foo. Fo, foo. Lkht! Wkht! Hweee, scri-bli-gli zaa-wiz, rt-tk! Lk-tk! Thro ciy twi, twi, twi. Ja bett czzzt, zip— ra, tis-d-d-d-d-d! Ri. Ri-hd! Spk-tk-rk-it-tk-rk-a, cr'g'hrrrud, hrrrud i'dk. Blee-sg pik-hs, es-soph-fk-fk, gus—bem, gus. K! Cwhd! St-t! Ty, wk! N'v, n'v, m-m-m-tk-a-tk-a. Wh? Scow! Tk? Scow! Ra, ra, sla-a-sby-tip, Ja bett nya, nya. Vek! Vek! Qk, sek! Hzch-st, seh'nin, tk, hud, hss'foo! N'fva! Hkk, law. Mn, mn, mn. Tk!"

The cacophony felt to Ry like pins into skin. His mouth fell open to let out a cry of pain, and that's when the cloud of sound and the stench of steer swirled up inside him, and when his senses finally cleared and he parted his lips to tell himself that he was all right, out came the wrong kinds of noises—Scowler noises.

Scowler tapped his metal leg against the floor, a call for attention.

For the first time in hours—no, days; no, years—Ry did not feel torn between competing personalities or destinies. He was a complete being with only one thing on his mind:

Tk. Lovely, lovely *tk, tk, tk.* When he looked at Scowler he saw someone just like himself: ugly, inconsequential, but possessed with a raw power that just might surprise everyone. Ry began to laugh, even though it felt like sobbing.

23 HRS., 6 MINS. AFTER IMPACT

Currents of energy screwed individual hairs deeper into his lip so that it felt as if his mustache were crawling back up inside of him. It was an exciting sensation. How could he have let anyone, much less that gutless kid, handle this glorious gem? Marvin squatted over it, basking in the creamy texture of the steam and how it packed like wet sand into his sinuses. It was a nice, heavy feeling. A feeling of gravity. Of consequence.

Scalper Jim lorded over the crater.

"I know, Jim, I know," Marvin said. "Just let me have this moment."

There was a breeze. He heard it rustle through Black Glade, then slalom about his bald head in a way that made him feel incomparably awake. Dawn's light was weak but when he spread his arms he could tell that his wingspan was wide enough to encircle the rock. Its porous surface likely meant that it was more awkward than heavy. And even if it was heavy, he was strong—there hadn't been much else to do in the pen besides pump iron. In truth, there was another, better reason he had never felt such strength: Scalper Jim. It was good to finally be joined by a worthy partner.

Marvin sat down and dropped both legs into the muddy water. He slid from the bank and held his breath until both feet finished sinking into the hot muck. The brown water sloshed just above his knees. He had expected it to have cooled since he last felt it, but it was still plenty warm. In fact, the pool's lowest level was downright scorching. He felt a twinge of unease. Unsure footing, heavy rock, hot water—was this even possible?

Scalper Jim's shadow struck the crater like a sundial.

With his old buddy Jim at his side, of course he could pull it off. A warm memory came to him: Scalper Jim emerging from the dust and smoke of the Bluefeather rubble, pointing the way out with his arms of impervious oak. Marvin had been pleased to see Jim, though not entirely surprised. He had been privately speaking to the Indian for years, much as other inmates murmured to Jesus. It's true, he had not confessed to Jo Beth that his escape had been orchestrated by a wooden Indian, but he knew that a master strategist like Jim would understand his reasons.

The memory segued into a second scene that was not as pleasant. Cutting through a field on the way to the farm, Marvin had come across a man. At first Marvin had been startled; to be totally honest with himself, he'd even been a little bit frightened. Were the police that crafty? Then he had locked eyes with the man and recognized him from Bluefeather. Jeremiah. Marvin never forgot a name. That was shock enough before he noticed the old man's clothes. They were *his*. He recognized the slacks, the long underwear shirt, the distinctive blots of his sweat stains. Marvin had felt sick to his stomach and had turned in the opposite direction.

But Scalper Jim thought differently and snagged Jeremiah as the old man darted past. Marvin stepped carefully into the next row, at least he thought he remembered doing that, and observed from a safe distance as Scalper Jim picked up the old man by his saggy jowls. Marvin was not sure this punishment was necessary but could not help but watch. Here was Scalper Jim, the best killer in the world, and Marvin had front-row seats.

It had been a textbook scalping.

Once they had reached the farm, Marvin had been left to handle his family alone. That he had failed shamed him to no end, but Scalper Jim did not appear to place blame. The team was back together—that was the important thing. On their way to the crater Jim had acknowledged the ugly yellow Beetle and Marvin had happily removed the battery cables. No one could be permitted to ruin the dream of him, Jim, Sniggety, and the meteorite driving off together into the sunset.

"Can't wait, Jim." Marvin chuckled. "So much to look forward to."

He sunk his arms below the surface and curved them around the circumference of the rock, but paused just short of grabbing hold. The heat was severe enough to make his palms perspire underwater. If the Professor, poor guy, were here, he would call this behavior reckless. Marvin appreciated that, but he also understood something that the Professor, for all of his book smarts, never could: what it meant to have waged a war against a piece of God's earth and won. It meant—it had always meant—sacrifice.

He hugged the rock with all of his might. The emotion he felt was wistful: Here was his final act as a farmer. But the true nature of the task did not reveal itself until he began to lift. The meteorite unstuck noisily from the mud, Marvin's legs tottered beneath the weight, and then heat began its fast infection. Oh, it burned, how wonderfully it burned!

And that wet sizzle, what a sound! But be calm, be steady, there was no reason for worry, because these arms were made of wood and one thing about wood is that it feels no pain.

23 HRS., 8 MINS. AFTER IMPACT

Ry believed that, given the chance, Scowler could devour entire worlds. What he could not do, however, was operate doors—he was just too short. Ry set him at the foot of the staircase and took a moment to deal with the front door. No one was getting out of here before Scowler's business was completed. He secured all three locks. Then he picked up Scowler, conveniently doll-sized again, and jammed his leg through a link in the chain lock. It made a statement, he thought.

A figure rushed across the dining room. Ry told Scowler that he would be back and began moving in that direction. His foot dragged a bit and Ry believed he could hear the metal of his exposed leg bone—he had an exposed leg bone, didn't he?—as it gouged Jo Beth's floor. He reached the edge of the dining room and paused to take in the scene. A fly flew into his open mouth, got lucky, and bounced off one of his teeth. He had so many of them, it seemed.

Sarah was wearing shoes for the first time in a day and moving around so fast she appeared to levitate. She spotted Ry while Jo Beth stood at the table before a lethal buffet of kitchen implements, trying to decide if the meat cleaver was the one she really wanted most.

"Mom." Sarah squinted into the dark dining room. "Mom, look."

Jo Beth's protective instinct defaulted to the back door.

When a threat in that direction failed to manifest, she followed her daughter's gaze until she, too, saw the figure looming from the adjacent room. Jo Beth forgot the cleaver and stepped closer, halting at the entryway right by the phone. Ry had a vision of blocking his mother with his arm at this very spot while she listed all of the reasons why they needed to leave the farm. The memory had to be fiction. No one would dream of abandoning this land before the harvest was in.

"He's chained by the doghouse," Jo Beth said. "I've got the spare car keys but we're going to have to circle way out by the machine shed because of the gun. Be ready to run. Ry? Got it?"

Jo Beth started to turn away, but her eyes had begun to adjust to the darkness of the dining room and she noticed something awry, the blots of blood that mosaicked Ry's jeans or the raspberry hue of his shirt or the orange coagulation that crusted his face and neck. Or perhaps it had something to do with her beloved gown, reincarnated as mangled bandages pasted to her son's head.

"Oh my—" Her tongue died halfway through the oath. "Oh my—"

"He looks dead." Sarah clutched her cheeks like a parody of someone in shock. "Is he? Mom? He looks dead!"

Jo Beth made a vague gesture in Sarah's direction.

"He's not." Her voice was not at all convincing.

Jo Beth inched closer, rapt by the snarl of fabric gathered at her son's forehead. One of her hands rose and Ry idly wondered if it were coming to rest upon his heart or head. Instead the fingers lighted softly against her own lips.

"Can you make it?" she whispered. "Tell me honestly."

Ry adjusted the giant cave of his toothed mouth.

252

"Hk-tk," he said. "Hk'a-tk."

Jo Beth's neck seemed to melt. "Oh, Ry."

"He's dead," Sarah said from somewhere in the kitchen.

"No." This time the denial was sterner. "Your brother is not dead."

Ry became aware of something incredible. This woman and this girl were both ready to cry. For *him*. He could hear the brittle respiration, smell the salty pulse in the wrists and necks, follow how the eyelids blinked to keep the ocular organs moist. These little biological events delighted him. Being made of liquid and bone rather than cloth and steel might make you breakable, but being breakable, he decided, was a thrilling thing. He thought he might block Scowler from his brain, just for a moment, and reach out for this woman to see if she did the same.

Then came the sound of the porch door being kicked from its hinges.

23 HRS., 10 MINS. AFTER IMPACT

Jo Beth spun around. Her elbow caught the phone, which clattered from its cradle and felled the miniature pine tree. Sarah was closest to the door, and the way that she looked at her mother, and the way that her mother looked at her, you'd think she was tumbling down the side of a crater instead of standing mere feet away.

Footsteps crashed across the porch. Dishes rattled in their cabinets. Each step took longer than the previous, as if the walker himself were constructed of solidifying cement. Jo Beth's paralysis broke and she lashed out with an arm, snatching Sarah's wrist and pulling her into the dining room.

Something thumped against the kitchen door and both mother and daughter cried out. Ry felt only a quickening of interest, and he moved toward the door just as Jo Beth and Sarah moved away. He shouldered by them without a look.

The knob moved, but it was a sloppy job and it rattled back into starting position. Jo Beth muttered something to Sarah, and Ry could sense how hard his mother was staring at the cleaver. There were reasons they did not run. This could be the overdue appearance of the police or a neighbor. Both were legitimate possibilities, if not for the coppery stink that even now crept through the windows. Ry knew who it was and could not wait—he even considered helping with the door. Then the bolt went flush with the faceplate and there was a soft, familiar *cluck*, and then the door swung wide along caterwauling hinges.

Marvin squatted upon the porch with his fingers dug into the crevices of the meteorite he carried. The steam gushing from the rock had scalded off his face so that his black mustache floated atop a glistening red mask. Against this open wound, Marvin's grin was blindingly white. The eyes, having lost most of their lids, seemed twice as large as was possible, and they swirled with what looked like childlike wonderment before zeroing in on Ry. Marvin's every muscle undulated with the effort required to handle such weight. The pause was charged and filled with the sound of sizzling fat.

"Very." The voice howled like a fugitive wind. "Heavy."

He baby-stepped outward for balance and the shotgun, pinned between chest and rock, crashed to the porch, the barrel blackened and smoking. With exquisite strain he stepped over it and into the kitchen. His lips were burned away but the skin around the mouth shaped into a grin anyway, and in the gap between the front teeth Ry could see steam rising from a fat purple tongue.

Marvin bent his quaking knees and allowed gravity to roll the meteorite from his embrace. The sound of pulling duct tape ripped through the kitchen as the skin of his chest and arms came off with it. The rock slammed to the floor with the sound of buckling wood and sat there steaming, its uneven terrain coated with what looked like lasagna—orderly layers of shirt, skin, and muscle. Marvin blinked at the meteorite, then at his own landscape of exposed tissue. He flexed an arm experimentally and the whole family watched the contraction of a gray tendon and the plumping of a blue bicep.

"Marvin!" The wife's panic was learned, instant. "Oh, God! Marvin!"

He staggered and runny blobs of flesh swung like taffy. It was a weak moment and looked wrong on Marvin Burke. After waiting for the flaps of skin to settle, he nodded briskly at the meteorite as if asking for one moment, please, while he caught his breath.

"Don't move," Jo Beth said. "Don't move."

The charred leftovers of his lips stirred as if he wanted a kiss.

Ry reached down to the table and took up the cleaver.

"Wait." Jo Beth waved her hands. "You don't have to. He'll just . . ."

The blade sang in Ry's palm and Ry sang back: *Tk, tk, tk.*

Further words failed Jo Beth. Instead she took handfuls of her son's shirt. He stiffened. He was kin to Scowler now, and those like Scowler were not to be touched, not unless you wanted to risk losing a finger, or worse. Ry swiveled upon the sharpened point of his steel leg—he had a leg of steel, didn't he?—and looked upon the one called Jo Beth, and behind her, yanking on her mother's arm as her mother yanked on Ry, the one called Sarah.

"Take the keys," Jo Beth pleaded. "Take the car. Send help. Ry? Ry?"

What he heard, though, was:

Reeeeeeeeeeeeeeeeeeeeeeeeeeeeeeeeee!

"Ry! Come on, let's go!" This is what Sarah said.

What he heard was:

Aiiiiiiii-iiiiiiiii-iiiiiiiiiiiiiii!

This is what monsters did. They misled. Ry did not appreciate such ploys, not one bit. In fact, they made his chest thicken with anger. But Scowler made it clear that the animal in the kitchen needed tending before other scores were settled. Ry grinned because he knew a thing or two about tending to animals, especially the bloodletting that came when they were done serving their purposes. Ry arranged the cleaver edge-out.

"Tk," he said.

The heat of the meteorite had whipped the puddle of Marvin's blood into pink fizz. The great farmer hunched and inspected this metamorphosis as he had once inspected proud seedlings. When he finally looked up, the swampy underside of his chin remained stuck to his sternum. With neck flesh dangling in ribbons, Marvin contemplated his son and the weapon he brandished. Placing a gluey hand to a knee, the man drew himself to full height. He would fight, despite how his body was melting. Ry could sense Scowler's high regard for such devotion.

The cleaver swung.

The aim was flawed and found only the last knuckle of

Marvin's right hand. A bit of finger was flung to the table, though Marvin chose not to notice in a way that was almost polite. Ry leaned over the pale hunk and experienced a storm of revulsion that was one hundred percent Ry Burke, zero percent Scowler. Would his father need to be disassembled joint by joint? He'd never be able to do it. A bead of blood squeezed from the nub and Ry looked away, feeling the same sickness that had paralyzed him nine years ago with the bat and the shears. Maybe Mr. Furrington and Jesus Christ were right.

Scowler chirped, urging him to look again.

The piece of finger had been replaced by a small nugget of wood, the drop of blood by a scattering of sawdust. Relaxation crashed over Ry like water. Scowler had gifted him with his special brand of blindness. He could see what he *wanted* to see and it was better, so much better. Chopping wood—that was something he knew how to do. He sighed and turned away from the table, eager to get started.

Marvin Burke had been replaced by a wooden Indian so tall the peaks of his headdress poked through the top of the ceiling. Ry nodded at Scalper Jim, a salutation between warriors. His appearance at this moment felt natural, though in truth Ry had not anticipated the Indian's size. Marvin's proxy was a goliath whose strength was derived from the simplicity of his formation; it would be difficult to break a hand that had no fingers, challenging to damage a chest that was but one solid block.

But he would try.

Ry attacked, only now it was Scowler, not Ry, and sawed-off steel, not a cleaver. The whetted edge struck Scalper Jim's defending elbow and cracked like an axe ricocheting from a tree trunk. Scowler's little body was shaken and as he recovered he heard the splintering sound of Scalper Jim's mighty limbs shifting into combat position. Jim did not go for the shotgun and this too Scowler admired. If there was anything that Marvin had made clear about his admiration for Jim, it was the Indian's disinterest in the white man's toys.

The tomahawk was at chest level and rising. Scowler spluttered excitedly and scurried to the right, coming in fast with another stab. This time the blade gouged across the slab of Scalper Jim's left arm, carving out a curled ribbon. Sawdust hit Scowler's empty eyes and coated his flashing teeth. He clucked in glee.

It was this injured arm that Scalper Jim extended with authority. His fist, the size of a breadbox, cracked the underside of Scowler's chin. Scowler reeled, feeling the collapse of his head's understructure, the snap of strings within his cloth neck, the loosening of nails all over. His metal skeleton began trembling, then shaking, then jackhammering with the punishing pulse of an Indian chant coming from inside the wooden colossus.

If one did not know better, the chant could be mistaken for a tuneless hum.

"Hmmmm hm hm hmmmm.

"Hmmmm hm hm hmmmm.

"Hmmmm hm hm hmmmm.

"Hmmmm hm hm hmmmm."

The story told by these tribal noises was a violent one with themes of loss, wrath, and revenge. It was almost too much to take. Scowler's head lolled on its busted neck and bled onto the floor a dozen seashell teeth. Certain emotions he knew well—rage and fury—but this thing called fear was new. There was no denying the truth that towered before him: Scalper Jim was bigger and stronger and had fought more bravely in larger numbers of fiercer battles. The cries of alarm coming from the human females made perfect sense because Scalper Jim was unbeatable.

That line of thinking did not last.

He was Scowler.

Scowler.

TK!

Scalper Jim's tomahawk dove and Scowler sidestepped it. He scampered face-first into the Indian's shins, clamped down with shark jaws, and began to climb the leg with his teeth, taking big bites of everything along the way, relishing the smooth coffee of maple wood, the bitter cinnamon of sandpaper. He munched thigh, groin, and stomach, while Scalper Jim flung his tomahawk at the height of his usual enemies. Scowler was no cowboy. For that matter, he was no neighbor farmer, no seed salesman, no jailer, no wife, no escaped convict encountered and scalped in the corn. He was Scowler, an uncategorizable thing of which there was no double or even words to accurately describe. He was brutality, he was pain, and this slothful redskin never even had a chance.

Scowler's teeth punched through Scalper Jim's throat and hung tight even as the Indian began to flail. The screaming from the humans in the next room increased, while Scowler's mouth flooded with wood chips and spilled over with sawdust. Finally the weight of this scrap wood became too much and he dropped to the floor. Scalper Jim had no knees but they buckled anyway—with two earsplitting pops both legs snapped in half. He fell, taking out the kitchen table in the process, landing so hard that his left hand and right arm broke off and a fissure rent his torso from neck to loincloth.

Scowler leapt, circled, and did what he did best: He ate.

The next few minutes were lost to him. His face was buried in (guts) wood, ripping past (skin) bark, and chewing up (organs) knots, though there were times when instead of the coarseness of lumber he swore his tongue tasted slick patties of warm meat and the spurt of tangy liquid. But he fought through it—he ate through it—and when he finally arose, smacking his damp cloth lips, he thought he had never felt so full and powerful, so quaking with the adrenaline of disaster.

But there was a funny feeling in his belly.

He recognized it and flashed his tiny teeth.

He was still hungry.

23 HRS., 19 MINS. AFTER IMPACT

Jo Beth took Sarah's wrist and darted through the dining room, into the hall, and up against the front door. The locks were in place but she might have had time to throw them if not for Scowler, the four-inch doll, jammed through the chain and beaming at them. It was a fright too many. She took Sarah's hand and they scrambled up the stairs.

Ry watched them flee. His eyes fell upon Scowler, beckoning to him from the front door, which meant he had vacated Ry's head, at least for now. Ry licked his briny chin and nodded. Yes, yes, he was coming. But as he made his way across the kitchen, he noticed a wadded matchbook with the logo of a tavern and a rumpled pack of Luckies. What was spread across the rest of the linoleum did not interest him, and he narrowed his focus to these discreet few inches. With his toe he pushed aside the matches and cigarettes, then nudged at the breast pocket of a prison shirt until it gave up its hidden cargo.

It was a small wooden carving of Scalper Jim. Marvin Burke, a man known for truth, had lied. He had not, in fact, put away childish things. Prison, Ry saw, had crushed the man until he had admitted to loneliness, the most shameful of things, and had found a way to craft a replica of his old friend from some esoteric scrap of wood. Using the bluntest of tools—Ry imagined the rounded edges of spoons, the harmless plastic of a toothbrush handle—the whittling must have taken an eternity. But it had been worth it. His father had clutched the toy warrior as Ry had once snuggled a turquoise teddy bear, and it had gotten the man through hell, out of prison, and then back into hell once more.

The figurine had broken in the skirmish. One hand and one arm had snapped off, and the torso was practically cracked in two. Ry felt his spirits taken by melancholy. Finding this speck of humanity was the last thing he wanted. His focal point widened enough to see that the floor, the walls, and even the ceiling were slopped not with the shavings of carpentry but the viscera of a hog house, and the carcass at his feet was a man who had been eviscerated, his chest cavity cracked open like a nut, dark currents still bubbling from the countless primitive gorings. There were sour chunks in Ry's cheeks and stringy fibers caught in his teeth. They were the flesh of organs, he knew that, just not which ones.

Ry turned away, vomit stewing in his throat.

Footsteps rattled across the second story. Ry's nose jerked upward, attuned to a predator's frequency: *Tk-tk-tk!* He scanned the ceiling, wondering where on earth they thought they were going: *Tk-tk-sh'sh!* Scowler cackled appreciatively. That was more like the boy he knew, the soldier he'd travel alongside into any glade of any level of blackness. Ry felt his nausea resolve into something warm, something close to lust but even more primal. Scowler was offering to climb into his head once more, but this time Ry wanted to do it himself, to show his brother what he was made of. He still, after all, had the cleaver.

Ry covered the ground floor in an instant and snatched up Scowler without slowing. Each staircase step was to be relished. The family photos opposite the banister were enjoyably insane, weird portraits of smiling buffoons with their arms around one another as if they had all the time in the world to escape doom. He tipped each one with a single finger until it slipped from its nail and exploded upon the stairs behind him.

The upstairs hallway was just as fascinating. He could see into Sarah's room, a pastel junkyard of jilted toys and kids' books; he could even see her beloved spiral notebook, right alongside a dog-eared volume titled *My Stars!: Asteroids, Comets, and Meteors.* Craning his neck, he could see through the ceiling door into the attic, where a piece of actual meteorite—not to mention some battered old dolls—lay forgotten in a nest of attractive though frivolous fabric. Scowler betrayed a single peep of nostalgia. He had spent a lot of time up there.

The one closed door belonged to his mother's bedroom. Ry sidled up to it and listened. Behind it he heard the rodent frettings of animals still clinging to life. Ry's mind was a hectic place now, but he seemed to recall standing in this spot many years ago while the one called Jo Beth lay on the other side making very similar, very desperate noises. It was funny, he mused, the difference a little perspective made. In a few moments the woman might remember those bindings and wish she had never been cut free.

23 HRS., 23 MINS. AFTER IMPACT

Scalper Jim had failed him.

It was enough to make even a man like Marvin Burke cry. Instead, translucent goo seeped from a ruptured eye. He did not remember that particular injury, but looking over himself with the eye that still worked, he found that he did not remember fielding the lion's share of these damages. Bones popped their white daggers through clothes and tender morsels of flesh were scattered as if by a storm. He looked bad, but he could not help but find the sight of his massacre comforting. It reminded him of the way soil used to look in the wake of the combine's tiller.

He flicked the remains of Scalper Jim from his chest. Nearby rested the stamped pack of Luckies and the match-book. He took them up in a fist. It would be nice, he thought, for his final inhale to taste of nicotine, and even better, he speculated, to watch the smoke escape through the new holes of his chest like his spirit lifting from his body. It was grand in a way—a lot better than wasting away in a cell.

His eye fell upon the pine tree.

The clenching of spiteful muscles squeezed blood from a dozen mortal wounds. Here he was, perfecting his death, and that tree lay there mocking him. It had been the first thing he had spotted when sneaking into the house, a sight so offensive it had all but erased the image of Jeremiah's scalping. With its dirty roots and brown needles and moronic sash of holiday lights, the tree represented all that had gone wrong with the model family that he'd tried to fashion. He'd made mistakes, sure, but none so unforgiveable as those made by his wife and son. The crops were dead, the counters were dirty, but still the imbeciles took time to dress up this piece-of-shit shrub.

The tree was on its side near his feet. He began to prop himself on an elbow so that he could reach it, but halfway up he felt a shift inside his torso cavity as his organs prepared to spill onto the floor. He lay back down. His skull felt lightweight and his vision was pinkish. At last, though, his headache was gone. It felt good to think so clearly, so good that he laughed. That meteorite to his left, sunk into melted linoleum, he didn't even want to look at it. Clarity snaked through his busted chest as if it had been trapped inside for days. Coming to the farm had been a bad idea. It was so obvious now. Once here he'd had an entire day to run, yet had not. Stupid, stupid. His mind, whetted for so long, had been dulled by the rock, or by Jim, and the most precious hours of his life had been squandered. For a man who prided himself on efficiency, it was the bitterest pill.

His body convulsed so violently that his fingers went rigid and brushed what felt like glass. Marvin gathered energy into his neck and took a look. It was a bulb at the end of the string of Christmas lights, which had unfurled when the tree had fallen. He extended his fingers—one of the tips was missing, he noted—and scratched them across the cord until it was close enough for him to take hold of the bulb. It was blue.

He instructed himself to flex his arm, while keeping his eye on the ceiling so that he could avoid the cutaway view of his bicep. Caught by the string of lights, the tree pulled closer. He employed his other hand too, the one threatening to shed its glove of skin, and was able to slide the tree alongside him like a wife in a marital bed. The topmost needles poked into the raw meat of his face and flaked away the charred crust of his mustache. Marvin sighed as deeply as he dared; it was pleasant to feel his mustache one more time.

Operating matches with the tip of a middle finger missing was surprisingly tricky. Finally he positioned a match sufficiently and flicked it across the graphite the same way he'd done it all of his life, and presto—a flame. He grinned. The heat warmed the enamel of his teeth. Not the same as taking a drag, but close. He brought the match toward the dry needles. It hovered too close; it drifted too far. Marvin chuckled up blood and felt sympathy for poor old Phinny Rochester—gauging distance with one eye was no mean feat.

Marvin was concentrating so hard that he missed the precise moment that his lungs failed to inflate. They settled like a wedding veil dropped to the floor. While registering this, he also missed the final contraction of his heart. He only noticed, seconds later, how the babbling brook of his blood had stopped.

Time to. Move. He touched the. Fire to the tree. It. Caught immediately. This would show. Him. The boy. Who'd fought him. Somehow won. Though there had been. Another one. Hadn't there? Hadn't he. Seen? A little? Beast? Chewing at? His Achilles tendon? As he had. Once. Cut a man's. In prison? He wasn't sure. Nothing was. Certain. Just. Smoke. And look—so. Much. Fire, so. Quickly. This. Would show. Them. What. Kind of. Man. He.

The secret key ring of Marvin Burke had never been found. Not during the trial, not after he had been sent to Pennington. So Ry did not make a big thing of it: He turned the bedroom doorknob and it opened easily. The one called Jo Beth and the one called Sarah both shrunk their shoulders and whipped their heads in unison.

They were trying to leave out the window. A sensible idea, given that the porch was right below; if they weren't too clumsy about it, they could escape without anything worse than a stubbed toe or a jammed finger. The problem was that Ry had nailed shut the troublesome window on Sunday afternoon. The room was a coffin.

Ry entered feeling like an owner. This bed, these walls, that window, this house, the whole farm—it was all at his mercy, just like Scowler said. He strode forward with the cleaver extended in one hand, Scowler in the other, and caught a glimpse of himself in the dresser mirror. He was coated with so much gore that it looked as if he had been skinned. He turned away from this promising vision and placed Scowler upon the bed, even taking a moment to situate him on a pillow so he could watch. Scowler whimpered and began burrowing. As surely as Sniggety could sniff out roadkill, Scowler could smell the old blood on the flip side of the mattress.

The one called Sarah backed herself into the corner nearest the window. The one called Jo Beth tore her eyes from the creature on the bed and moved an arm's length from the pane so that her body stood between her two children. She held up a hand as if believing that the cleaver wouldn't cut through it like butter. *Tk-hraw! Tk-tk!* Ry advanced and thought how wonderful it was that their final confrontation would take place here, in this room, the secret dark heart of the farm. The females would be split open and who knew if sawdust or something else would fall out.

"Stop," Jo Beth said. "You stop right there."

Ry did stop. Her voice had changed since he'd last heard it. It puzzled him. The tone was not the delicate china arrangement he recalled from the crater. Nor was it the screeching falcon from when she had slapped him. He searched his memory, an act now as effortless as paging through a phone book, and traced the tone of voice back to nine years ago in this very spot.

Things that emerged stronger from suffering were to be mistrusted.

"Now you're coming after me." Her voice was as flat and simple as a plate. "I understand that. I hate what I did to you. You should know that. I hurt you—you think I don't know that? When the teachers stopped believing in you and the therapists stopped believing in you, I stopped believing in you too. That's all there is to it. All right? Now put that thing down."

On the bed, Scowler ceased his hunt for blood.

Jo Beth's lips curled up against her teeth. She looked ready to bite. This right here, her normal face, Ry realized with fright, was the woman's monster form. It had been brazenly displayed right in front of his eyes all these years.

"I kept you here when you should have been out there, moving on, doing I'm not even sure what. College?" She shook her head once, and the sweaty mat of her hair flung and returned like houseflies caught on flypaper. "That's my fault and I know it. But it's your fault, too. You understand? If enough time passes, the world ruins everybody."

Scowler broke his silence with a lowing. His cornmeal guts began to rattle.

Sarah appeared to hear it. Her nose crinkled and she flapped her hands as if they were covered with wasps. Ry took a step back, the cleaver growing heavy in his fist. No one but him, the special boy, the one true fighter, was supposed to be able to hear Scowler. But that wasn't what Sarah was detecting.

"Smoke." She was sniffing the air. "Mom, smoke."

Jo Beth's hand veered toward the girl, but her eye line did not shift.

"You need to lower that," she said to her son. "You know who you're acting like?"

Scowler's lowing intensified. Ry remembered a snippet of something a therapist had once suggested, a ridiculous assertion, that Scowler, more or less, was Marvin. If that were true, who killed whom downstairs? And if Ry was becoming Scowler, didn't that mean . . . Ry pressed a hand to his forehead. A strip of crusted dress fabric fell away. The wound beneath had scabbed, though when he touched it the scab slid away on mucus.

"It's outside," Sarah said.

Ry gazed out the window, and yes, there was smoke, mushrooming upward along with the soft whooshing and crackling munch of fire. He contemplated whether all of them should take this outside and sift through their complaints while at a safer distance, but Scowler brayed, digging into Ry's mind with a single desire: Blood. Ry's vision paled with the overlay of Scowler's blindness, and his teeth began to divide, multiply, and sharpen.

"Ry, you look at me. You listen to me. I had Sarah to protect. I had me to protect too. Just because you're about twenty years younger than me, that means I don't matter? I'm all alone out here. In the middle of all this worthless dirt. I'm practically old. And what have I done, what do I have to my name? And still, *still*, I know that I must matter to someone. Doesn't that have to be true? Isn't it possible it's you? I needed you here, for me, for *me*, and if you had to be hurt some of the time, well, so did I. We took turns, Ry. Now put that *down*."

"Oh, no!" Sarah pointed at the floor. Wisps of black smoke were eking through the warped boards, and she danced to avoid stepping on the slithering plumes. It looked like fun and Ry felt a brotherly compulsion to play along. His feet—his feet of flesh, not steel—were leaden, but they began to run through the motions, up, down, up, down.

Scowler shrieked his displeasure at this juvenile behavior and Ry clutched at his skull, the cleaver nearly performing a self-scalping. He felt the beast tightening the marionette strings of his arteries and veins. His skeleton was manipulated and the cleaver began to rise. Ry fought it; his whine became a cry. Sharpened seashell teeth began to emerge from his gums and he bit down on his lips to delay their arrival. The pressure built. His lips began to peel apart and quickly, bloodily, in the seconds before Scowler's jaws took over, he mouthed Sarah's word: No. No. No. Its repetition made it come easy, as easy as *tk-tk-tk*, as easy as an Indian chant, as easy as recited facts about meteors that would never, ever fall. Blood poured from his right nostril before he could finish. He licked it from his upper lip, feeling against his tongue a single remnant of a phony mustache.

"Fire! Fire!" Sarah's exclamations came rehearsed from school safety lessons. "The stairs! The hall! Fire!"

"That doll on the bed." Jo Beth's voice was strained. "That stupid doll."

Ry sobbed in pain. The soft marrow of his bones was being threaded by serrated steel. He doubled over—he was shorter now, much shorter—and watched his nosebleed pour into black smoke until the drainage ceased because he no longer had a nose, while his head—top-heavy, conical—swirled with noises every bit as compelling as Jo Beth's. *Tk-ch-hwr'ch-tk-tk!*

"You think I kept those dolls for you." Her every word dizzied the smoke. "You're so wrong it makes me sick. I kept them for me. I kept them to cover my ass, because I was worried I'd fail my kids as bad as I failed this shit-hole farm. I kept them as a way out. For me, Ry. Not for you."

The fire in the hallway ate some floor, rolling their way. The heat doubled.

Smoke could not hide Jo Beth's heartbroken expression. "It was that goddamned woman, Linda. That woman who barely knew us. She was a better mother than me; she's the one who convinced you that you were special and smart and had a future and could do anything you wanted. And I hated her for it because you believed every word."

Was it true? That Ry had ever had such uplifting thoughts?

Even more incredible, was it possible such things were true?

Jo Beth nodded. "That woman was right."

Scowler's shriek shattered the mirror. Ry recoiled and spotted the tiny troll pulling himself across the bed the fastest way possible—by his two withered arms, his razor leg halving the mattress behind him. The carnivore mouth widened, nearly ate its own head, but its hysterical sounds were swallowed by the hurricane howl of the blaze. All at once the fire was everywhere, twisting like serpents over the floor, reaching like vines across the ceiling.

Sarah screamed, threw herself at the window, and tore at the sill.

Jo Beth grabbed her son's collar. Here was the physical contact Scowler had wanted. The parts inside of Ry that pined for violence, the bones and the teeth, drew together like magnets and the cleaver hopped to striking position. Ry clenched his muscles but some of them had turned into traitorous, jellified cancers. The blade teetered in the balance.

"I've kept you in a little box, just like them, so you couldn't escape." Jo Beth's forearms extended from the smoke, took his face, not caring that his teeth were sharp, his skin leathered and frayed. "But I'm letting you go. Right now. This is your chance, baby. Make me proud."

The wall cracked in two. Patterns of wallpaper became instantly mismatched. The lamp swinging from the ceiling tore free, its electrical cord ripping from the plaster across the ceiling, down the wall, an endless umbilical. The floor opened up with an elephantine sigh, and decorative lamps, a jewelry box, and a half-dozen dusty bottles of perfume skidded across the surface of the dresser as it pitched. Red embers billowed up from the first floor and attached themselves to everything like hellfire insects. The dresser dipped like a seesaw, then paused on its fulcrum. Floorboards caught beneath the weight snapped and fired across the room like spears. Sarah took one in the back, Ry the shoulder.

He straightened, for a moment a man and nothing more or less. Death, violence; survival, violence. These equations were jumbled, had been in his classroom history books, would be till humankind's dusk. The meteorite had changed nothing about these problematic rituals; its silt had merely acted as the sugar that made ordinary poisons go down easier. The decisions, all of them, remained his, and Jo Beth was right. It was now or never.

Long ago in this room he had cut his mother free.

At last she was returning the favor.

The cleaver flung backward, slicing the smoke into two continents. Ry hurled himself forward, the blade taking only a few hairs off Jo Beth's head and a single button from the sleeve of Sarah's jacket. The edge of the cleaver struck the very center of the window. Glass shattered, hot wind sucked inward. Ry reeled and Scowler leapt onto his back, sinking one thousand teeth into his spine. Ry went blind and clung to the frame, gobbling down noxious fumes, anything to suffocate the parasite. The initial implosion of smoke roared over his head, and he felt an inrush of cooler temperatures and glimpsed only stray tongues of fire below. The north side of the house had a favorable wind. They could still make it.

More of the floor caved in with the sound of steers making a final mad dash through the corn.

Scowler tunneled inside of him. Bones were chipped, organs pierced, fluids boiled. Ry kept focus by taking advantage of Scowler's finest classroom talent: Math. He counted the curved segments of glass still clinging to the frame and recalculated them into fractions. One-third of the surface area of the window still survived, sharp enough to bleed all three of them. He raised the cleaver to do some simple subtraction but Scowler took hold of his rib cage and rattled it. Ry gasped and the cleaver toppled from his hand, cartwheeling over the sill. For a single moment he knew absolute loss. Then he saw a faraway flash, the cleaver stabbing into the lawn below, and realized that all he needed to do was follow suit.

Ry backpedaled for a running start. His final step landed upon air where there was no more floor, and he tipped backward to meet the firestorm, the meteorite, what was left of his father. But Jo Beth's fingers snatched his wrist and pulled with canny timing, and he found himself balanced upon the same heel that nine years ago was broken and minutes ago had been savage metal but now was a man's strong and healthy foot, and he turned on it and drove from it, and did so without a word or look of thanks, because such manners were unnecessary between mother and child. Lost deep inside, Scowler continued to scarf his host's intestines, but it was a loser's feast. Ry had the advantage of glorious momentum, God's gift to the young. He wondered if he always had.

His form was spectacular. Not a single inch of his tall-for-his-age body touched the frame. What glass remained was blown outward by his elbows and shoulders and hips, and the storm window never had a chance. Ry went head over feet, end over end, and before landing believed that he glimpsed his mother, way up above, already helping Sarah through the opening.

Why was the air so much cooler on his trip back down to earth?

Why was the weight of the world finally gone?

Life drained from him as steadily as if from a spigot. The last memory he carried, the one of impact, was no different from the ash raining all around him, picked up in the breeze and stolen. The only impressions left were sensory. How the breaking of bones sounded like the rending of steel, how the scuffing of skin felt like the tearing of cloth.

But he was not scared—angels were smiling at him. Their eyes were crazed and imploring. One of the angels was called Sarah and her words were too quick and too many to follow. The other was called Jo Beth, and she slapped his cheeks and through a manic smile moved her lips in the same pattern until Ry picked out the syllables: *Stay with me. Stay with me. Stay with me.*

Her face was painted with soot and she held in one hand the shotgun. This detail mattered to Ry; it meant she had dared to sprint onto the back porch of a burning house. There was a time, only a few hours ago, when he would have viewed such action as proof of her need to salvage the meteorite, to turn it into cash. The mother he believed in now was better than that. She, the greatest hero of them all, had braved toxic smoke, disfigurement, death. And all because the gun meant safety for her children and there was no telling what fresh dangers the new day would bring.

Far across the yard the fire continued to burn, insinuating itself into the daylight. The weathered dairy barn, the wilted chicken coop, the leaning corn crib, the corroded silos—all were revealed as structures of utility and grace. Someone must have rigged Ry's perception so that he had spent his whole life seeing only the ultimate futility of these structures while concealing what made them worthy, the struggle itself, the striving for a better day.

Ry would give anything for one more hour in this paradise.

He tried to raise an arm to touch their faces. The arm went nowhere. He traced his mother's panicked lips—*I shouldn't have moved you, but the fire*—and he tried to shake his head to tell her that she did right, she had always done everything right. The head did not shake. Frustration pricked at his mouth, the only part of him he could feel. He gathered his energy and pursed his lips. They leaned in, wild for his words.

And there was so much he wished to say! Troves of wisdom and insight were suddenly available to him to spend as he saw fit. He was Mr. Furrington: He believed in his mother and sister and during dark times this belief ought to light their way. He was Jesus Christ: His sacrifice would remind them of the wisdom they held like doves and how rewards would be theirs when they let those doves use their wings. He was Scowler, too: They could not let any future Marvins stand in their way, no matter what town or city or path they chose. There was a new talisman for Jo Beth and Sarah to carry and its name was Ry Burke. Please, take of him what you need.

None of this made it across his tongue. Jo Beth wiped his forehead and mouthed sympathy—*Shhh, baby, don't try to talk*—and he had no choice but to comply. After all, he was tired. He had never been so tired.

He let his neck slacken so that his right cheek dropped into overgrown grass he could not feel. The sight line did not include the blazing house, but there was plenty else to appreciate. There was the garage, a grain bin, the junk shed, the machine shed, the McCafferty Forty, even Black Glade. All things considered, not a bad final view.

At the closest edge of the field, trudging back to the crater hand in hand, were the Unnamed Three. They had not perished; Ry admonished himself for having entertained the thought. What's more, they were no longer pale or gnarled or burnt. They stood at their full, proud heights and moved like happy toys, if toys could move at all, which, of course, they could. Scowler was in the middle, swinging from the arms of his taller companions, his head bowed as if smarting from a recent scolding. On the left, Furrington hopped on one leg, his progress tireless and ebullient. On the right, the long banner of Jesus Christ's body flapped in the occasional gust. Birds, their numbers growing every second, circled the Three, the gentlest escort.

They were twenty feet into the McCafferty Forty when, one at a time, they turned around.

Furrington touched a paw to his bowler, as if to say: *Farewell, lad. We had some fun, didn't we?*

Jesus Christ pressed an open palm to the air, as if to say: *If thou needest us, thou knowest where to look.*

Scowler made no such special address. For some time he stared with blind eyes and a gaping mouth before turning away and pulling his companions in the direction of the crater. Ry thought he saw Furrington's paw touch Scowler's back with shy affection; a few seconds later, he was almost positive that Jesus Christ touched his stigmata to the top of Scowler's pointed head. Scowler's malformed feet picked up speed, began to skip. Ry could not help but smile. After so

276

much excitement, the little guy must be looking forward to lying down.

Ry would have enjoyed watching their slow act of disappearance but his body did not cooperate. His eyes closed. He felt a plummeting sensation—or was it a rising? He felt his mother's touch, just barely, but it was enough to guide him softly along an unlit path. There was a sorrow that came with entering into this void, but he told himself that was a good thing, even a great thing. You can't recognize sorrow, he reminded himself, without having first known joy.

The Soft Ear

TUESDAY, AUGUST 25, 1981

26 HRS., 0 MINS. AFTER IMPACT

He was wrapped up to his neck in a blanket so natty and hay-threaded it must have been peeled from the floor of a barn. It smelled sharp and real, and he pulled it tight around his shoulders. It was midday and Ry found himself sitting against the side of the block shed on the farm's eastern end. At his side was a mason jar filled with pump water, and from the looks of things he had drank over half of it. He had no memory of rebirth.

The house was cinder. Though it had been one of the property's smallest buildings, its obliteration made the farm look empty. Within the black smolder, white fires burned with persistence, billowing forth brown flakes that could have been flayed from Sarah's notebook. It was impossible to reconcile this modest pile of rubble with the proud house he

279

had lived his life inside, with all its familiar labyrinths and infinite dead ends. He considered the possibility that this was a dream, but he tossed that idea away upon noticing shapes inside the wreckage that did not look like wood or furniture.

A car horn honked. It took Ry a bit to appreciate the significance of the sound. He tore his eyes from the debris and watched as a dust-caked four-door sedan pulled into the grass thirty feet away, ignoring the gravel driveway because of its proximity to the house. He heard shouts of hello and saw Jo Beth approaching from the direction of the garage, clutching the shotgun in her left fist, Sarah's hand in her right. Both of them were clad in old jackets Ry had last seen housing spiders in the garage. Jo Beth waved the gun in a salutation.

Quite abruptly Ry became aware that it was a gorgeous day.

The car door opened and Kevin Crowley, a short, pudgy fellow with pale skin and curly red hair, exited. He held a weapon of his own, a rifle. He walked up to Jo Beth and extended an arm. Jo Beth hesitated, then accepted the offer and moved in for a sideways hug. The two weapons clacked in a duck language. Upon release, Kevin looked dazed but still managed to muss Sarah's hair. He said something; Jo Beth nodded and said something back. She gestured at the house. Kevin pointedly did not look at it.

Ry heard other car doors open and watched as an astonishing number of Crowleys unfolded themselves from the sedan. Kevin's wife, Peg, was the first out, followed by an indeterminate amount of girls and a single boy. They wandered closer to the remains of the house as if drawn by an interstellar magnet still possessed of a degree of power. Ry considered the trail of smoke feeding up into the sky like a twister and wondered what would happen when this meteorite dust was rained back down upon Iowa.

Ry drew the blanket close to his chin and let go of the macabre thought. Finally one of the Crowley kids began to approach. He recognized her, felt a fluttering nervousness, and almost laughed at that reaction. Still, he touched his nose to check on that zit and was relieved to find that his coat of dried gore was plenty thick enough to conceal it.

Esther Crowley stared down at him with concern.

"Ry," she said. "Are you okay?"

He nodded. It hurt his neck.

"I'm sorry," he said. The words came out mushy.

Esther cocked her head. "About what?"

Ry shrugged. "College," he said. "You were supposed to be leaving."

Esther looked at him strangely.

"It's all right," she said. "But thanks."

Even disheveled, she was a knockout. Ry licked his lips. "You all right?"

Esther shrugged. "What happened to your hair?"

Ry reached a hand up and touched the bare, scabby skin.

"It's gone," he said with wonder. He saw her worried expression and tried to sound reassuring. "It'll grow back."

Peg was suddenly there, kneeling at his side.

"Esther," she said. "Hush."

"We're just talking, Mom."

Peg's hands felt nothing like how Ry remembered Esther's hands, though they displayed similar confidence. With a thumb she pulled up his eyelids one at a time, then used her fingertips to probe his neck. Sliding her hands beneath the blanket, she pressed gingerly at his ribs and shoulders and wrists. Peg Crowley was a nurse, a fact he remembered out of nowhere, and he happily gave himself over to her satisfied nods and disapproving tsks.

Additional shadows fell over them.

"He all there?" Kevin asked. His eyes bugged at Ry's bloody visage.

"He's got a broken rib or two, maybe a fractured collarbone. His wrist here is swollen and so are both ankles. And he's cut up. . . ." Peg twisted around and squinted up at the other adults. "Jo, he's sliced to pieces. This cut in his forehead is serious. What happened here, honey?"

Jo Beth shook her head vaguely.

"It was a bad night," she said.

Peg stared at her. After a moment, she nodded. Her eyes held tears.

"I understand," Peg said. "We had a bad night too."

Ry swept his gaze across the congregated Crowleys: Esther, her dirty-faced sisters, the lone six-year-old brother with what looked like a smear of dried blood matting his arm hair. Ry was not positive, but he recalled there being eight Crowleys. He counted, got mixed up, counted again, but kept coming up with seven. But he could not trust his math, especially in this condition. It had never been his best subject.

Peg stood and wiped her hands on her dirty slacks.

"I did turn on the television, Jo, after you called. And they did eventually break the news about the prison and the . . ." She waved a hand at the clouds. "The things from the sky. I tried to call. I did. It didn't go through."

"One of those rocks hit the bridge," Kevin said. "On Route Nine. Emergency vehicles haven't been able to get through. We couldn't get through either; we were as good as trapped

282

over there. We had to go halfway to Bloughton and swing around the reservoir to get here. Otherwise we would've come earlier. It's just, we . . ."

"I know," Jo Beth said softly.

She reached out and took Kevin's shoulder, which trembled.

Peg took Jo Beth's other arm, put a palm to her filthy cheek.

"Oh, honey," Peg said.

The Crowley boy made an impatient cheep. Everyone was brought forth from their trances of apology and forgiveness. Arms dropped, understanding nods were exchanged, and together, as equals, they scanned the farm, looking for anything of value that needed to be brought along.

"Our car is dead," Jo Beth apologized.

"Figured as much," Kevin said. "Not sure how we're going to cram everyone in, but I suppose we'll manage."

"We Crowleys are used to close quarters," Peg added. "We pack like sardines."

On cue, the Crowley kids began drifting back toward the sedan. It was time to go. Ry put both palms to the ground and began to push himself upward.

"Oh, no," Jo Beth said. "Ry—"

"I can do it," Ry said.

"Let me—"

"Mom." He raised his eyebrows at her.

Her mouth closed. She nodded.

With Jo Beth and Esther hovering close, Ry gritted his teeth and went over the muscle groups he'd need to pull this off. He felt nothing but confidence. Standing up, moving on his own, returning to life, all of it was going to take three things he was newly rich in: hope, judgment, and courage. These qualities paid immediate dividends. His thighs performed their duties and his abdomen muscles held steady. The blanket slipped from his shoulders and he heard Esther gasp at the blood crusted to his clothes.

"It's . . . ," he started. "I . . ."

"Idiot," Esther said. "Let me help you."

She held out an arm. Ry sent up a prayer and let her wrap that arm around his shoulders. There was nothing else to do but take hold of her waist. Their first step proved that Peg had been right—there was something wrong with his ankles. But it was not an entirely unpleasant thing, taking his time arm in arm with Esther Crowley. There were worse fates everywhere, he thought. Just look around.

Everyone was piling into the car through multiple doors. As they waited, Jo Beth joined Esther to hold up Ry and he sensed excitement in her touch. He did not blame her. At long last they were leaving. It was not exactly as planned; she wore no smart ensemble and her cargo did not include the dress of her dreams. But a clean slate, thought Ry, was worth something too. Off to their right, the For Sale sign swung in the breeze, smoking.

With one foot already in the backseat, Sarah gave her brother a long look.

"You look like a terror man," she said.

Ry creased his forehead. The hole did not hurt much anymore.

"A what?"

"A terror man." Now she looked uncertain about her terminology.

"A terror man?"

"You know." Sarah made an impatient gesture. "A horror man."

Ry shook his head and discovered with some surprise that he was laughing.

"Fine," he said. "I'm a horror man."

Her eyes narrowed suspiciously—she knew she was being made fun of. But then she brushed her blond hair away from her face with two fingers to show that she was grown-up enough to let it go. Looking pleased with herself, she took one last look up at the sky and clambered over at least three bodies until she was just a face among other faces, no longer the youngest or most special. The other kids' elbowing caused her to cry out and elbow back.

"This is bullshit," she muttered.

"Sarah," Jo Beth warned.

Sarah lowered her voice. "This is *dog*shit," she clarified.

One of the Crowley girls guffawed. There was a pause as dangerous as a dare and then Sarah giggled, carefree and clarion. Ry's heart soared—it was like the birds returning all at once in a flock of astronomical size, the insects pouring back home with the sound of one hundred resplendent choirs. He thought he might wilt with the majesty of it all, but Esther and Jo Beth were there at both sides to keep him propped, while Kevin stood by the driver's side door, overseeing the stacking of bodies.

"All right," Kevin said. "All set back there?"

Jo Beth began to work with Esther to lower Ry into the passenger seat, but Ry dug his stiff ankles into the grass. Their progress was halted; all three faces still outside of the car asked for explanation. Ry swallowed and tried to think of the right words. The last time they had tried to leave this farm they had almost forgotten the same thing.

"Sniggety," Ry said.

Jo Beth's face softened. Her lips pressed together.

"Sniggety's . . . tired," she said. "Let him sleep."

The lie was all over her voice. Too tired to stop herself in time, she glanced at the doghouse. Ry wrenched his neck to get a better look. A mist of smoke forced him to squint, but yes, there was the old mutt lying on his side next to the scanty wooden box that had sheltered him for nearly two decades. Ry leaned forward, tried to see if the animal's ribs were moving. He could not tell.

He pulled away from the women's grip.

"Ry," Esther said.

"Son," Kevin said.

Ry reached into Jo Beth's arms and wrapped his fingers around the shotgun barrel. Her eyes widened and she pulled back. There was no forgetting the postures Ry had struck near the end, the threat that had blazed from his eyes and the nightmare noises that had gurgled from his throat. She stared at him a good long while, transferring her trust slowly before letting up on her grip.

He checked the safety, arranged the stock so that it was planted firmly into the grass, and just like that the proper operation of crutches came rushing back from where he'd stored it along with sundry other fifth-grade memories. The Winchester was more the proportions of a cane, but the idea was the same, and once he was balanced on his swollen ankles, he struck forth. Stab, swing. Stab, swing.

Everyone was watching his every move, but he did not care. In fact, he welcomed it. From their shell-shocked silence he could tell that these people would forever divide time into before the rocks fell and after the rocks fell. But under no circumstances would he allow the events of the past two days to define him; he'd spent nine years defined by a single event and had learned that it was a terrible way to live a life. With each stabbing, swinging step, he visualized himself: five years postimpact, ten years, twenty.

It took him not much longer to reach the doghouse than it would someone of perfect physical health. Sniggety remained on his side in the dirt. His paws were not twitching. His lashes and whiskers did not flutter from the usual canine fantasies. Ry grimaced and took a knee. The pain became sharper, just a bit. He let his heart rate settle, placed a hand atop the dog's ribs, and concentrated.

He felt it: Breath.

But it was weak. Ry gently pulled the skin back from one of Sniggety's eyes, just as Peg Crowley had done to him minutes ago. The cornea was milky and unresponsive. He let the lid slide shut and then carefully lifted the freckled edge of the animal's lip. The dull pink tongue pressed heavily against a row of grimy teeth.

A burden lowered itself upon Ry's shoulders. It might have been smoke inhalation that had done this to the dog. It might have been two days of being rattled by the unfamiliar emotions of elation and panic. Or it might have been nothing more than the years sneaking up on him on a glorious morning complete with perfect round clouds and blowing grass and green leaves waving from the highest branches.

Sniggety would not wake again; these final long hours would be dementia followed by death, and there might very well be confusion and pain.

Ry checked the shotgun. It was heavy with bullets.

The others could wait. No one would bury this dog but him.

He stroked Old Snig's neck, put his lips to the soft ear, and whispered.

"Good boy."

ACKNOWLEDGMENTS

Thank you to Richard Abate, Joshua Ferris, Alison Heryer, Beverly Horowitz, Amanda Kraus, Dale Kraus, Craig Ouellette, Grant Rosenberg, and Katie Ryan.

ABOUT THE AUTHOR

Daniel Kraus is the author of *Rotters* and *The Monster Variations*. A writer, an editor, and a filmmaker, he lives with his wife in Chicago. Visit him at danielkraus.com.